D1245397

YA Rials
Rials, Hannah
Ascension : a novel

$10.95
ocn984342284

Hannah Rials

Aletha Press

Ascension is a work of fiction. Names, characters, places, and incidents either are the product of the author's imagination or are used fictitiously. Any resemblance to actual persons, living or dead, events or locales is entirely coincidental.

Copyright © 2016 Aletha Press
All Rights Reserved.

Published by Aletha Press an imprint of Audrey Press LLC.
No part of this book may be reproduced or transmitted in any form or by any means, electronic or mechanical, including photocopying, recording, or by any information storage and retrieval system, without written permission from the publisher.

For information address:
Audrey Press/Aletha Press
P.O. Box 6113
Maryville, TN 37802

Printed in the United States of America
August 2016
Signature Books (www.sbpbooks.com).

Editor: Mallory Leonard
Book Design by Roscoe Welply

ISBN 978-1-936426-00-3
Library of Congress Catalog Card Number on File.

www.audreypress.com/alethapress
www.audreypress.com/ascension

To my parents,

for always believing in me, supporting me,
and loving me.

To Pam Hix,

for helping to shape Cheyenne and me
as we grew up together.

Your perspective on life
comes from the cage
you were held captive in.

-Shannon L. Adler

// Acknowledgements //

With Much Gratitude ~
There are too many thank yous to be given! So many people have influenced, helped, and changed both me and this book, but I guess I better start somewhere!

Thank you to my boss and publisher, Valarie Budayr, for giving me a chance as an intern and then taking an interest in my book. There aren't enough thank yous for all you've taught me.

Next to my wonderful editor Mallory Leonard, who's jetting around the world. You just fell into our hands thanks to fate, and I'm still amazed at how well you get both me and Cheyenne. You're amazing!

To my graphic designer Roscoe Welply, you're just wonderful! I'm proud to say that I've shown you the world that is vampire novels.

To my copy editor Peggy Carrouthers, you made me do a lot more work, but you also made this book a whole lot better!

To all of my friends who have ever laid eyes on a draft of this book and told me to "keep going, it's good, maybe change this"--thank you!

Thank you to my original readers for your wonderful opinions and encouragement!

To all of my English teachers through out time who have nourished my love of reading and writing. I might've struggled in class, but all those years of papers have paid off!

To my sister from another mister-thanks for listening through all the tears, doubts, and highs. I'll always appreciate that brutal honesty!

And lastly a big thank you to my puppy dogs. No, they haven't actually read the book, but they've sat beside me through it all!

Contents

Prologue

Every young girl has that one day that she's been looking forward to since forever. For some, it's her first kiss, her first cell phone, or her sweet sixteen party. For me, it's my Ascension, and it's happening tonight!

The Ascension is only the single most important thing that ever happens to a Deuxsang. That's what I am, a hybrid of human and vampire. Get it? The French for two-blooded? Until now, my vampire blood has been dormant. But tonight, on my thirteenth birthday, I'll go through a ceremony that will awaken my vampire side. After I ascend, I'll be able to flit, which is basically flying super fast, if only six inches off the ground. Throughout puberty I'll develop one of the four mental powers that vampires have, and I'll become stronger than any human. I can't even begin to describe how amazing my life will be.

My family has a special dress that every girl wears at her ceremony, and now I'm wearing it—crisp white, too much taffeta, a high collar, and a crimson sash around the waist. The taffeta is kind of itchy, but I can forget about that since I can't *stop* thinking about the fact that my mom let me wear make up. I was sure she'd say no last minute, but here I am, looking like a china doll—face painted as pale as the moon, eyes lined in black, and lips coated scarlet. For the first time in my life, I feel beautiful, like I'm coming into my own.

Slowly, my family arrives—my sister, aunts, uncles, cousins, Gramps, Nana, Grandpa, Grandma. They're all here for me, for my day. My sister Kara offers me an uncomfortable hug and a stiff smile, but her uptightness is easy to ignore. My cousins surround me. The younger ones are asking me if I'm nervous, and the older ones brush them off saying, "It's no big deal." The buzz of life in the room excites me.

Everyone chats easily while we wait for the sun to go down. Mom and Dad quiz me one last time on the material I need to know for my pre-ceremony interview. Nana makes sure I look perfect, adjusting the sash, wiping at my make up. I can't take my eyes away from the window, watching as the sun sinks below the trees and the sky turns darker and darker.

We all stop as four sharp knocks echo through the living room. Dad crosses swiftly to open the door for the Council representatives assigned to our family, bowing to them as they pass. The lead vampire is an extremely terrifying man. His dark eyes are set deeply in his skull, casting shadows over his face. Two women with striking blonde hair and crimson eyes follow him. They are tailed by three more men who could be triplets—same black hair, beady eyes, and meaty features. All of them wear identical, crisp, black suits. I've seen these vampires several times over the past thirteen years, but they still make me uneasy—especially the leader. He looks at us like we're hamsters in a cage.

Without a word to anyone in the family, the vampires follow Dad into the dining room and promptly shut the doors. This always happens. Dad, being the alpha of our family, has to give them the status report on all of us.

A few minutes later Dad reappears with a broad, proud smile on his face. My mom squeezes my hand and kisses my forehead. My turn. Dad takes my hand and leads me into the dining room where four of the six vampires are seated. I take in everything—the black tablecloth, the golden chalice filled to the brim with fresh cow's blood, the drawn curtains, and the files resting in front of each vampire. I turn around and meet the eyes of two of the men, arms crossed over their chests.

I feel the vampires' eyes on me and try to stand taller. The leader flicks his hand—Dad's signal to leave. He squeezes my hand one last time, and then the two vampires follow him out and close the doors.

For a moment, the four just stare at me. Then the leader opens his mouth. "Cheyenne Marie Lane, daughter of Samuel and Lisa Lane, sister of Kara Lane." His voice is booming, intoning the phrase as a question. I've been trained for this, but some big part of my brain is panicking. So I just nod. All four narrow their eyes.

"Let us begin the interview. Cheyenne Lane, *what* are you?"

I close my eyes, calm my breathing, slow my heart. "I am Deuxsang. In my veins runs the blood of humanity and of the superior race." I clasp my hands behind my back to hide the trembling.

"What must you hide from humans?"

"My mental ability, sir. Before my eighteenth birthday, I will discover whether I am a dream-walker, an illusionist, a compeller, or an inflictor. Also, my need to drink blood. I will drink only after sunset, and only the blood given to me by the Council."

"What separates you from the superior race?"

"I blend in with humans. I walk in the day and eat human food. I will never bite a human or consume human blood. The vampires are my protectors. I owe them my allegiance and obedience."

"Finally, what *is* the Ascension ceremony?" The leader asks, his empty eyes having a curious glint to them.

"It is the process through which I will surrender my humanity to release the vampire within me and fully embrace the two bloods running through my veins. From now on I will subjugate my humanity in favor of my vampire nature."

"I believe that's enough questions." The leader stands, and the others follow. "It is time to the begin the ceremony. Cheyenne Lane, please step forward."

I walk up to the table, trying to quash the fear screaming in my head. This is my moment. This is what I've been waiting for.

"The Deuxsang came into being through an accident of nature. Humans can never know of their existence. The Deuxsang live under the protection of the vampires. They live under oath of silence. Do you, Cheyenne Lane, now swear to keep the secret of your people?"

"Yes, sir."

"Do you, Cheyenne Lane, pledge loyalty to the vampires?"

"Yes, sir."

"Very well. It is time to embrace your dual nature."

I try to still myself as the leader walks around the table to stand in front of me. The second woman, the one who tries to smile, carries the chalice. The scent of the blood is overwhelming. I take my last necessary breath as the leader grabs my shoulders with beautiful, timeless hands. I'm ready. I'm not scared. This is my time. My moment. I am ascending.

Then his fangs pierce into the skin between my shoulder and neck. My eyes blast open as a head splitting shriek erupts. I can see the confusion in the vampires' eyes. I know this is wrong. Why is this wrong? Why does it hurt? I try to pull myself away from his bite, but the more I struggle, the stronger the pain becomes.

I gag as his fangs slip out of my neck. Simultaneously we fall to the floor, convulsing. One of the women rushes to him, steadies him, pulls him to his feet. No one comes to help me. I'm shaking so hard I can't even scream. I'm trapped inside my body.

"What are you saying, Mirnov?" I hear one of the females asking over my screams. "You think she's like him?"

I want to pull at my dress. The neck is choking me. The taffeta is making my sweaty skin itchy, but my arms feel useless. They just lay numb at my sides.

"I think she might be. She definitely tastes different. Her blood is—intense. Go ahead. Try her. Just be careful."

Through my tear-filled eyes, I see the first woman bend down beside me. I try to push myself away, but my body is betraying me. My insides are on fire, and everything else is numbing pain. I feel her lift my arm, and another round of screams erupt as her fangs suck the blood from my wrist. I squeeze my eyes shut as she pulls away. Before I can even think, two more sets of fangs bite my shoulder and my bicep. I can't do anything. Tears fall down my face. I want to scream. I want to die.

"Good God, Mirnov, you're right. You must tell the chairman immediately."

When they've had their fill of me, Mirnov scoops me up in his arms and holds my head up. He takes the chalice and puts it to my lips.

"Cheyenne Lane, take your first drink of life." He holds the chalice to me, but I can't move. I try, thinking maybe it will help. It has to. Nothing could be worse than this. When I remain still as a corpse, one of the women opens my mouth and pours the entire chalice of blood down my throat.

Suddenly my body is on fire. I thrash, gag, scream, cry. Why is this happening? Daddy said it would be easy! Daddy...where's Daddy?

I throw myself toward the door, but a blinding pain shoots all the way through my body. I scream, nearly choke, as some invisible force wraps itself around my heart. I hurl my arm over my chest, clawing at the spot where my heart is struggling to beat. My eyes go blind. White noise fills my ears. I can't even hear my own screams. I can only feel the string, pulling tighter and tighter on my heart.

Why is this happening? This was supposed to be easy—no pain, Rove told me. Dad told me. Everyone told me. And why so many bites? Why is my dad not here? Why hasn't he stopped them from doing this to me?

My mind goes blank as the string constricts on my heart. I scratch my nails into the floor, tears burning down my cheeks. I try to yell for my dad, but I can't find the air for the words.

As the minutes pass, my heart slows. It beats two times. Then once. And then I die.

...

When I wake up, I'm in my own bed. Sweat pastes the dress to my body and my hair to my face. There are no vampires. There's no pain, no burning, no string. I feel fine—better than fine. But then I remember everything—the disapproving looks, the pain, the conversation, and all the bites. Most importantly, I remember that I'd been alone. I'd called out to my dad, only to be answered by my own screams.

I've been waiting for this moment my entire life. I'm finally a true Deuxsang, but all I feel is disgust, anger, and complete loneliness.

I flinch at the knock on my door. For the first time, I am able to hear every gear click as my dad turns the doorknob and steps into my room. "Hey, Cheyenne. You ready for school?"

Some piece of me was hoping that he'd rush in here apologizing, holding me as I cried. He just smothered that hope.

I don't try to hide the shadow of anger that passes over my face. "Leave me alone," I nearly growl, turning away from him and pulling my knees into my chest.

"Excuse me, young lady? What did you just say to me?" He steps closer. I can feel the anger radiating off of him. Yesterday, I would've cowered and apologized. Today, I would rather eat nails than apologize to him.

"Don't talk to me!" I yell, whipping around to glare at him full-force. "Don't ever talk to me again." My jaw clamps shut as I try to control myself. "And don't ever think I'll forgive you because it will never happen." I can taste the bitterness in my voice, and I refuse to look him in the eye. Those aren't the same eyes I've always trusted.

His face fades from anger to confusion to utter defeat. He opens his mouth, but then, without a word, he backs out of my room and closes the door. I curl back under my covers, unable to escape the horror of last night, and cry until I run dry.

One

Again, Cheyenne. I want to hear it again. You have to get ready for your Affirmation interview. If you don't pass the interview, then you won't be acknowledged as a full citizen of Deuxsang society. Instead of going to Clandestine University with the rest of your peers, you'll be stuck here with us, learning this all again. Is that what you want?"

My dad looks like he's about to have an aneurysm. As of late, most of our weekly Council-mandated lessons end this way. He has to teach me, but I have no desire to make it easy for him.

"Why? It happened two-hundred years ago. And you know what? The story doesn't even make sense."

"You need to watch your mouth, young lady. I don't care what you think about our history, you must respect it. You accepted this duty when you ascended." My nostrils flare when Dad brings up my Ascension. We don't talk about it anymore because it always ends in a huge blow up that takes a long time to recover from, not that we've ever recovered. I don't really think we ever will.

"Fine. Until two-hundred years ago, the Deuxsang lived in an isolated town outside of New Orleans. *Unbeknownst* to us, some local witches had discovered a way to use Deuxsang blood in a magic spell that would give them our mental abilities—vampire abilities. Armed with this power, they would finally be able to face the vampires—their mortal enemies—in open combat. Our ancestors weren't expecting the attack. When the witches struck, they set the town on fire and wrapped it in a wind tunnel. Most of the Deuxsang rushed out to fight while the rest took as many children as possible to a safe location." I lean back into the couch, crossing my arms over my chest. I know this. I know the tale of the Massacre. I just don't care.

"The Deuxsang leaders called their protectors for help, but by the time the Chairman of the Council and the rest of the vampires arrived, all the Deuxsang were killed. The witches, unaware that the call to the vampires had gone out, were still in the town, draining their victims. They were no match for the vampires and were quickly wiped out. The chairman felt responsible for the orphans, so the vampires raised them in a secure location, then disseminated our people around the country so another massacre could never happen. Witches are monsters, and we are thankful to the vampires for saving us, even though they couldn't save the older generation."

"You forgot something," Dad snips, miffed by how robotic my speech is.

"After hearing what the vampires had done to those witches, the rest went into hiding. No one has been able to locate them since."

"Good. I guess. Could be better."

I just roll my eyes. I'm never going to be good enough for him.

"I just don't get it. The story seems too tidy."

"I will not have you disrespecting the defining moment of Deuxsang history. You know my grandfather was killed that night. Gramps always talked about what an inspiring Deuxsang he was—one of the first to run out to fight the witches."

"Yes, Dad, I know. You tell that story all the time, but another thing I don't get is why all the witches are in hiding everywhere."

"Because they're terrified of the vampires, as they should be. The vampires saved us, saved our future. We are grateful to them for all they've done for us."

I have nothing to say to that. I don't see why I should be grateful to the vampires who bit me over and over again, who just stood there talking as I writhed in agony. I owe them nothing.

I can tell he's getting fed up with my questions, but I don't really care. "Dad, won't they ask me about the Chairman in my interview? He kind of seems like someone to know about."

"No, the Chairman is a mystery to all of us. We know he exists, but none of us have ever met him, and I assume it'll stay that way."

"But why?" I press, knowing full well that I'm pushing my luck.

Dad's face turns an unnatural shade of red that only I create. "Because that's the way things are, Cheyenne. The Chairman saved us, so we respect his privacy. Do you understand?"

No, I don't understand. I don't understand why Dad, our alpha, has to report to The Council every month on whom the children are associated with, what our studies are, how much blood we're consuming nightly, and how our abilities are developing. I don't understand why we can't get our own blood. The vampires don't trust us at all, so they deliver four gallons of blood per person per month. They come after we're all asleep, and when we wake up the next morning, there's a box of fresh blood waiting for us. It's like Santa Claus, only creepier.

"I guess I'm just going to have to understand."

I smirk. "Am I free to go? I have to get ready for work."

I stand up.

"What? You're not working. Tonight's Marilyn's Ascension."

"Well, that's too bad. I'm scheduled to work tonight, so I'm going in to work." I cross my arms, ready for the battle.

"Cheyenne, there's no question," my dad roars, his eyes flickering red. "You *will* be present at Marilyn's Ascension. You'll just have to call your boss and tell her you have a family obligation."

"I can't do that an hour before my shift. How unprofessional is that, Dad?"

"I don't care!" He slams his large hands down on the tile of the counter. "Do you know what it would look like to the Council representatives if you weren't here? That's just not acceptable."

"Tell them that I'm sick. I don't know. Make something up, Dad. I'm not missing work."

"Oh, yes you are because I say you are. You have a duty to this family and to our community. I know you did this on purpose, but your attempts to miss your cousins' ceremonies will not work."

My shoulders slump in defeat, not that I thought

I'd win. I'll never win. "Fine. I won't go to work, okay? Are you happy?"

"That's my girl," Dad rumbles, rounding the counter to wrap me in a bear hug that I used to find reassuring. Now it's just a reminder of his betrayal. "How about you help your old man and start setting up for the Ascension tonight?"

Sam Lane is hardly an old man. Dad looks like he could easily be in his thirties. Forties would be completely out of the question. I've never even seen a wrinkle on my parents' faces except when they're frowning or yelling at me. I'm not actually sure how old my parents are. After Deuxsang turn eighteen our aging begins to slow down. Dad looks thirty, but if I had to guess, I'd say he's just over one-hundred.

"I would, but I have to make a phone call." I smirk at him and make a mad dash for my room before Dad can stop me, trying and failing to flit.

My boss answers on the first ring. "Hello, thank you for calling Allpets! How may I help you today?" Jamie asks with her forced cheery voice, one that I'm very familiar with.

"Hey, Jamie, it's Cheyenne." I already feel horrible for what I'm about to ask her. I know I should go ahead and say I can't work on days of my cousins' Ascensions, but I always hold onto the hope that my dad will let me skip. Just once—that's all I ask, but it's never going to happen.

"Oh, hi! What's going on?" The cheeriness disappears from her voice, and I can hear the exhaustion that she tries to hide so well.

"I really hate to say this, but…"

"Let me guess, you have another family thing?"

I cringe when she asks. I really need to start using a different excuse. "Yes, unfortunately! I'm so, so sorry! I really hate doing this to you. I can make up for it anytime."

"It's fine, Cheyenne. You can come in tomorrow morning. You're off school, right?"

"Yes, today was my last day."

"Great. Be here for opening. I'll get someone else to cover your shift for tonight."

I can't even describe my relief. Thank God for humans. "Thank you so much, Jamie! I swear this won't happen again."

"Mmm hmm." With that, the line goes dead, and I'm left in my depressing bedroom with no homework to be done and nothing else to do either. Great.

Luckily, I hear a car pulling into the driveway. I focus my ears just enough to listen to the nearly silent engine of Rove's sports car before leaping out of my bed to meet my favorite cousin. I'm out the door and in front of his car before he even has time to turn off his music. He looks up at me lazily from his low-riding seat.

"What's up, Munchkin?" he asks, nonchalant and completely ignoring the fact that we haven't seen each other in way too long.

"Don't Munchkin me, you jerk. You can't just disappear off the face of the planet and expect a warm greeting!" I cross my arms over my chest, waiting for him to apologize.

He pulls himself out of his seat and throws his arm over my shoulder in one swift motion. He's been much more successful at growing into his Deuxsang speed and grace than I have. "Don't give me a hard time, Cheyenne. It's the last month of school. I've been busy."

"Oh yeah, you were busy with school. Likely." He narrows his eyes and pushes me ahead of him.

"Shut up. I happen to take my school work very seriously, for your information." We both laugh at this. "Alright, I'm sorry," he admits. "I've been a bit busy with a new girl." He shrugs like it's nothing. It's not nothing. Dating is never nothing with Deuxsang.

He doesn't look at me, and it makes me nervous. "Rove, is she…?"

Rove shoots me a silencing glance as Dad walks up to us with his arms open. "Hey, there's my long lost nephew!" They pat each other's backs in that awkward guy-style. "How've you been, son?"

"I'm good. Just getting ready for my final exams. How are you, Uncle Sam?" Rove and I are already inching toward my bedroom before Dad can respond.

"Yeah, you two go catch up. We'll get you once everyone's here." Rove flits down the hallway before I even have a chance to blink.

When I get to my room several moments later, Rove is lounging on my bed. "Okay, answer my question, Rove. Is she human?" My eyebrow rises to a sharp angle.

Rove waits an unnerving minute before responding me. "Define human?" he challenges.

"Not funny, Rove! You could get in serious trouble," I whisper, afraid that the walls have ears in this house.

"Calm down, Munchkin. It's not a big deal. She's just some girl to pass the time with." It's comments like this that make me wonder how we get along so well. He can be so chauvinistic.

"A—stop being an idiot, and B—it doesn't matter! She's still human, and you know the rules. It's way too dangerous." Despite my complete distrust of my parents and the contempt that I have for the vampires, I still respect their rule. No matter what, Deuxsang can *never* expose their true identity to humans. The stories my family have told me about what the vampires on the Council have done to Deuxsang who have strayed send chills down my spine every time. I don't want anything like that to ever happen to Rove. I don't even want to think about it.

"Cheyenne, relax. I'm sure I'll get bored soon enough. You're making a big deal out of nothing."

"Sorry, I don't want to see my cousin slaughtered by a bunch of blood thirsty vampires. I'm *so ridiculous.*"

"Good. I'm glad you admit it. And speaking of blood..." I can smell it too. Dad must have set out the pitchers already. My throat burns as thirst takes over. It's so easy for me to forget about having to drink blood during the day—I enjoy my sandwiches and bacon breakfasts. Then the sun starts to set, and it's like a switch flips. The vampire half takes over, and I am overwhelmed by the need for blood. Except tonight. Tonight I'm thinking about the Council representatives and my cousin Marilyn. Is she excited, like I was?

"So, is that guy still hassling you at school?" Rove asks, knowing the topic of Erik Ashford will get me off his case.

"Why would you bring that up? I don't want to talk about this right now."

"Why? What's going on with this dude that you can't tell me about it?"

"Because it's embarrassing, Rove, and not a big deal. I really just need you to drop it, okay?" I feel a headache forming above my eyebrow already, and the ceremony hasn't even started.

"I'm not dropping it until you tell me what's going on, Cheyenne. I'm like a dog with a bone, so you might as well give up."

I bite my lip, regretting ever telling him that Erik Ashford was harassing me. "Look, I don't know. The guy just has it out for me. He's a jerk, and he picked me as his target. It's seriously nothing I can't handle." I note his white knuckles. Rove's the closest thing I'll ever get to a sibling since my sister has been pretty much absent from my life.

"What does he do?" he mutters through his teeth.

"Sometimes he'll call me names or shove me in the halls. Let it go."

"I don't believe you. Tell me. What has he done?"

"Okay, well, there is this one thing. A while back, my geometry teacher assigned us a million proofs for homework. It took me *hours*. Anyway, I put my math stuff in my locker the next morning, then got it out again for fourth block. When I opened my folder to turn in the assignment, I found a bunch of ash instead of my homework. I can't prove it, but it had to be him."

"This guy broke into your locker and set your homework on fire? That's not no big deal. That's insane." He stares back at me, and for this first time I remember, there is no hint of joking in his eyes.

Before I can respond, a blonde head pops into my doorway. "Cheyenne!" Kara, my sister, opens her arms to me with her usual thousand-dollar smile plastered on her face. "How are you, baby sis?" I hug her stiffly. I'm never sure how to act around Kara. There's such a big age difference between us that there's no real connection, as much as she tries to pretend there is.

"I'm good. Where's Thomas?" I peer around her to see my towering brother-in-law. Together, the two make a shockingly contrasting pair. Thomas is tall with slicked back dark hair and sharp features. Kara is shorter, not much taller than me, with perfectly styled blonde hair and a warm, round face, though they both dress nicely, no matter the occasion.

"Right here, Cheyenne." He leans down awkwardly to give me a side hug and pat my shoulder. Despite the fact that Thomas has unofficially been a member of this family for too many years to count, he still hasn't settled into the role. I guess having to situate yourself into a new family would be intimidating.

Normally, Kara would join Thomas's family, instead of the other way around, but Thomas is an orphan. He's never told us what happened. "How have you been?"

"Same old, same old." I smile encouragingly, trying to make him comfortable. Rove isn't helping things at all. He's always given Thomas the cold shoulder, and I've never been able to understand why.

"Well," Kara sighs. "Dad wanted us to let you know that everyone's here, so you should come join us in the living room. I'm sure you two are getting thirsty anyway." Again, Thomas looks at her, but she ignores him and just smiles at us.

"Yeah, we'll be out in a minute. I just wanted to show Rove something." I nod, reaching for my laptop.

"Okay, but hurry. You don't want to keep everyone waiting." She squeezes my hand in what I'm assuming is supposed to be some sort of sisterly gesture, but it just comes across as pushy and weird. She and Thomas leave just before I roll my eyes, unable to contain it any longer.

"Chill out, Munchkin. She's just being Kara." Rove whispers, laughing at me.

"I know. That's the problem."

"What did you want to show me?" he asks, nodding toward my laptop.

I glance down, confused. "Oh, nothing. I just wanted her to leave." This time, it's his turn to roll his eyes as he pushes me out of my room.

I follow Rove to our usual seats beside the window trying to ignore the pity glances thrown my way, and I think about how different I am from everyone else in my family. On top of what happened at my Ascension, I still haven't learned to flit or come into my ability. Rove is getting really good at controlling his powers of illusion. Kara is a dream-walker, and Thomas is a compeller. Then there's Lilith, who has the power of infliction. She can inflict excruciating pain on anyone just by willing it. My parents have tried to teach me how to tap into my ability, but it just ends up giving me a headache.

Our cousins Drake and Marilyn, brother and sister, are already waiting for us. Marilyn is wearing the same dress that all of the women in my family wear for their Ascension. I remember the constriction of the turtleneck and the itch of the taffeta. Already, I'm in a bad mood, but the fear in Marilyn's eyes softens me. I sit beside her, and she instantly reaches for my hand, squeezing harder than she realizes.

"I can't do this, Cheyenne. I can't. I'm not going to make it. It's going to kill me; I just know it," she whispers, not wanting everyone to overhear her worry.

Drake reaches for her other hand and shakes his head. "No, it's not. You can do this." Drake, who just went through his Ascension a few months ago, has adapted the best of all of us. He's already learning about his compelling ability, and he always knows the right thing to say.

Rove leans forward to look Marilyn in the eyes, and he smiles. The fear vanishes from her face as some sort of pleasant vision dances through her head, thanks to Rove.

"Rove, stop. She needs to focus." Drake shoves Rove's shoulder, knocking away the connection with Marilyn.

"That beach was beautiful, Rove. Thank you," she sighs, remembering the slight escape she had for just a few moments until the fear returns. "It's gonna hurt like it did for you, Cheyenne, isn't it? I just know it."

I don't get to respond before four knocks rumble against the front door. Everyone stops and turns toward Dad crossing the living room to invite the vampires in—the same vampires that almost let me die. Mirnov, the leader, followed by the same two women and the other three men. They look exactly like they did two years ago for Drake's ceremony, the same as when they all bit me. The last and newest member of this party makes me want to throw up. Lilith, my older cousin. She was recruited by the Council after graduating from university, so I guess she's been working for them about three years. She's basically their lackey, but she blends in beautifully with those monsters—cold, calculating, and basically flawless.

I watch them all glide into the room silently except for the clicks of Lilith's heels. They're looking at us like they always do—like we're guinea pigs, like property, except for Lilith. While the vampires continue to observe us, Lilith's eyes have not strayed from Mirnov's stone face. I almost catch a trace of emotion in that blank slate of hers. I didn't think she could sink any lower.

Almost instantly Mirnov's eyes land on me. His eyes don't move from mine. He just stares like he's looking for something inside me, but I don't know what he could be searching for.

I remember that the vampires had some discussion during my ceremony, but I can't remember what they said. I wish I knew. Maybe then I'd understand why he's looking at me like this—why they're all looking at me. They pause in the middle of the living room, their eyes switching from me to Marilyn, probably curious about whether or not Marilyn will be the same as me. For her sake, I honestly hope she's not.

Hesitating at the dining room door, Dad stares at them staring at us. Marilyn squeezes my hand harder than normal. Satisfied with the show, the vampires turn away in sync and follow Dad into the dining room. Lilith stays with us, taking a seat next to my mom, forcing herself to chat casually with her brother Magnus and her parents. But she watches the door like she can make it open. Too bad her abilities don't work like that.

Everyone's staring at Marilyn now, who looks after

the vampires in sheer panic. All I can hear in my head are my screams. I feel phantom pain from the string around my still heart. Marilyn jumps to her feet, pulling me with her. She looks to Gramps, who's second in command since he was the alpha before Dad. "Gramps, can I use the bathroom?" she asks, her voice barely coming out.

He glances at the closed door, listening carefully to the voices on the other side. After a moment, he nods, turning to us. "Be quick, hon. They're almost done."

Without hesitation, she drags me with her down to the end of the hallway, slams the bathroom door behind us, and crumbles to the floor in a mess of heavy breathing and tears. "Cheyenne, help me! I can't do this. I'm not as strong as you." I kneel down in front of her, pulling her hands away from her tear stained face.

"Marilyn, listen to me. If I can make it through the ceremony, you most certainly can. You are made to do this." Her tears slowly start to recede, and her breathing calms. "Are you ready?" I whisper.

She nods, throwing her arms around my neck. "Thank you, Cheyenne. I love you," she mutters into my hair. I smile at those three words. Deuxsang don't say "love" too often after we ascend. I rub her back before lifting us both to our feet.

"I'm gonna head out there," I say, straightening her dress and fixing her dark curls. "You take as long as you need. Don't let those vampires pressure you, okay?" She nods solemnly, still holding onto my hand. She almost doesn't let me go when I open the door and step out into the hallway. I can feel her eyes on my back as I return to the living room. Every head snaps in my direction in an eerie synchronization. "She's using the bathroom," I say when Dad gives me a panicked look.

He huffs, stomping down the hallway to pull her out. A moment later, he's dragging her behind him. There are tears in her eyes as she glances first at her parents, at her brother, then finally at me. My eyes follow her through the open doors where Mirnov and the rest of the vampires wait for her. When Dad comes back out, two of the men follow him and pull the doors closed, standing guard in front of them. Their eyes don't look at us, but just graze over our heads.

My hearing has started to improve, thank goodness. At least one thing's working in my favor. I can almost hear everything they're asking her. Rove tries to chat casually with Drake and me, but I can't focus. My mind is four years in the past right now.

With every question they ask Marilyn, I flash back to standing there thinking I was completely prepared, proud of my answers. I see shadows move as the ceremony begins. Marilyn's voice is quiet, but I hear her shaky "yes" as she takes the oath. There is no choice. We either ascend, or we die. If we don't go through the Ascension ceremony, if the vampire in us isn't allowed to manifest alongside the human, our bodies will be consumed by necrosis, one organ at a time. I've never actually known this to happen to anyone. It's just what we're told, and it's scary enough not to attempt it. No is not an option in our world.

I shudder when I hear Marilyn gulping down the cow's blood. Then my body tenses, preparing for the screams, cries, anything, but all I hear is a little gasp and then a gentle thump as they lay her on the floor to ascend.

And again, same as when Drake ascended, I'm reminded of how completely isolated I am from my family.

When the doors open Aunt Luna, Uncle Miles, and Drake jump to their feet. The female vampire smiles when she addresses them. "Your daughter did wonderfully. She will be healthy and strong. Her body was ready to accept the Ascension, and she will become a worthy Deuxsang. Congratulations." They bow, thanking her. For what, I don't know. That woman didn't do anything. She turns to glance at me with a curious glint in her red eyes. I almost look away, but I make myself keep eye contact.

After an unnerving moment, she smirks and opens the doors to Uncle Miles, who scoops Marilyn up in his arms. The vampires are the first to leave the house. They, including loyal Lilith, follow single file behind Mirnov, not pausing to say anything to any of us. As suddenly as they appeared, they are gone. Then slowly, everyone else follows until there are only a few people left.

I wonder if they came out to announce my Ascension. I shudder to imagine how that went. How do you even describe that? It never happens. I can just picture my mom and dad shaking their heads in shame, the rest of the family holding back their shock and embarrassment.

And I *am* an embarrassment. I can't flit. I haven't even felt a flicker of my ability. How much more of a failure can I be?

Two

Rove follows me as I close the door on the last of my family members. My head feels like it weighs a thousand pounds. I just want to go to sleep. But he has that look that makes me think he has something he wants to talk about. Great.

"You alright, Munchkin?" He asks, picking up on my less than excited expression. I nod, though the movement feels like my brain is an earthquake in my skull.

"Yeah, what's up?"

"Well, I have something to ask you. I meant to ask you earlier." He pauses, waiting for prompting or approval. When I don't say anything, he continues, "Since you seem so interested in my love life, you wanna meet my girlfriend?"

My lips part in a sigh, shoulders slumping. "Rove, are you sure that's such a good idea? If she's human..."

"Seriously? Who even cares? It's not like I'm marrying the girl. We're just dating." I note the defensive shift in his voice, warning myself to tread carefully.

"I'm sorry, alright? I just don't get why you have to do this."

I can practically hear his eye roll. "Do what? Date? Be a teenager? Maybe you should try it sometime."

"We aren't exactly normal teenagers, Rove. If we break the rules, we don't just get *grounded*," I pucker at the bitterness in my voice.

"Hey, I follow the Council's rules. We're not forbidden from dating humans, just from mating with them."

I bite my lip before I say anything he can use against me. "Never mind. I'm sorry, okay? I won't say anything else about it. I'd still like to meet her."

He doesn't say anything for a minute, his version of sulking.

"So, when?"

"Tomorrow night at Lily's. Seven o'clock. Don't be late." His voice is clipped, but I can hear that he's a little bit happy.

"When have I ever been late?" I open the door for him, but Kara comes scurrying into the room, ushering us into the kitchen with some big announcement.

"Rove, you can hear this too. Hurry up!" We straggle behind her, just to make her mad. It's not really difficult.

Everyone else is already in the kitchen, huddled around the island in the center of the room.

I lean against the island beside Rove and grab a glass of blood. "What's going on?" I ask, downing it in one gulp.

"Well, Thomas and I have two things we wanted to talk to you guys about," she smiles eagerly, making me nervous.

"First of all," Thomas says, startling all of us, "I got a new job—an assistant professor's position at Clandestine." Everyone erupts into congratulations, shaking Thomas's hand. Clandestine is the Deuxsang university in New Orleans, basically my only option for college. "We'll be moving down in a couple of days, and we'd like to invite Cheyenne to come stay the summer with us." I look up sharply at the two of them, at the eagerness in their young, beautiful faces. I'm confused. "We figure, you'll be down at Clandestine in a year anyway, so you might as well come down and get a feel for the city."

"You'll love it, Cheyenne!" Kara squeals, squeezing my hand again. I'm speechless, as are mom and dad. When they don't respond, Kara frowns. "Come on, Dad. This is a great opportunity for Cheyenne. Plus, she'd be a great help in getting us settled into our new home. Say yes," she prompts, winning them over with that charming smile of hers.

Mom and Dad look at each other, a silent conversation passing between them, before Dad smiles reluctantly. "I honestly can't think of a reason why not. It does sound like a good opportunity. I'll file a request for the Council's approval, but I don't see why they'd reject this." So apparently everyone gets a say in the matter except me?

"Perfect!" Kara shrieks, bouncing up and down on her toes. Thomas puts a calming hand on her hand to stop her. I look between my family—the young, eager to prove themselves couple, who are offering an exciting new city with the possibility of freedom, and the old, stuck in their ways, restrictive parents that I've been eager to escape for years now. I guess my decision has been made for me. Kara's been waiting for my smile, and when it comes, she throws her arms around me, swinging me from side to side. Gramps nearly has to pry her off of me.

"What about me?" Rove asks, that sly smirk of his making an appearance.

Kara laughs like he's the funniest person in the room. "Rove, I don't think I could handle you for a whole summer." I glance up at just the right time to see Thomas's jaw tighten and his eyes roll way far back in his head. Well then. "But we'd love to have you down for a week. I mean, I think everyone needs to visit New Orleans before they start at Clandestine." She smiles genuinely, but her husband looks anything but pleased.

"Awesome! Thanks, Kara. I'll mention it to Dad." He turns to me. "Double Trouble taking the Big Easy!" I feel so cheesy high fiving him right now. He's such a dork.

"And we have some more news, something else that Cheyenne will be helpful with, or should I say...someone," she grins, winking at Thomas. When we don't say anything, she yells, "I'm pregnant!"

Mom and Dad sputter. My eyes drift toward Kara's stomach, and I notice a little bump. "Pregnant, as in with child?" I ask.

"Of course, Cheyenne! Don't be so dense." She looks at Thomas, a nervous laugh escaping her pink lips. "You could say something," she whispers.

"I'm sorry, honey," Dad finally says. "You just shocked us. That's great news!" He walks around the counter and hugs Kara. "Congratulations."

Everything about Mom's face screams happiness. A tear leaks out of the corner of her eye. "I'm so happy for you! How far along are you?"

"Four months," her hands unconsciously fall to her stomach, stroking the small bump.

"Oh, honey!" Everyone crowds around her, even Rove, touching her stomach, hugging her, and then Dad and Gramps rush to shake Thomas's hand. I hang back, staring at my empty glass. Kara glances at me over Nana's shoulder and simpers, urging me to smile back. I nod, then walk back to my room. A moment later, I hear a knock on my door.

"It's open," I call.

"Wow," Kara says, picking up a stray book on my desk and staring around the room. "I can't believe you've kept this horrible wallpaper."

"Not like I had much of a choice," I mumble, turning my back on her.

"So what's up, sis? Did Marilyn's ceremony upset you?"

"The ceremonies always get to me. You know that," I mope.

"Is that the only reason for your mood? I was hoping you'd be happier for me," she admits, looking down at her stomach.

"I am happy for you."

We're avoiding each other's glance. Neither of us really know how this sister thing is supposed to work. It's like we both want to be closer than we are, but the age difference makes it hard. She's just so much older than I am. I'm not even really sure how old she is anymore. I guess she graduated from Clandestine before my thirteenth birthday, and now she has her own family. We can't really relate to each other. I still haven't fully grasped the fact that I've only lived a very small portion of my life. Two-hundred years seems like such a long time when you really think about it. Two centuries of watching your world and your life change, twice as fast as you. I'm seventeen, and after I graduate college, my aging will slow down gradually. It's amazing. I don't think my parents were planning on a second kid, and then I happened after Kara was basically on her own. She always seemed like she enjoyed spending time with me during the scheduled monthly visit that she mostly kept to. Mostly, our hanging out meant her talking and talking, trying to fill the gap of silence that always found its way into the room.

"I'm glad you're coming to stay with us this summer," she says, breaking the familiar silence. "I'm hoping it'll give us the chance to get to know each other better."

"Plus it couldn't hurt to have an extra set of hands when you're getting ready for the baby," I joke.

She chuckles. "That part will be fun too."

I smile, but then remember something that makes me wonder, "Was it your idea for me to spend the summer in New Orleans?"

She looks stricken, like I've hurt her feelings. "That's a strange question."

"Kara, we should be going," Thomas calls from the foyer.

She nods in agreement and looks at me one more time. "Well, I'll see you soon, Sis." Then she turns and leaves. When she's gone, I lie back on my bed and hear the good-bye chatter through the door, thinking about how she didn't, and probably never will, answer my question.

...

It's my last day at the pet store before I head to New Orleans. I'm going to miss this place. I really love my job. Some parts of it are sad, but I love animals. I know this quirk makes me a bad Deuxsang. We're typically a detached breed, calculating and logical.

I'm just about to close up my register when a guy my age runs up and slams a big bag of dog food down on the counter. I take a step back, locked into place by his forest green eyes. A tingling feeling rushes over my body, and a flame sparks in my throat. I can feel the tips of my fangs stabbing into my gums. No. *Not now.* I suck in a deep breath, willing my fangs to stay hidden.

"Hi there," he says.

"I'm, uh, closed. Sorry," I mumble, not able to look away from him.

"Please? All the other lines are busy, and I really need to get home. My dad sent me out for dog food. He's putting me to work while I'm in town." He looks down at me through thick eyelashes that make his face even more charming. I sigh, reopening my register, and he smiles. "Thanks a lot for doing this." He narrows his eyes at my nametag and reads, "Cheyenne. I like that name."

I bite my lip and scan the dog food. "Your total is ten dollars and fifty-two cents." He fumbles around in his wallet. "Are you new around here? I don't recognize you," I say, studying his face.

"No, I grew up in Louisiana. When my parents split, my dad moved up here. My older brother and I stayed with Mom, but my younger brother chose to live with him. I visit every once in a while." He scrounges through his jean pockets.

"Why'd you choose to live with your mom?" The question pops out of my mouth before I can stop it. "I'm sorry, you don't have to answer that."

When he smiles, a dimple pops into one cheek. "That's okay. It was a pretty nasty divorce, and sides had to be chosen."

I've crossed into extremely personal territory. Must change course. "So where does your brother go to school? I might know him."

"Uh, I actually don't know. That's embarrassing. I don't really keep up with him. We don't get along well either." His hands jam into every pocket as he continues his search for the money. "Sorry. I know I have it. Aha!" He pulls a crumpled ten-dollar bill and some change out of his back pocket and holds it out to me. "Knew I had it, Cheyenne." I try not to grin when he says my name, but it's really hard.

"I don't think I can accept this," I say, shrugging my shoulders as I reach for the bill.

"What?" His green eyes double in size. "Come on, now. I mean, it's a bit worn for the worse, but it's not unusable."

I just shake my head, looking down at the bill, but I can't keep up the façade for long. I start laughing as I open the cash register and print off his receipt.

"You're a funny one." But he's smiling as he says it.

"Have a nice night," I hand him the receipt and smile at him.

"I'm Eli, by the way. Just in case you were wondering who you nearly gave a heart attack."

I look up at him, my lips pressed together. "Sorry, I couldn't help myself."

He rolls his eyes, but his gaze never leaves mine. "Well, I hope to see you before I leave. Thanks for the favor. I owe you one."

"Goodbye," I say as he hoists the bag up over his shoulder.

"Good night, not goodbye," he winks, giving my heart a little flutter.

I nod my head once before turning away to close the register. I see him smile again before turning around, and I'm left with a horrible burning in my throat.

I walk to the back and hang my smock on the designated hook. All the dogs and cats have settled in for the night, curling up together against the glass windows. My boss is sitting at her desk, twiddling a pencil between her fingers and quietly reviewing the day's total sales on her computer. "How'd we do today?" I ask as I pull my keys out of my purse.

"Not too shabby! Is your shift already over?" Jamie looks up from the screen and glances at the cages when one of the cats hisses.

"Yeah, I'm going to meet my cousin for dinner." A breeze rushes through the store as the next-to-last customer leaves, bringing a chill into the room.

"Fun. Well, have a good summer. Let me know when you're back in town, and I'll put you back on the schedule." She smiles, the dark bags under her eyes prominent in the dim lighting, and looks back down at her computer, shifting uncomfortably in the wooden chair.

"Sure thing. Have a good night!" I rush out of the room, happy to get some fresh air. The sun is still shining brightly as I climb into my car. I pull my phone out of my pocket and dial Dad's number.

"Hi, hon. How was work?" He answers on the first ring.

"Fine, Dad. I'm just letting you know I'm meeting Rove for dinner." I throw my purse on the passenger seat and watch as a group of junior high kids walk down the sidewalk.

"Where's dinner?" I hear Dad grab a pen out of the metal container sitting on his desk. The kids stare at me as they pass. One girl leans over to her lookalike and whispers. They both glance at me before bursting into giggles.

"Lily's, where I always eat. Do you really have to ask that question every time?" I can hear the scratch of his pen as he scribbles the name down on a piece of paper.

"Just don't stay out too long, hon. You've gotta get home to pack for your trip. Remember, your flight is at nine tomorrow morning which means that we have to be at the airport at eight, which in turn means that you have to be up at seven!" he yells through the receiver, anticipating me hanging up on him.

"You got it. I'll be home by curfew." I start to pull the phone away from my ear when he stops me.

"*Before* curfew!" he exclaims, exasperated.

I glance down at the clock in my car and roll my eyes: 6:50. Good thing nothing in this town is more than ten minutes away. My car pulls out of the parking lot, and I speed down the empty road. By now, humans of Winmore, Virginia, are either snuggled up at home, or they're at Lily's.

I have to park my car in the back. The lights on the "i" on the sign are out, and the letter hangs off the marquis. Kids from school and from the next town over have formed cliques around their cars, occasionally laughing a little too loudly. The front door jingles when I push it open. I scan the room looking for an empty table and notice the back of Rove's head. Beside him is a dark brown mass of curls sticking out in every direction. I weave my way to their booth in the back of the room and slide into the ripped, faded red vinyl seat across from them.

"Hello, how are we this evening?" I ask, forcing a jolly smile onto my face.

The second I sit down, Rove scoots away from the girl. "Jillian, this is my cousin, Cheyenne. She's more like a sister, actually. Cheyenne, this is Jillian."

I lean across the table and shake Jillian's hand. "It's nice to finally meet you! Rove doesn't really talk about his family, but I've heard some about you. That's gotta say something, right?" A blush rushes to her cheeks as she sneaks a suspicious glance at Rove.

I try not to show my relief at Rove's discretion. "Really?" I smile at Rove and then turn back to Jillian. "Well, Rove's a really private person. I only just learned you existed!"

"Cheyenne, can I see you for a moment over here?" Rove mutters.

"I just got here, Rove. I can't have already embarrassed you?" I meet his glare across the table.

"We'll just be one second." Rove smiles at Jillian as he kicks my shin and slips out of the booth, grabbing the back of my collar.

He stops near the front door where I can finally wrench myself free. "What was that for, Rover?" I jerk away from him, straightening my shirt.

"Do you have to be a smart ass? Can you just relax and act normal for five minutes?" he huffs, crossing his arms over his puffed out chest.

"Alright, but five minutes is all you get. After that, I go back to being the weirdo of the family. Got it?" I try to fight back a smile, but it breaks through.

He rolls his eyes, but he's grinning back at me. "If you think you can manage that." I glare at him but say nothing. "Anyway, here." From his messenger bag, he hands me a bottle of warm blood just as my throat begins to pulse. "Here's my thank you offering. Be careful when you drink around Jillian, and be *nice*. I know you have a hard time getting along with people, but this is something you're going have to get used to."

Is he saying what I think he's saying? Surely he knows he can't actually have a long-term relationship with a human. The Council would make sure of it.

"And don't start on me with the whole 'she's human' thing. I know this, and I don't care. So please, just go over there and play nice."

"If you hadn't interrupted me I would have said, 'Sir, yes, sir!'"

"Whatever." He ruffles my hair and lightly pushes me ahead of him. As we walk back to the table I fake a limp, and laugh when he shoves me one more time.

We slide back into the booth where Jillian is looking over the menu. "So what's good? I've never been here before." It's a good thing she doesn't look up because Rove and I exchange a humored glance. The only things we've ever had to eat here are rare steaks and hamburgers. Deuxsang need to consume blood in the evenings, and those are the only options we can stomach, literally.

"Um, I hear the garden salad is really good!" I bite my lip to hide my sarcasm. Rove kicks me under the table, and my smile falters. "But I'd try the chef's special, whatever it is tonight. He always whips up something delicious."

"You're so lucky you get out of school a week before

us," Jillian chimes. "I am so ready for summer!" She sets her menu down on the table and looks first at Rove, then at me. "I'm so glad you could meet us tonight! I've wanted to meet Rove's family for too long, but he's always avoided it."

"And how long exactly has he been avoiding it?" I unscrew my bottle and sip the blood, sending the soothing liquid down my aching throat.

"A year! Rove didn't tell you?" I cover my mouth as coughs wrack my body, blood forcing its way back up my throat. "Are you okay?" She leans forward, concerned, one hand gripping the edge of the table, the other interlocked with Rove's.

"Yeah, I'm fine!" I smile weakly. "Just a little shocked to hear that you've been going out for a whole year, and no one knows anything about it." I turn to Rove, whose eyes are just as wide as mine. What happened to this just being a casual thing? "What's wrong?" I turn to Jillian, who is whiter than paste.

"You—you have red stuff on your teeth." Jillian sputters.

My hand flies up to my mouth, and I wipe the blood away with my napkin. "Oh, sorry. Tomato juice." I shrug my shoulders and steal a quick glance at Rove. "So a year, that's...wow! How'd you meet?"

"Cheyenne," Rove stares at me incredulously, "we go to the same school."

I stop, sarcastic words frozen in my mouth. "Thank you for taking the question so literally, Rove. What I mean is, how did you start dating?" I glare at him and take my turn kicking his shin.

"Well," Jillian glances shyly at Rove, "I was new

last year."

"And I was her guide through the school," Rove smiles. I cannot figure this out—he says it's casual, but they've been together a whole year? He seems like he really likes her, yet...

"I guess, we just kind of hit it off, and we've been dating since." She leans against him, wrapping her arm through his.

"You two look like you were made for each other." A high-pitched, grating voice mauls my ears. Dread seeps into my bones as I turn to face my *dearest* cousin.

"Lilith." I bounce out of my seat and pull her away from the table, spinning her away from Rove and Jillian. "What are you doing here? Weren't you supposed to go back to New York?"

"The representatives asked me to stay behind to make sure Marilyn ascended properly. Didn't Aunt Lisa tell you? I stopped by the house, and Uncle Sam said you were meeting Rove here. I thought we could catch up, since we didn't really get a chance to chat last night." She leers at me condescendingly, hands on hips.

"There's a reason for that, Lilith."

"Oh?"

"No one wants to feel like they're being watched by the Council. Besides, when have you ever wanted to talk to me?"

"Well, aren't you just in a delightful mood, Cheyenne? Anyway, I'm here now. There is no point in my leaving." She drags me back to the table, completely ignoring everything I've just said, her nails pinching against the skin of my forearm. I slide in first, across from Jillian, whose face is a mixture of curiosity and fear.

"Um, hello?" Jillian says.

"Hi, I'm Rove's older cousin Lilith. Who might you be?" Lilith places a scrutinizing eye on Jillian, linking her hands in front of her tight mouth.

"I'm Jillian. Rove didn't tell me I was meeting two cousins today." She looks sideways for help, but Rove is completely horror-struck, his mouth hanging wide open.

"Why are you here, Lilith?" he asks, finally closing his mouth and turning red in the face.

"Cheyenne's here," her screeching voice gnaws away at my brain.

"Cheyenne was *invited.*" He's clearly using all of his will power to control his anger.

"Rove, it's okay." Jillian places her right hand on Rove's arm and squeezes. "The more the merrier!" She's so innocent. Poor girl. She has no idea what she's getting herself into.

Lilith smirks at Jillian with disdain. "So Jill, tell me, how long have you known my cousin?"

"Well we've been dating about a year now."

Lilith's already sharp gaze turns absolutely lethal. I feel her stiffen beside me. Her nostrils flare, and she snatches the bottle out of my hand, taking three large gulps and emptying the bottle before dropping it onto the table.

"As a matter of fact we were just telling Cheyenne about how we first met," Jillian says, pressing closer against Rove.

I'm pretty sure Lilith just crossed over into hysteria.

"I would absolutely *love* to hear this story," she screeches and turns to squint at me. "Wouldn't you, Cheyenne?"

"No, I just heard it." I glare at her and jab my elbow into her ribs.

Lilith crosses her hands in her lap and waits for Rove to tell the story. "She was new. We liked each other, and now we're dating. End of story."

She raises her eyebrows. No one says a thing. All eyes are glued to the checkered blue tablecloth in front of us. Lilith grasps the empty glass, her knuckles blanching as her grip tightens. "Dating. Dating, dating, dating. Isn't that just *great*?"

"Ow!" Jillian drops her head into her hands. She looks like she's trying to hold her skull together. "Oh, my gosh! What's wrong with me?" She closes her eyes, pressing her hands even harder against the sides of her head. "Rove—"

I realize what's happening too late. I shove Lilith out of the booth just as the glass in her hand shatters. Her concentration is broken.

Shards fly across the table. Jillian shrieks, and Rove raises his arm in front of her as glass shoots toward them like bullets. He doesn't flinch as a shard buries itself in his bicep.

Lilith picks herself up off the ground, dusting herself off. "Oh, my goodness; I am terribly sorry! Rove, would you come with me to find a waiter, please?" Lilith's words are apologetic, but her voice and face are anything but. I hope Jillian won't notice the lack of blood that should be spurting from Lilith's hand and her boyfriend's arm.

Rove stares back with wild eyes. "I don't think so, Lilith."

A silence settles over the restaurant after Rove's voice drops. Every head turns to our table to observe the broken glass and steaming heads. Lilith narrows her eyes, and I hear a guttural crack come from Rove. He gasps, gripping the table to hold himself up. His jaw is clenched so tightly that he might just shatter his teeth. Reluctantly, he follows her out the back door.

I slide out of my seat and take Rove's place beside Jillian. "Are you okay?" I ask, picking minute shards of glass out of her curly hair as she lifts her head up. Her expression is totally confused as she fights to keep back her tears.

"I guess so." She shakes herself and more glass falls off of her shoulders. "What just happened to Rove?"

"Oh, I think he was just trying to be intimidating, you know? Cracking his knuckles, blah blah," I try to laugh. If only she knew. I don't know what Lilith cracked in his body, but it didn't sound good.

She laughs nervously, wrapping her arms around herself. Her eyes trail to the door as she strains to hear what they're saying outside.

"Don't worry about Lilith," I lie. "She's the radical of our family."

"What do you think she's saying to him?" Her eyes are glued to the back door.

"Probably nothing. She's always mad about something, and she just kind of yammers on."

"Whatever you say," Jillian says, half laughing.

I slide out of the booth to *actually* get a waiter. A guy from school follows me back to the table with a trashcan and wet rag. His shoes stomp against the floor as if they weigh a thousand pounds.

He stares at the watery mess, his eyes bugging out of his head. "What did you chicks do?" He rubs his free hand through his shaggy hair as he looks me over from head to toe. A shiver runs down my spine when his eyes start to linger.

"Will you please just clean it up?" I say, clenching my hands behind my back. He places the trashcan at the end of the table and swipes the rag across the top, collecting glass shards in the crook of his hand. He pulls another cloth out of his back pocket and begins to mop up the water. As he wipes his hand over the top for one final check for broken glass, his palm gets caught on a shard that pricks the skin, and a drop of blood falls onto the clean table.

"Shoot!" He recoils, gripping his hand to his chest. Unfortunately, that only increases the blood flow; it now streams steadily down his hand and over his forearm. The scent knocks me backward. Fresh *human* blood. I take a step toward him, holding my hand to my mouth.

"Cheyenne, are you okay?" Jillian yanks me out of my trance.

My body jerks as I take a step back, smiling behind my hand. "Yeah, I just don't like blood. I think I'll go check on Rove and Lilith. Be right back." I stride the distance to the door and yank it open. Flames kindle deep within my throat.

I allow myself a moment to calm down once I'm outside, and a moment is all I get. I follow the screaming to find Rove cringing on the ground, gripping his head while Lilith stares at him with ice. I walk up behind her and shove her out of focus.

"What are you thinking, you idiot? A human? I should dispense of you right now and not even give the Council a chance!" She shrieks.

"Lilith, let it go!" I shout.

She turns on me. "I don't want to hear a word from you. You're bringing as much disgrace to this family as he is. You two are absolute failures, and you're going to get yourselves killed."

After a moment, Rove stands up and focuses on Lilith. Her head snaps down to look at her arms and legs. Then she screams, brushing at something on her body. "Rove, stop it! I hate spiders!" But he doesn't stop. When Lilith's shriek pierces the night, I stop him.

"Rove, she's had enough. Come on." His nostrils flare, and I can tell he doesn't want to listen to me. I have to say, the sight of Lilith squirming on the dirty alleyway ground, brushing off imaginary spiders is pretty hilarious, but still cruel. We're not supposed to use our abilities on each other, even if we can.

Finally Rove releases her. She jumps to her feet, still shaking off the spiders. When he can breathe again, he yells, "Go back to New York, Lilith. That's obviously where you belong. Up there with your vampires."

Lilith rolls her eyes and laughs sardonically. "Could you be any more ignorant? You know nothing of my role or my reason for taking it."

"Sure. Whatever you have to tell yourself to get through the day." Rove spits, glaring at our cousin.

"Tell yourself this, you parasite: You are lucky *I* am the one who caught you. End it. Now." After an icy stare that lasts forever, she turns and walks away from us. I don't know what she meant just then, but I believe her. I hope Rove does too. We both stand stunned for several seconds before returning to the restaurant.

Jillian is on edge as we slide back into the booth with

her. Rove puts her at ease with a shrug. "So what do you say we actually get some dinner?" He raises his hand and the same boy who cleaned our table walks over, hesitation in his eyes.

"What can I get ya?" he asks, pulling out his notepad but keeping his eyes on us.

"I'll have the chef salad," Jillian says and hands the boy her damp menu.

He turns to me. "A hamburger steak, rare please. And yes, that's all."

"And I'll have the same," Rove says, rubbing his throat.

"So what was your cousin's problem?" Jillian asks, lacing her fingers through Rove's after the waiter walks away.

"Oh, don't worry about her. Lilith is just—I don't quite know the word to describe her," I sigh.

"I can think of a few," Rove grumbles. "Don't worry about her, Jill. You don't have to deal with her anymore."

"What did you guys say to her to get her to leave?"

"She left of her own accord. We think she might be mental, but don't say anything to our family. They'll go ballistic," I wink at her and make her laugh.

Just when I think the night can't get any more exciting, the bell on the door rings announcing two new customers: one I've known since fourth grade, the other a newly familiar face. Standing there together I see the cute guy from the pet store and the guy that's been harassing me for years, Erik. I slump down in my seat and look out the window, turning my back to the rest of the restaurant.

"Cheyenne, what are you doing?" Rove asks, raising his eyebrows at me, a glimmer of amusement on his face.

"Nothing, just enjoying the view."

"Of the parking lot?"

I squint out the window again, pretending to notice all the cars. Why does he have to be a smart ass all the time? "I thought I saw someone by my car. I was making sure they weren't breaking in."

"Right." Rove rolls his eyes and turns to Jillian.

From the reflection on the glass, I keep my eyes on Erik and watch him find a table as far away from us as possible. Eli doesn't look like the same person from the pet store. He looks angry now, frustrated. I know Erik's spotted me. I can feel his glare on my back, but I won't do anything if he doesn't. Rove keeps looking at me curiously and follows my gaze to Erik's table. "Who's that?" he asks.

"Well, that's…uh."

"Wait a second." I can see recognition in Rove's eyes as he remembers what I've told him about Erik. "It's him, isn't it?" His fists clench on top of the table. He starts to stand up, but I grab his arm and pull him back down.

"Don't. I don't want to start anything here." Rove is not even looking at me. He's glaring at an ignorant Erik.

"But, Cheyenne, when am I going to get the chance to confront him again? He needs someone to teach him a lesson. He can't bother my baby cousin and get away with it."

"Okay, well that someone is not you. He's always the one who starts something, and I'm not going to change that now. Just let it go. I can handle it myself."

"But..."

"Let. It. Go." I narrow my eyes at him and kick his shin yet again.

For the next few minutes, Rove, Jillian, and I make

forced small talk. I learn about her family and about her summer plans, what colleges she's looking at. Before she has the chance to ask me the same, our waiter brings out our food. Rove and I rip into our nearly bloody burgers while Jillian picks daintily at her salad. I really wish Lilith hadn't finished the rest of my bottle now.

I clear my plate, and excuse myself to go to the bathroom. As I leave the booth, I realize that Erik's table is right next to the bathrooms. I stop, trying to decide if I have to pee that badly, but my bladder feels like it's going to explode. I guess that's my answer. Rove watches me move silently across the restaurant and try to slip into the bathroom unnoticed, but Erik's not at his table.

Eli looks up as I pass their table and calls after me, "Hey, Cheyenne, remember me from the pet store?" I ignore him and keep walking. When I turn the corner, I slam into the very person I was trying to avoid.

"Lane? I thought I told you to stay out of my way this summer." Erik's deep, threatening voice breaks the noise of the crowd. My heart sinks to my toes as he corners me by the door.

"I was here first, Erik." I'm as close to the wall as I can get, and he's way too close to me. His piercing eyes meet mine without a hint of hesitation.

"I don't care if you were here first. I want you out. You're hogging my oxygen and tainting the view."

"What's your problem?" Eli jumps up from his seat and shoves Erik's shoulder. "Why are you bothering, Cheyenne?"

Erik turns his blazing glare away from me to Eli. "How do you know her?"

"None of *your* business, and you didn't answer my question." Eli takes a threatening step toward Erik.

"Well, that's none of your business, brother." I look up sharply at Eli who makes a face at the familial term.

"Erik, get away from me. I just need to go to the bathroom." I shove him away and dash into the bathroom, thinking he won't follow me. But, of course, I'm wrong. A moment later, I hear the door swing open and the lock click. "Erik, get out of the girls' bathroom." I hear someone pounding on the other side of the door, but Erik ignores him.

"How do you know my brother?" He takes a step toward where I'm resting against the cold, tile wall.

I feel blood rising in my throat as he gets closer. "I don't. He just came to my register today. Stay away from me." His glare narrows. In a matter of seconds, he is right in front of me, his arms locking me in a cage. "Get off of me," I growl. His body odor mixes with his awful breath to create a putrid stench that fills my nose.

"You stay the hell away from my family! Do you understand me?" He shakes my shoulders, making my head hit the wall. I want to fight back. My hands ball into fists beside me.

"Erik, open the door!" Eli yells. Erik rolls his eyes, grimacing down at me.

"Answer me! Do you understand? You stay the hell away from my brother, you slut."

I try to stop myself, but it's too late. I slam my fists into his gut and move out of the way just before he doubles over, his nose slamming into one of the sinks sending spurts of blood everywhere.

"Bitch!" he shrieks, wiping blood away from his nose. He grabs a fistful of my hair into his hand and pulls me to the floor.

"Let go!" I stomp my heel into his shin and wriggle in his iron grip. He gasps but doesn't release me. This time I kick his kneecap, and he falls to the ground beside me, shoving me onto my back.

Out of the corner of my eye, I see the bathroom door fly open, and Eli and Rove leap into the room grabbing Erik. Rove slams a punch into Erik's jaw just before Eli throws him out of the bathroom. Rove helps me to my feet, but before my senses come back, Erik lunges at me and strikes my cheek barely scratching my thick, Deux-sang skin. When Erik raises his hand for a punch, Eli grabs his wrist and pushes him away.

The manager rushes from the kitchen, shouting, "Break it up, break it up!" He steps between the two of us, turning his head left and right. Erik and I glare at each other in silence, neither one of us moving. He sneers at me with the smug confidence of a declared victor. I step around the manager, narrowing my eyes as I jerk my arm back and slam my right fist against his eye and my other into his stomach.

"Stay away from me," I whisper as he falls, groaning, to his knees. *If my dad finds out what I did, I'm dead.*

Rove and I walk back to our table, past the onlookers, past Eli, past the shell-shocked manager.

"I think I'm going to head out. I have to pack for tomorrow," I say, giving a tired smile to Jillian. "It was nice to meet you, Jillian. I hope you have a nice summer." I can't read her face—a jumbled mess of fear, sympathy, and confusion. I walk up to Rove standing beside the front door. "I'll see you when you come visit New Orleans in a few weeks, Rover. Don't go on any adventures without me." I try my best to avoid looking at the gaping crowd.

The bell jingles when I push the door open, my eyes glued to the ground, my keys ready in my right hand. As I reach my car, someone grabs my shoulder from behind. I swing my arm back, ready to take off a head.

I hear a whoosh of air as the person dodges backward out of my reach, which is strange. Deuxsang reflexes, even mine, are way faster than any human's, yet there's Eli standing right in front of me with his head on and everything.

"Sorry, I thought you were Erik." I turn away from Eli and unlock my car.

"It's understandable. Heck of a swing you've got there," he says as he moves closer to stand beside me.

"What do you want?" I ask, opening the door and looking up at him. His forest green eyes stare at me, a single eyebrow raised. A sense of unease washes over me, like when I know Erik's planning to do something to me.

"I just wanted to apologize for my brother's behavior. I didn't realize."

"Seriously? I don't want empty apologies." I whisper through gritted teeth and step up into my Jeep.

"Hey, give me a break. I don't live here, alright. I'm just trying to do the right thing." He looks offended, but I don't buy it. "Besides, it looks like you can take care of yourself."

I ignore him, still angry at myself for losing control. "You have no right to apologize for him." I rub a hand across my aching head. It's so annoying. I can't bleed; I don't have to breathe, and yet I can still get a headache.

"I'm sorry, Cheyenne, I don't know what else to say."

"Then don't say anything. Why do you care anyway?" I rev the engine, but Eli steps around the open door.

He dips his head to my level, holding on to the top of the car. "I don't know what all Erik has done to you, but I'm sorry. Trust me, I'll deal with him when we get home."

What does this guy want from me? "And I should trust you because?" I ask, catching my breath as he leans closer.

"Because I'm not like my brother," he whispers.

"Yeah? Prove it. Leave me alone." I reach around him, close my door, and grab the steering wheel to steady my hands.

Eli leans through my open window and says, "I wish I could." I hate the fact that he looks genuine. He's related to Erik, so that's not possible.

I slam my foot on the gas, forcing him to jerk back. Then I'm out of the parking lot and on the road trying to ignore my tight, burning throat.

Three

"Cheyenne, wake up." Dad's voice cracks through my thick wall of sleep. "Cheyenne, it's seven fifteen. We have to leave in fifteen minutes."

"What are you talking about?" I groan, pulling the thin comforter over my head, rolling away from his voice.

"We have to be at the airport in forty-five minutes! If you don't get yourself out of bed, I'll drag you to the airport in your pajamas." He rips my yellow comforter off me and pulls me to a seated position. I narrow my sleep-filled eyes at him. "Get. Up." All the lights are on in my room, the blinds are pulled back, and music blasts from my speakers—anything and everything to wake me up. "Let's go!"

The airport is thirty miles away in the next town over. Dad's old, comforting jazz plays quietly through the scratchy radio. He's loved it ever since I can remember. I'd come home from school with the house rocking to the sound of Louis Armstrong. I rest my head against the back window, watching the world slip behind us, the hills of Virginia a blur.

Goodbye Winmore. No more school for the next three months. No more Erik. No more parents or ridiculous family meetings.

"Cheyenne!" My dad yells.

"What?" I wince as my head bangs against the window,

and I stare at the back of my dad's head.

"I asked you if you are excited about your trip?" He sighs, a wrinkle forming between his eyebrows as he glances at me in the rearview mirror.

"Yes, sir." I rub my hand over my head and turn my eyes back out the window.

"Well, be sure to take lots of pictures. Call us as often as you can and *think* while you're there. Don't make any stupid mistakes," he says, massaging the back of his neck.

"Isn't this the speech you're supposed to give at the airport as you see me to my gate?" I ask. I don't know why he's nervous. He's not the one who has to fly. I'm seventeen, and I've never flown before. I'd prefer not flying today, but my parents don't want to drive ten hours.

"Well, it won't hurt you to hear it twice," he grumbles.

Mom smiles beside him and grabs his free hand. "Don't worry about her, Sam. Thomas and Kara will take good care of her."

I've always wondered what kinds of relationships other kids at my school have with their parents. I understand that all families are stressful and have their own problems, but I feel like my family kind of tops the cake. Our people have this huge secret hanging over our heads, a lethal secret, and until we're adults, no one trusts us to keep it.

I think it's worse for me. My parents are afraid that since my Ascension was particularly horrible that I now harbor this hatred for our people and the vampires, and they're not totally wrong. I can't imagine how wonderful it would be to not live under the microscope of the Council, to not have to see them for my cousins Ascensions. But I don't hate my people. It's not the entire Deuxsang race's fault what happened to me. There's just one Deuxsang that I can't trust anymore—my dad.

I used to be such a daddy's girl. My mom and I never got along because she always wanted me to be different—to be interested in dresses and pigtails and pink. My dad didn't care as long as I did what I was supposed to. I leaned toward him and away from my mom. But then I turned thirteen and watched helplessly as four vampires bit me while my dad waited in the living room. He should've stopped them. He should've saved me, and he didn't. I can't forgive him. The same goes for my mom. They could've at least tried.

They know I don't trust them, and I can't really tell if they care or not. I follow the rules. I keep my curfew. I'm a good Deuxsang daughter, but there's nothing between us now. I can't hold more than a five-minute conversation with either of them without it ending in some sort of argument over something ridiculous. All conversations about my Ascension are put to a halt before they even begin. It's not even an option.

Plus, they treat me differently now. They act like they have to be careful about what they say, like I'm afraid of who I am. I'm not afraid of being a Deuxsang. I'm still proud of it, but I wish being who I am wasn't such a struggle.

Rove, who's only a few months older than me, already knows that he's an illusionist and has already gotten pretty good at controlling it. He flits everywhere. There's no explanation for why I haven't developed as I should have, so we just don't talk about it. My dad teaches me the history and culture of our people as if I am a completely normal Deuxsang, and it kills me because I want to know. I want to understand why I'm different and why I can't do everything that my family can.

And I can't tell whether to be excited about this trip. Yes, it's a chance to get out of the house and away from my parents, but I'm just stepping into Kara and Thomas's lion den. Is that going be any better? Especially now that she's pregnant? They're basically younger copies of my parents. Who knows—maybe they haven't been wound so tightly just yet? Kara's already wound pretty tightly, just in a different way.

But it doesn't really matter. This summer is going to be great with or without my family. I'm going to be in a new city. I'll get to see Rove. It will be great.

They've remodeled the airport since the last time we were here, which was two years ago when Mom's parents moved to Winmore. Now the building is bleached white. The floors look clean enough to eat off, not that I want to try it. All of the attendants at the check-in desks have fake smiles and grande coffees within reach.

Dad checks all three of my bags while Mom and I stand back staring at TV monitors set up around the lobby showing arrival and departure times and gates. I locate my 9:00 a.m. flight, which departs from Gate C, the smallest and final gate in the airport.

There are only three people going through security, and this is thankfully as far as Mom and Dad can go. I drop my backpack on the ground as Mom pulls me in for a hug. "Now, you be a good help to Kara. Help her with her pregnancy. Don't be a nuisance. And take care of yourself, too. Don't make stupid mistakes, and *never, ever* go out into the city by yourself. Do you hear me, young lady? And if I hear that you've been walking down Bourbon Street... " Her eyes squint as she pinches my cheeks together in her hand.

I try to say "yes, ma'am" but that's not exactly how it comes out through my squished mouth. She reluctantly releases me, and Dad envelops me in one of his famous bear hugs. I hug him stiffly, patting his back as he kisses my cheek.

"I'll call you guys when I get to the house." I pick my backpack up off the floor and secure both straps on my shoulders.

"Thomas is picking you up, right?" Mom asks, a frantic note in her voice.

"Yep, he'll be there. Bye." I walk into the security line, slide my flip-flops off, and push them and my backpack down the conveyor belt. The guard smiles kindly at me as he motions me through the body scanner.

"You have a nice day, little lady." I nod and smile at him. Stepping back into my flip-flops, I grab my backpack and walk toward the end of the airport. I know my parents are waving, but I can't force myself to turn around. I'm too distracted—New Orleans, here I come.

...

The airplane attendant seats me in an aisle seat three rows from the front beside a man with a bad comb-over, behind a mother of two, and in front of a man who looks on the verge of a heart attack.

The attendant smiles at me with forced charm, instructs me to stuff my backpack beneath the seat in front of me, then walks away to help a man with his carry on. The plane seems too small for such a long trip. The door isn't even closed, but I can already feel my throat constricting. I snatch the Sky Mall Magazine out of the pocket in an attempt to distract myself while the rest of the passengers board. Two guys around my age walk past me sparing only a glance in my direction before moving to the back of the plane. No surprise there.

"Ladies and Gentlemen, welcome to Flight 1280 to New Orleans. Allow me to make this a comfortable experience for you; please look to me for your safety instructions." I zone out during her instruction session and let my eyes wander over every inch of the plane. "We will arrive in New Orleans in three hours. Please enjoy your flight."

I glance past the comb-over out the window and grip my armrests as the plane shifts into motion. The engine whirs beneath me and my head begins to pound. I close my eyes and suck in a deep breath of oxygen to open up my throat. Suddenly, the front wheels lift off the runway, and we are in the air, heading down toward the bayou.

...

I'm so grateful to be off the plane that I nearly fall to the ground at the gate entrance, but I have some restraint. I walk through the empty gate, smelling of sweaty workers and old paint. I navigate my way through the huge airport, amazed by how clean it is and how friendly all the workers are. Riding down the escalator, I catch sight of Thomas and Kara. My sister, I can tell, is jumping out of her skin and literally jumping in the air. Thomas places his hands on her shoulders to keep her still.

Kara barely lets me get off the escalator before throwing her arms around me. "I'm so glad to see you! Did you have a nice flight?" she asks, squeezing me against her protruding stomach. Thomas stands protectively behind us until Kara releases me and then leads the way to the baggage claim area.

"My flight was smooth. I made it alive. Let's just say I'm not ready to fly again any time soon."

"Well, that's nothing to worry about right now. I'm just glad you got here safe and sound." Kara wraps her arm around my shoulder, partly because she doesn't want to lose me in the pressing crowd. "I think you'll like the house; it's magnificent—it's one of those old Victorian homes with a wraparound porch and creaky floors. Oh, it's just perfect! The moving truck arrives tomorrow, so the house is kind of empty. But that just means that you can help me design the baby's room, and you can pick out the colors for the guest room, which is where you'll be staying. Oh, this is going to be so much fun!" she squeals.

"Wait, how big is your house?" This sounds a little extravagant for a young, expecting couple on a professors' salaries.

"It took us forever to find this place, but we had a little help. Thomas's family left him everything when they died. They owned a sugar cane plantation down here, and their savings were..." She looks gratefully to her husband, but Thomas is avoiding her sympathetic glances. I can see the bitterness in his face.

"You still didn't answer my question. How big is it?"

"You'll just have to wait and see!"

I'm surprised. Normally, she'd be busting a gut to tell me every last detail of her dream home.

"Well, maybe *I* should marry old Southern money," I joke. She rolls her eyes as we approach the baggage claim. I spot my three matching green suitcases, accented by the neon orange ribbons that Mom triple knotted on the handles, and yank them off the conveyor belt with Thomas's help.

The airport is filled to capacity as Kara and I elbow people to keep Thomas in sight. Faces are a blur until we are literally pushed through the sliding doors onto the louder and even busier sidewalk. "Get used to it, Cheyenne. Welcome to New Orleans," Thomas says looking back at me.

"I'll adapt." I smile, rolling my eyes at Kara who stands unruffled with her hands perched protectively over her stomach.

"Thomas, why don't you find a cab for us," she suggests, grabbing one of my bags from him. He sets my other bag down, his jaw set. Within ten seconds, he's hailed one. I guess even drivers can tell he means business.

"Thank you," Kara sings, grabbing my bags and walking to the door Thomas is holding open for us. He throws the bags effortlessly into the trunk, a permanent frown etched on his face.

The driver stares warily at us as we climb into the cab, Thomas in the front. A proud smirk rests on Kara's lips as we buckle our seat belts and Thomas gives the driver their address.

It takes ten minutes to get out of the airport, even

with taxi drivers honking and swearing in French at other drivers. The traffic isn't much better once we get into the city either. Taxi drivers must just honk their horns for the fun of it.

I roll down my window and stare out into the sea of tourists, watching as they navigate easily down the wide sidewalks, exchanging pleasant smiles with passersby entering and exiting famous restaurants and unique boutiques that stand next to each other in tall, colorful buildings lined with Spanish iron rails. Carriage drivers lining a main road shout out prices for rides around the French Quarter, not taking it personally when people brush by them with no notice. Young men and women play jazz on their guitars and saxophones while keeping a close watch on their upturned hats and opened instrument cases lying in front of them, overflowing with coins and bills. Our taxi only stops for a minute before the traffic light turns green, and the rest of the sounds of New Orleans are drowned out by the cacophony of honking horns.

"So," Thomas turns around in his seat to see my awed face, "what do you think of the big city?"

"It's amazing! So much better than Winmore" I sigh.

"You said it, sister!" Kara laughs, glancing out the window as the cab pulls to a stop. I narrow my eyes at her forced sisterly affection. I can tell I'm going to have a whole summer of this.

We pull up to a house, and Thomas pulls out some bills, slaps them into the driver's palm, and swings the door open, helping Kara and me out. We each grab a bag out of the trunk.

"Jeez, Cheyenne, how much did you pack? You don't

own this many clothes!" Kara says, brushing her blonde hair out of her eyes.

"Hey, that one's just books. Be careful with it!"

The cab speeds away after Thomas slams the trunk closed, and we stop on the sidewalk to stare up at their gargantuan home. Two stories loom over me as my eyes run over the pale yellow stucco, accented with pristine white shutters. The green yard is filled with towering oaks and blooming magnolias, their thick leaves shading the wrap-around porch, home to three, white rocking chairs and a wooden swing. I glance at my beaming sister and smile. It's ridiculous, but it's perfect for her.

I follow them up the porch steps into the grand foyer. A magnificent, dark oak staircase with an ornately carved banister winds its way up to the second floor. The entrance is empty except for a few scattered boxes. The deep maroon walls fade into crimson as I walk into the sitting room. A white mantel surrounds a wide, sooty fireplace on the far wall. The living room leads into the white dining room, which holds a long, dark wooden table that runs from one end of the room to the other. *How many kids are they planning to have?* An empty sideboard rests against the wall.

Kara puts her hands on my shoulders and leads me quickly through Thomas's empty study before pushing me up the stairs. I reach the top of the stairs and follow her down the hallway. At the second door on the left, she turns sharply as I walk into the room with my bags and sigh at the sight of the hideous yellow wallpaper sprinkled with pink gladiolas covering the walls.

"Thank you, Kara," I call sarcastically, grimacing as

my sister giggles in the doorway.

"I thought you would appreciate the paper," she smiles, a little sarcastically. Thomas appears behind Kara, placing his hand protectively on her shoulder. He grimaces at the tragedy that is my rental room.

"It's only for three months," I mutter, turning to inspect my bed, thinking I can manage for three months. So much for escaping from home. The bare mattress and boxed springs stand taller than my waist. The wide floorboards creak as I walk around the side of the bed and throw myself onto the mattress.

"Why don't you get yourself settled? Call us if you need anything." Kara closes the door behind them, leaving me alone in my new room. I look around, imagining how to cover up the wallpaper so that I will barely have to look at it.

Kara and Thomas have moved down the hall, but they're not far enough away that I can't hear them. "When are you going to talk to her?" I can hear her seething voice.

"I will, but not today. Being down here will be good for her. She can learn to be successful in our world. Your family is very respectable, but they have done a horrible job of raising Cheyenne, especially after her Ascension. Let me handle this." The chilling tone of Thomas's voice sends a shiver down my back. No wonder Dad's worried about him taking over as alpha. He's definitely got the attitude.

"I know. I just want everything to be out in the open, so that we can focus on *our* family." *Ouch, Kara. Thanks.*

"I'm a competent man. I can handle two tasks at once." A door opens and slams shut. Thomas mutters something then storms down the stairs.

I collapse onto my bed, rolling over their argument in my head. I know Kara and I aren't the best of friends, but does she really actually want me here? Was this her idea, or Thomas's? And what do they need to tell me? What's so important?

I pull myself to my feet and step through the double doors leading onto the balcony, staring out into a huge courtyard filled with rosebushes, fountains, a small table and chairs, and a path leading into thick woods. A rickety, white rocking chair sits in the corner of the balcony beside a small, metal table. The iron railing seems to be a motif of New Orleans.

The next house over must be a five-minute walk, leaving plenty of space between us. That house through the trees appears to be no less magnificent than this one, although I bet it will lack the charm that Kara will bring to her home. A hint of color catches my eye as I turn to look at the monstrous oak tree webbed with Spanish moss leaning over the top of the balcony. Stray strands of gold and purple beads hang in the top branches, carelessly forgotten by the previous owners. A warm breeze rustles my hair, and I smile at the sound of the magnolia leaves brushing together. *Welcome home, Cheyenne.*

Four

It's done. I'm finally finished unpacking. I didn't bring enough posters or pictures to cover up the vomit-inducing wallpaper, but I still have time for that. My armoire is filled with my clothing. The desk stores the few pieces of makeup and jewelry that I own, along with my laptop and everything electronic. My favorite part, the bookshelf built into the left wall, is only a fraction full of books. I wonder how hard it would be to convince my mom to let me build this bookshelf at home. Probably impossible. But for now, this makes me happy. I've stapled icicle lights to the ceiling so that now I can stare up at the stars without going outside.

The moment I sit down to take a breath, my phone in my back pocket starts ringing. "Hey, Dad."

"Don't sound so excited. We never heard from you yesterday. How was your flight?"

"Fine. I'm sorry I never called, but everything was just a blur yesterday. How are you?"

"Not too bad. Your mother's a nervous wreck, but with you there safe and sound, maybe she'll calm down. What did you do today? I want the full report."

I collapse into the pale green cushions of my reading chair and sigh. "We've been unpacking all day. I'm sure Kara and Thomas still need help downstairs, so I'll probably need to hang up soon."

"Well, that sounds like fun. How's the house?"

"Oh, gorgeous, naturally. Nothing but the best for your oldest daughter, right?" I didn't really mean it sarcastically, but it kind of came out that way.

"Hey, watch your tone, or you'll find yourself on a plane home."

"Sorry." I press the phone tightly against my ear when the other line settles into silence. I hear muffled murmurs in the background but no coherent words. They have gotten good at masking their voices. "Dad?"

"I'm here. Do you want to talk to your mother?" I can hear her heels clicking as she walks across the floor to take the phone from Dad.

"Actually Thomas just called me, so I better go see what he needs. Just tell Mom I'll talk to her tomorrow."

"Okay, have a good day."

"Bye." I end the call and slouch into my chair, a huge smile on my face.

"Are you done unpacking?" Kara asks from the doorway, leaning against the white frame in her dirty, old overalls.

"Yep, all done."

She sighs and looks around the room. "Nicely done. I wouldn't mind living in here."

Thomas suddenly appears behind her, wrapping his arms around her stomach. "Now you wouldn't want to go and do that," he whispers closely to her ear. Kara giggles, her eyes squinting mischievously.

"Okay, if you two are gonna start doing…whatever… you need to get to your own room."

"If you say so," Thomas shrugs and pulls Kara into

the hallway and out of view, even though I can still hear her giggling all down the hallway. I hope these walls are soundproof.

I glance at the clock beside my chair. It's too late to start unpacking the baby's room. It can wait until tomorrow. I spring out of the chair and carefully open the towering armoire and grab my fuzzy pajama shorts and an old tank top. Ready to settle in for bed, I grab one of my books and do just that. My eyelids start to fall when I reach the next chapter, and I'm no longer able to focus on the words. I close the book for the night, setting it on the corner of my vanity. I drain the last few drops of blood left in my cup and sit it beside my book. My eyes weigh a ton by the time I finally lie flat on my back, and the moment my head hits the pillow, I'm out like a light.

...

When my eyes open the next morning, the room is dark. A ball of panic forms in my chest. Then I remember the curtains surrounding my bed. My body relaxes into the mattress, and my fists release the blanket. Suddenly, the curtains swing open, and Kara is standing at the end of the bed with an annoyingly bright smile on her face.

"Wake up, sleepy head! We are going to finish unpacking the house. Plus, we'll have guests coming over. They have a daughter around your age, so maybe you'll make a friend." She pulls the curtains all the way around until they stop against the headboard.

"What time is it?" I rub my hand across my eyes and blink.

"It's 10:00. You have no idea how hard it's been for me to let you sleep in. Now come on." She rips the blanket off me and opens the doors to the balcony. A melody of birds' chirps floats into the room accompanied by the brush of the leaves against the roof and the whirring of car engines.

"Yeah, yeah. I'm up, I'm up." I stiffly swing my legs over the bed and let my shoulders hunch as I stretch down to my toes, pulling the aches from the new mattress out of my back. "I still have to get ready, Kara." She sighs impatiently and walks out of the room, but I can still hear her breathing behind the door. "Go."

First I need a nice, warm shower. As the water heats up, I brush the putrid smell out of my mouth with mint toothpaste. I turn the showerhead to the strongest level and let it beat the knots out of my back and neck. My body begins to relax, muscles loosening, kinks uncoiling. I faintly hear Kara calling my name, but I choose to ignore her. She can wait another twenty minutes. I make sure the shampoo is thoroughly rinsed out of my hair before turning off the water and stepping onto the cool tile of the bathroom. A shiver runs up my back, and I quickly wrap a freshly washed towel around my clean body. I run the blow dryer over my hair until only the tips and underside are still wet. I pull on a pair of old jeans and an overly worn, incredibly soft t-shirt that I have loved for years.

"Cheyenne, honestly, this is getting ridiculous," Kara says from outside my door.

"Come in, if you must." The door swings open immediately, and Kara falls into my chair.

"Goodness, you take forever!"

"Just calm down. It's not like we have anywhere to be."

"No, but I'd like the house to be in order before the Lacroixs come over this afternoon. We have to make a good impression," she mumbles, stomping out of the room and down the stairs.

Why are they so important, I wonder? I pull the door closed and trail after her. Thomas is in the dining room, a small glass of blood in his hand and a newspaper on the counter.

"Good morning! Sleep well?" Thomas asks.

"Why are you drinking blood in the *morning*?"

He exchanges a furtive glance with Kara, who surprisingly shrugs without a word. "Why not start off the day with a dose of life? Here, enjoy."

As far as I knew, no Deuxsang drinks blood before sunset. I take the small, clear glass filled halfway with cool, red liquid. I lift it to my nose, take a hesitant sniff, and place it to my lips. Normally the smell of cow's blood is appetizing, but this is different. Maybe it's because my body is programmed for human nutrition in the morning. The blood slides onto my tongue, and it tastes so *different*. Could it be pig's blood? It's definitely not the same blood I drank in Winmore. "Are you sure about this?" I grimace. "It's sorta..."

Thomas cuts me off, "You'll get used to it." I wrinkle my nose and nod my head, not fully convinced.

"So we're having company?" I ask, slightly annoyed that I hadn't been told earlier.

"Yes!" Kara chimes in, elated. She can't wait to be a hostess. "The Lacroixs are very active and prominent within the New Orleans Deuxsang social scene. It's a big deal that they've agreed to call on us, so I need you looking and acting your best. This could really help put us on the ladder."

I roll my eyes. "Why do I have to be there? I don't need to be on any ladder."

"Because," Kara snaps, "they are bringing their daughter, who is a year older than you."

"Kara and I think this'll be good for you," Thomas interjects. "The Council put you in human schools, and your parents never introduced you to other Deuxsang. We want you to know someone before you start school here next year."

I'm confused. "Isn't that what the point of college is?"

"Yes, but she'll already be at Clandestine when you get down here, so I'm sure it'll be nice to know someone. You could just say thank you." He waits for me to respond, and when I don't, his jaw tightens.

"Alright, enough chit chat." Kara hands me a cloth and wood polish, and we set to cleaning the whole house.

It takes forever, but finally Kara looks at her watch and realizes the guests should be arriving. She has a mini panic attack and shoos me to my room to get dressed. I roll my eyes as I walk to my room, selecting a dress from a wad of clothes on the floor just in time to hear the doorbell.

Kara is showing the family into the living room as I slide down the banister, knowing it will irritate her. She turns around stiffly and smirks at me over her shoulder. I straighten a photograph of my grandparents hanging on the wall before sitting down with everyone. Thomas and Kara share the love seat, hands locked together, while the other family sits on the couch. The daughter is sandwiched awkwardly between her parents. She looks like she's as happy about this as I am. Her untamed red hair and oversized band tee stand out against her blond parents' ironed collars. She sits with her knees pushed together and her hands crossed in her lap.

Thomas stands and gestures to me as I walk across the room. "Cheyenne, I'd like you to meet the Lacroix family. This is Mrs. Gail and Mr. Griffin Lacroix and their daughter, Ginger." *Ginger*? Some parents are just plain cruel.

Judging by her wince, Ginger seems to think so too. "Actually, I go by Anne—that's my middle name." I smile at her.

"I think the name your parents gave you is lovely." Kara's the queen of backhanded compliments.

"Mr. and Mrs. Lacroix, thank you so much for coming to our home today. I must apologize. We've just moved in and haven't had time to become fully settled in our new home," Thomas says.

"It's a lovely home, Mr. Burns. I think Griffin and I actually looked at this house when we were first married. I'm sure you two will add your own charm to it." Mrs. Lacroix smiles a full, white smile. Anne rolls her eyes.

"Mr. Lacroix, I've heard so much about the advocate work you've done for our people with the Council. It's absolutely inspiring." Thomas is making a fool out of himself, and it's making me sick.

"Oh, thank you, son. That's kind of you to say. Are you well versed in the advocacy issues?" Mr. Lacroix sits forward in his seat, his interest piqued by Thomas's brown-nosing.

Kara jumps in before I get caught listening to a boring conversation. "Cheyenne, why don't you take Ginger up to your room?" she suggests nonchalantly. I smile and nod, then take bottles of blood from the hostess tray on the coffee table, check to see that Anne is following me, and bound up the stairs two at a time. I switch on the overhead light in my room and close the curtains. Anne trails in slowly behind me.

We stand in awkward silence for a moment, neither of us sure what we're supposed to do. Eventually I offer her a bottle, and she takes it before perusing my library.

"I love your books," she says quietly.

"Thanks. I wasn't really able to bring all of them on the plane."

She snorts and nods, seeming to understand my dilemma. "So how many play dates have you been forced into?" she asks, not looking up from a book now open in her hands.

"Um, none actually. This is kind of new for me." I take a sip of blood and sit cross-legged on the bed, comforted by Anne's bluntness.

"Well, you're lucky. I've lost count, but they're always horrible. Have you noticed how snobby our people can be?"

"I actually don't know any Deuxsang outside my family."

Anne turns sharply to stare at me. Clearly, I'm an anomaly in even more ways than I already knew. The shock passes quickly though, and she smiles. "Well, now you know me," she says. "So, what are you?"

"Excuse me?" I ask, thoroughly confused.

"You know, what's your ability—dream walker, compeller, illusionist, yada, yada, yada?" She slouches in the lounge chair across from me, observing me with her cool, green eyes.

"I haven't really...I don't know. I haven't really been able to tap into it yet." The familiar blanket of shame washes over me even though Anne smiles, and not in a mocking way.

"Whatever, it's no big deal. How about flitting?"

"I haven't been able to do that yet either." I blush, expecting judgment.

"You'll get it. I mean you have to sometime, right?"

I don't want to share my doubts with this girl I just met, so I change the subject. "So who's the band?" I nod at her shirt.

"Oh, it's my boyfriend's jazz band. Totally original for New Orleans, right?" She laughs and glances down.

"Wow, I've never heard of a Deuxsang band before."

"Yeah, wouldn't that be something?"

I start to laugh but stop myself. Then I realize what she's saying. "He's human?" I mouth, aware of the open door. Even though we're on the second floor, I've learned how words can travel in this house. She nods her head nervously, biting the edge of her lip. Anne's wild hair falls into her eyes, and she brushes it away with an exasperated hand swipe. I say the only thing I can think of. "My cousin's in the same situation."

"Has he told your family yet?" she asks, her green eyes growing wider.

"Um, no. Well, he hasn't *told* anybody per se, but one of my cousins happened to find out before I left, and let's just say she didn't take it well."

"Yeah, no one knows about us yet, so I'd appreciate..."

I smile and mock zipping my mouth closed.

"Thanks."

Two hours later, Anne and I are still talking, something I haven't ever done with anyone but Rove. We've discussed everything from her boyfriend to books to controlling parents.

"Isn't my name just awful? I don't know what my parents were thinking!"

"Maybe they didn't see the irony?" I suggest, taking a sip from my second bottle of blood.

"Maybe, but it's the worst type of irony possible. I guess that's the story of my life. I'd prefer dramatic irony. You know, like in *Romeo and Juliet*," Anne intones the title with a flourish of her arms.

"That's my favorite!" I pull my worn copy of the play out of my purse.

Anne grabs it and flips through the pages. "This is so great. Did you know that a local acting company's actually performing *Romeo and Juliet* on the square tonight? Want to go?" She glances down at her watch and looks back up at me.

"I'd love to! What time?"

"In about an hour."

"Let me just tell my sister." I bounce out of the room and down the stairs. Kara, Thomas, and the Lacroixs are still chatting quietly in the living room. Kara looks up when I walk in.

"Hey, Cheyenne, where's Ginger?"

"She's upstairs. I just wanted to let you know that we're heading out. She invited me to go see a production of *Romeo and Juliet*."

"How about you ask if you can go first, Cheyenne?" Thomas levels his gaze with mine before Kara can speak. I glance between them, hesitating before I answer.

Biting back the curse in my mind, I respond, "May I please go see *Romeo and Juliet* with Anne?"

"That's fine. Have fun." Kara tells me, ignoring Thomas, who seems less fine with it.

"Great. I'm just going to go change." I race out of the room and leap up the stairs.

"Cheyenne, where is it?" Thomas calls.

From the top of the stairs I yell back, "Ask Anne!"

I rip a t-shirt out of the armoire and slip on my oldest pair of jeans. I untwist my braid and let my hair fall around my shoulders. My crossbody lands on my shoulder as my foot hits the foyer floor. Anne is waiting at the door, texting. Thomas walks out of the sitting room and hands me some cash.

"This is for emergencies only. Got your phone?"

"Yep," I pat my back pocket and smile as I snatch the money out of his palm and stuff it into my bag. "Thanks, Thomas. I'll see you later."

I grab Anne's arm, shocking her out of a dazed state, and drag her out the open door. The sun is falling lower and lower below the horizon as we make our way out of the Garden District. We jump onto a streetcar that leads to the French Quarter and find a seat near the back.

I stare out at all the spectacular houses that line St. Charles Avenue with their looming privacy walls and trees as old as the city itself. People are starting to emerge from their homes, heading downtown for the nightlife. The city is a different place when the streetcar rolls to a stop on

Canal Street. Anne and I leap down the stairs onto the busy sidewalk and turn onto Royal Street. The multicolored buildings are lit up along their roofs with twinkling lights. Saxophonists, guitarists, and small bands have claimed every street corner. Some of their hats and cases are bulging with money, while others are disappointingly bare. I stare into the illuminated windows of boutiques that are open late on Saturday night. My hand grabs Anne's arm as she pulls me through the busy sidewalk.

"Anne, where are we going?" I call over the music.

"Jackson Square—but we're meeting my boyfriend at Preservation Hall first. He had a gig."

We stop in front of a building that looks like an ancient abandoned club. The old wooden walls are falling apart in front of us. The place is the farthest thing from my idea of a club, but inside the place must be hopping. I can feel the vibrations of the bass, and my ears are flooded with saxophone runs. A young guy leans against a rickety wall of the club, his guitar case standing next to him.

"Mason!" Anne calls over the music. He grabs his guitar case, and his eyes light up as a smile stretches across his handsome, freckled face. He stoops to place a kiss on Anne's cheek as he wraps his free arm around her waist. When he pulls away, Anne introduces me.

"Mason, this is my friend, Cheyenne. She's new here."

He shakes my hand and winks at me. "A friend? You? I don't believe it for a second."

"Oh, you're so funny. How'd your set go?"

"Oh, you know...we killed it."

I glance over Mason's shoulder at a figure walking toward us. I can't see his face yet, but something about him seems familiar. Mason follows my gaze and laughs.

"Dude, over here," Mason beckons and pulls the guy into our group. "Eli, this is Cheyenne. Cheyenne, this is my drummer, Eli." Eli slides his sticks into his pocket and locks eyes with me, matching my confusion.

"What are you doing here?" I say, trying to keep my gaze steady, at the same time he says, "You're here!"

"You two know each other?" Anne asks, slightly amused.

"You didn't mention that you were coming down here," Eli's trying to smile at me, but there's almost a hint of cockiness to his tone.

"Well, normal people don't share their summer plans with complete strangers, especially considering the circumstances." Eli flinches at the harshness of my voice, but the cocky façade doesn't fade away. I can feel Mason and Anne looking awkwardly between the two of us. I cross my arms and take a step away from the group, looking down at my shoes.

"Well, as interesting as this reunion has been, we've got a play to get to." Mason claps his hands together. "Why don't you come with us, man?"

"What play?" Eli asks.

"*Romeo and Juliet*," Anne says, sparing a sideways glance at me. She looks at the body language between Eli and me and raises an eyebrow.

"Sure, why not," Eli decides, sounding less than enthusiastic.

Mason and Anne seem happy with the addition. They each wrap an arm around the other and start walking toward the busy square leaving Eli and me to follow. He doesn't look at me as he walks with his head down.

He's lost all his obnoxious bravado, and I find myself unexpectedly disappointed by this.

Before I know it, we've arrived at the square. We push our way through the crowd to find a place near the front of the stage. Mason pulls a blanket out of his backpack, and we all sit down. Anne leans against Mason, smiling as the narrator walks onto the stage in his Renaissance costume. I settle stiffly beside Eli, crossing my legs, linking my fingers in my lap. He leans back on his elbows, his long legs crossed at the ankles stretching out on the grass.

The narrator steps on stage, tapping the microphone gently before announcing the famous first lines of *Romeo and Juliet*: "Two households, both alike in dignity, in fair Verona, where we lay our scene."

"What's your favorite scene?" Eli whispers to me.

"The ball, but it's all brilliant," I whisper, although I don't know why I'm even responding to him.

"I see someone thinks highly of the bard."

"Who doesn't? He's the greatest writer in history. Basically every play since covers one of his themes."

Eli half-grins at my enthusiasm. "Plenty of people would take offense at that opinion."

"Well, they don't particularly matter to me," I mumble, hugging my knees to my chest.

He smirks, "You're right. They're all idiots."

He's mocking me. "Just shut up and let me watch the play."

A smile creeps onto his lips as he glances sideways at me. He leans over and whispers in my ear, "You know what I think? I think fate has brought us both to New Orleans."

Five

"Cheyenne, if you don't hurry, we're going to be late!" Anne calls from downstairs. I prance around my room, filling my bag with a book, wallet, and anything else I think I might need for the day. I hop awkwardly down the stairs as I strap on my sandals. Anne gives me a "once-over," since it now seems to be her job.

"Eh, it's alright for a coffee shop," Anne shrugs her shoulders, a barely satisfied glimmer in her clear green eyes.

"*It's alright*," I mutter under my breath. "Kara, Thomas, we're leaving! Call me if you need something,"

"Cheyenne, come here for a second please," Thomas's voice echoes through the wooden house, and I hold up my index finger to Anne. Thomas and Kara are lounging at the dining table. Thomas holds out a glass of blood to me. "Drink this before you go."

He has made me do this every single morning. I've gotten used to the taste, even though I still think it's weird. Surely I can skip one day. "No, thanks. I'll just get something at the coffee shop. Bye."

"Remember to be back by four for Rove," Kara calls, not glancing up from her cereal.

"I won't forget," I turn to go, but Thomas stops me.

"Cheyenne, I told you to drink the blood before you go." The intensity of his voice freezes me in place.

Slowly, I turn to face him.

"Why?"

His eyes narrow. "Doesn't matter why. As long as you are in New Orleans, I'm your alpha, so you follow my rules."

I look to Kara for support, and I can see she's surprised by Thomas's demand. However, she's powerless against the alpha card. I take the glass from him and sip from it. I'm surprised to find that this morning it actually tastes good. I guess blood in the morning is an acquired taste. I empty the glass, and when I do, I wish there was more. I set the glass on the table and look at Thomas compliantly. He looks pleased.

"Cheyenne, let's go," Anne calls from the foyer.

"Mustn't keep Anne waiting," he says, shooing me from the dining room. Kara looks from him to me and nods. I walk to meet Anne, plastering a smile on my face. She grabs me, and then we're gone.

Once we're a few houses down the road, Anne releases my arm. "So, Eli was asking about you last night." She observes my general indifference to the subject and presses further. "You never did say if anything happened during the play."

"That's because there's nothing to tell," I shrug, avoiding her piercing eyes.

"Really? I kind of felt some chemistry between you."

"Or you were projecting your own raging hormones onto everyone in sight." The hunger for more blood has made me grouchy, but she's too caught up in her own imagination to think anything of it.

"I think you fell in love with him at first sight and

are just afraid to admit it to anyone—even me, let alone, to yourself," she declares in her soap opera voice.

I muster a grin I don't really feel. We walk in silence for a moment before I can get out my next sentence. "Anne, there's something that makes me not trust him, okay?" I consider for a moment. "Alright, so Eli has a younger brother who's my age."

"Yeah, Erik," she grimaces. "We've met him unfortunately. Enough said"

"Right. I don't know what his deal is, but as long as I've known him, he's made my life hell. I'd rather keep my distance from him and anyone who shares his genes." I grimace, finally looking at her.

"Seriously, Eli's nothing like Erik. I can attest to that. I've met the twerp. You can't judge people based on their families. I mean, if you judged me based on my parents, would you be hanging out with me right now?"

I laugh, shaking my head at her. "Yeah, yeah, yeah. Whatever." I roll my eyes and walk past her as she stops to retie her Chuck Taylors. The streetcar pulls up just as we arrive. I slip my fare into the toll box, and the driver hands me my all-day pass. The car is completely full, so we have to stand in the front. Passengers' chattering drifts through the open windows as a cool breeze from the gulf surrounds us. It's easy to tell when we're getting close to the French Quarter—the music gets louder, and the food smells become stronger.

"Seriously though, Eli's a great guy," Anne says. "He'll grow on you, I'm sure."

"I don't really plan on getting to know him."

"Well, that's going to be a problem if you hang

around me, that is." She's got me there.

"I could always *stop* hanging out with you." I suggest, a sarcastic smirk on my lips.

"Yes, but then your New Orleans social life would be dead. Besides, you'd be completely lost without me."

"I think I could manage well enough," I retort, turning away from her to stare out the window. The city passes by slowly, and every hundred feet, the car stops to let off passengers and receive new ones. The seats fill up before Anne and I have a chance to snag them.

We jump off when the car reaches Jackson Square, along with a horde of tourists with their cameras and fanny packs. I follow Anne down the sidewalk even though I know where I'm going. New jazz bands are on the street corners with their guitar cases and hats open for donations. I throw a dollar into the bucket of a young girl with a perfectly scratchy blues voice. Her lips break into a smile at the sight of my dollar, but her voice never wavers.

The smells of chicory coffee, fresh baked bread, and Café du Monde's beignets float through the air. We walk past the bustling café and turn onto Decatur Street. Brennan's is almost a full house this morning. Mason already has a booth saved in the back corner for us with three steaming cups of coffee waiting. Anne slides in beside him while I take my place in the opposite seat, wrapping my hands around the coffee and closing my eyes as the fresh steam wafts into my nose, replacing the smell of blood.

"What time do you go on?" Anne asks Mason, and I notice his guitar case beside him.

"Not for another hour. I just want to hear the people before us."

Mason isn't very tuned into people around him when there is music playing. If Anne says something to him, he just kind of nods and groans a response.

"What time is Eli supposed to be coming?" Anne faces Mason, but I can see her squinted eyes pointed at me.

"Soon, I guess." He takes an absent sip of his coffee and crunches on chocolate biscotti. Watching the crumbs falling onto his plate makes my stomach growl.

"I think I'll go grab something to eat. Anne, do you want anything?" I ask, but she just shakes her head, her loose red curls bouncing wildly. I order a chocolate muffin and a slice of banana nut bread. It's amazing how pastry tastes so good at this time of day, yet I won't be able to stand to be near the stuff in a few hours. When I walk back to the table balancing my two plates, I stop when I see Eli sitting on my side of the booth. He taps his thumb and forefinger against the wooden table and stares absently at the photograph hanging on the wall of a blue werewolf. I sit down on the outer edge of the seat as quietly as possible.

"Good morning, Cheyenne. Fancy bumping into you here!" He turns around with a cheery smile on his tan, charming face.

"Fancy isn't the word I'd use," I mumble, stuffing a piece of muffin in my mouth. I turn away from him, looking for anything around the room to distract me when my eyes land on something, or someone, even worse. Erik is sitting at the table farthest from us, watching the room like a hawk.

Eli notices where my eyes have landed. "I swear he won't bother you."

I roll my eyes and turn my back on him, reaching occasionally for a bite of my food. The current band is good but uninspired. Eventually they stop playing, and I force myself to participate in the half-hearted applause. Then it's time for Mason and Eli's band to play. When Mason steps up to the microphone, his deep voice sends French lyrics into the sunny atmosphere of the restaurant.

"I wrote these lyrics," Anne whispers to me.

"I didn't know you like to write."

She nods shyly, dipping her head a little to stare at her empty coffee mug. "I mostly write poetry, but I occasionally spurt out a short story or a song."

"Well, you're very talented."

She looks past me up to Mason, her eyes glazing over. I can tell I'm not in the room anymore. I wonder what it's like, to be in love like that. Too bad it'll have to end.

I try to focus on the band, but knowing that Erik's just a few feet away is unnerving. I feel the air changing. I don't know why, but something's off about everything. Erik suddenly glances up at me, his cold, gray eyes meeting mine. A charming smile ripples over his perfect features. He winks at me, his pearly white teeth flashing in his mouth. I stifle the urge to punch him and quickly turn away.

When the band finishes playing, Anne and I wait for Mason and Eli outside the restaurant, people-watching and listening to the street music. They appear a few minutes later, Mason grasping his guitar case in his callused hands.

"How'd it sound?" he asks, wrapping his free arm around Anne's waist. She answers him with a kiss. A really long, uncomfortable one.

"Okaay," Eli says in attempt to break up the awkward moment. "How 'bout we take Cheyenne to the Cemetery?" He turns to me with an eager grin on his face. "I think you'll enjoy it."

"I've seen a cemetery before, thanks."

"Not one that's the final resting place of the Voodoo Queen of New Orleans. Come on, it'll be fun," Eli's already broad grin stretches, and he nudges my shoulder. I immediately take a step toward Anne.

"I've never actually been," Anne says. "My parents never thought it was proper to say the least. I hear you're supposed to break bricks off of other tombs to scrawl something onto the Voodoo Queen's, and you can leave her offerings."

Eli knows he's won. "I think that settles it. We're going."

The cemetery is within walking distance, just farther down Royal Street than the trolley goes. I wouldn't necessarily call this path the beautiful part of the city. The buildings back here are dingy, some decorated with graffiti—symbols with meanings I don't want to know. Music coming from the French Quarter, the sounds of mules' hooves clacking against the pavement as they pull their carriages through the Quarter, the smell of shrimp frying and spices simmering in gumbo grow fainter as we move through the abandoned neighborhood.

"So what school are you looking at down here?" Eli asks, slowing down to walk beside me. I resist the urge to speed up, even to try flitting. Anything to not be standing beside him.

Kara's told me that whenever humans ask me what school I'm applying to, I'm supposed to say some human school. "Uh, Demond University."

"Oh, cool. I applied there."

"But you don't go there?" Why am I asking him questions? I don't care.

"Nah, Mason and I decided to take a gap year to work on our music and to help Mason's mom."

"Why does she need help?" I ask, genuinely curious since it's not about Eli.

"She's just pretty sick. So she needs a lot of stuff done for her." There's pain in his voice that I can't place, but I'm smart enough to not say anything stupid or disrespectful. I keep my mouth shut.

All of a sudden, I feel eyes watching me. Eli is in front, leading the charge. Mason and Anne are behind me chatting about new song ideas. I turn to my right and find eyes. Several children stand side by side on a rickety porch, the house's roof caving in behind them. Their clothes are filthy and look several sizes too small. Mud streaks their faces, creating distorted shadows. The tops of their heads look like they've never seen hairbrushes. I can't say how old they are: children, tweens, and teenagers. A dozen brown eyes, narrowed to slits, stare at me as I move down the street following in Eli's footsteps. Suddenly, he drops back beside me, moving as silently as a cat.

"Don't let them bother you, Cheyenne."

"Maybe they need help."

"All they have to do is ask."

"It's not that simple." I stop, glancing up at his disconcerted face. "Some people, as much as they want to, can never ask for help." I stop talking and find his brown eyebrows knit together, wrinkles forming on his forehead.

"You can always ask for help," his whisper is harsh, insistent. His eyes search my blank face.

"But there's not always someone there to help you."

He stops walking but continues to stare at me with disapproval or pity, I don't know. But I don't like either option. I stop too, meeting his gaze evenly, coldly. He's not getting anything out of me, no matter how much he probes.

I glance back at the kids one last time and almost have a heart attack when I do. Their lips are raised to a snarl. But it's almost as if they're smiling. And their eyes are red—like a vampire's.

"Why so serious?" Mason asks as they approach us, goofy smiles matching their giggling. They haven't noticed the kids.

Eli shudders and turns to them, smiling brightly. "Just trying to solve a riddle." He looks down at me quickly before moving forward again. "We're almost there. I think I see the cemetery a little ways down." We all begin walking again. I hang back with Anne and Mason, absently listening to their conversation. The picture of those kids is imprinted in my mind. I try to blink it away, but it won't budge. I was imagining things. They're just sad, lonely kids.

The cemetery is as unnerving as I'd imagined it would be. The rows of decrepit tombs are encased by a short brick wall. It's not much protection from intruders, but by the looks of it, intruders seem welcome. We walk into the cemetery, and an unusually long shiver runs down my body. Tombs, some as tall as Eli, are side by side, barely inches apart. The bricks are crumbling, falling to dust once they hit the ground. Every muscle in my body is tense and knotted. Every sound makes me flinch. Something isn't right.

"Hey, check this out!" Mason calls from a few rows back. I walk toward his voice, my eyes surveying the path before I step out from behind a tomb. "It's the Barbarin family."

He's standing in front of tomb 218, a white, unkempt tomb with dark spots where the bricks have crumbled. "This family was a jazz dynasty—they were amazing!" Mason touches the white bricks affectionately, staring at the plaque. I roll my eyes and keep walking, wrapping my arms around myself. A flash of light catches my eye. I look past the rows of brick and stone structures, trying to follow an image, but then it's gone. A chill reaches to my core.

The newer tombs are in better condition than the eighteenth and nineteenth century tombs, but they're still dilapidated. Some of them have flowers and pictures in front of them. Then I come to a large tomb near the back of the cemetery: The Voodoo Queen of New Orleans—Marie Laveau, Eli explained to me on the way over here. It stands much taller than I, made of soiled white concrete with several lines of three consecutive red X's on the front. Money, candy, cigars, bottles of rum, and jewelry lie in a heap at the tomb's entrance. I walk around the side and run my hand over the etchings from past visitors.

"Wanna leave an offering?" Eli leans against the tomb, holding out a piece of candy.

"You brought a Jolly Rancher to offer to a Voodoo Queen?" I snort. "No thanks." I shake my head, trying to hide my trembling hand. I don't want him to see how unsettled I am. I don't have to think about death. I know it'll come eventually, but that eventually is hundreds of years from now. But in this cemetery, I don't know, that hundreds of years doesn't seem so far away. And it's like I can feel the magic in the air—whatever kind of magic Voodoo is: good, bad, in between. It's here.

"Alright then. I'll make an offering. Me and the queen are old pals." Eli kneels in front of the tomb with a handful of Jolly Ranchers and places them in the semi circle of other offerings. He closes his eyes like he's praying.

I freeze when all of the junk offerings start to rattle, quaking against the ground. Eli's eyes snap open and he leaps to his feet. "Did you see that?" he whispers, his eyes searching wildly around the tomb.

"See what?" I say as a cloud wisps around the tomb and encircles us, pushing us closer together. I feel something stirring in my blood when I look up at Eli. He's smiling like he has a secret. Then, just as quickly as it appeared, the cloud is gone. Everything looks normal. For a moment.

I quickly take a step back from Eli, pulling at the end of my shirt. "What the heck?"

Eli laughs. "Seems like Ms. Laveau is offended that you don't want to offer her anything."

He's completely unbothered. That cloud came out of nowhere. Like magic. But that's impossible. There's no way a dead Voodoo lady could have cast a spell to freak me out. Then suddenly the bush to my right goes up in flames. I scream.

"She can make all the offerings she wants," Erik's familiar voice pierces the air like a knife. "Who would ever listen to *her* prayers?" The disgust in his voice makes me turn around stiffly, the hair on the back of my neck standing on end.

"I told you to leave us alone." Eli steps in front of me to face his brother.

The bush fire roars taller than both of them. "Nah, I think I'd rather keep my eyes on this blossoming relationship." Erik kicks a bottle out of the semi-circle, and it rolls through the dust. Breaking the Voodoo Queen's circle can't be good karma.

"Keep it up, Erik. I would love to give Mom a reason to put you on a plane home."

"Ah yes, because we know she would be happy to take the side of the son who's so much like her." His face drops. I watch Eli's shoulders tense. His neck stiffens and his knuckles whiten on his clenched fists. Then as quickly as the fire started, it's gone, leaving only smoking bushes.

"Get out of here." Eli reaches for Erik's shirt, but he ducks out of the way and slides toward me.

"I mean, what do you see in this anyway? There's something very wrong with her, and you know it."

His words make me feel ill. They're words I've thought over and over, a truth I've seen in my family's pitying eyes. Hearing Erik say it is too much to bear. Involuntarily, my hand tightens into a fist, and I slam my knuckles right into Erik's protruding jaw. He stumbles back but grabs my hair, pulling me down with him. I land on top, mindlessly swinging my fists. His arms come up to protect his face, but I beat them away. Blood spurts out of his nose. Human blood.

I've never tasted human blood before, but now I'm consumed with a need for it. I feel my fangs pierce through my gums behind my canines. His neck is clear, unguarded. His arms are busy trying to push me away in vain. I pin his shoulders to the dirt, watching carefully as his jugular swells, available and vulnerable. I lean down. My mouth parts just slightly.

Suddenly, two strong arms wrap around my waist. I pull Erik upright with me, my hands still gripping his shoulders. "Cheyenne, let go," Eli whispers in my ear. Slowly, I pry my fingers off his shoulders and drop my arms. Erik falls back to the ground, staring up at me with eyes as wide as full moons. Suddenly, a tunnel of wind wraps around us. What is happening here?

Eli's arms are still wrapped around me. I run my tongue over the points of my fangs. Erik gasps as he squints at my mouth. "You better watch your step, Lane."

He disappears behind the tomb just as I squirm out of Eli's iron grip. I sprint behind the tomb to find nothing. Erik's gone, completely vanished. I turn my head wildly, searching for him, my throat burning like the bush. He couldn't have gotten out of the cemetery that quickly.

"Cheyenne, what's going on?" Anne calls. I turn on my heel, brushing my hair out of my face and taking a deep, unnecessary breath.

"Nothing," I say as I turn the corner, pretending to brush something off my knees. "I just tripped over something and fell." Eli looks from me to Anne and back again before walking away, his hands stuffed in his pockets. Anne watches him, one eyebrow arched to a sharp point.

"So, you and Eli?" She smiles at me, wiggling her eyebrows, and giggling—an action I find annoying.

"No, not Eli and me. I told you what happened.

I tripped."

"Yeah, *that's* why Eli looked so guilty and suspicious when I walked over here. It's okay. If you don't want to tell me, I understand. It's none of my business." She holds her hands up in surrender and walks back to Mason without another word.

I jog to catch up with her. "I'd tell you if anything happened, so you can trust me when I say that *nothing happened.*" Anne stops, turns to face me, and stares at me with her hard, green eyes. After careful consideration, she nods curtly and turns away satisfied.

"So can we leave now? I'm starting to get the heebie-jeebies in this place," Anne says loudly, already moving toward the exit at the back of the cemetery. *She has no idea.*

"If you insist. My stomach's starting to growl anyway," Mason says from behind a tomb. "Who's up for some lunch?" I glance down at my watch: 1:00.

The vision of the cloud, the feeling of magic, the weird fire and wind. *I almost bit a human.* There's something wrong with this place, and I want to get as far away from it as possible. "I should probably be getting home. My cousin's arriving today."

"Don't try to get out of lunch, Cheyenne." Anne narrows her gaze at me, an unspoken question in her statement. "I heard Thomas. You don't have to be home until four. You're coming with us."

Six

We walk to the last stop and wait until a streetcar arrives and begins boarding new passengers. Mason and Anne snuggle together in the back, while I sit as close to the front as possible, my head still reeling.

Eli sits in the seat behind me, his back resting against the window. He hasn't said a word. He stares absently out the opposite window, past a woman with a pink mohawk. I try my hardest to ignore him because every time I look at him, I see his eyes wide with shock, and I see that wind tunnel whipping around him. And I see Erik. And I feel the bloodlust. There's no way he could have known what I was thinking, but still, if anyone ever found out what I almost did, I'd be dead.

"Riverwalk stop. Passengers, we have arrived at the Riverwalk. Please watch your step," the driver yells down the car. Passengers shuffle down the aisle and down the steps. Mason and Anne file by us last. Anne grabs my arm and pulls me out of my seat. The wooden bench creaks as Eli stands up and follows behind us. The Riverwalk is as busy as ever. We walk past the crowded entrance of the strip mall, past the always-illuminated casino.

"Anne, where are we going?" I call from a few feet behind her. Eli is lagging behind me, but Mason is ahead of all of us as he makes a left on Poydras Street.

"Mother's," she yells back.

"What's Mother's?" Just as I ask, we stop in front of an old, tall red brick building. A line runs from a brown awning on the building's side, halfway down the block. All who are lined up face away from the glaring sun, staring intently at menus. Mason grabs three for us as he skips to the back of the line. "So what's good here?" I ask, gazing at the menu.

When there's no response, I glance up. Three pairs of eyes are glaring at me over their menus. "Are you kidding me?" Mason says, lowering the plastic rectangle. "You've never heard of Mother's, the birthplace of po'boys?" I shake my head innocently, staring around the circle.

"Mason, give her a break. She's a tourist," Eli says, grinning for the first time in an hour.

I glare at him, pursing my lips to hide my smile. "I'm not a tourist, thank you very much. I'm just new."

"Mother's is where you get the most mouthwatering po'boy you could ever imagine. You've never tasted anything like this. It's just..." I can practically see the drool spilling out of Mason's mouth as he yammers.

"Alright, sweetie," Anne coos and touches Mason's shoulder, "I think she gets the point." He opens his mouth to say one more thing, but Anne's hand acts like a mute button, thankfully.

"Get the Ferdi Special with debris and fully dressed," Eli whispers as Anne and Mason turn back to their own menus. A rock forms in my stomach as his face leans close to mine. "You can't beat it. When you come back here, you'll never order anything else."

"Yes, but what is it?" I ask, regaining composure and shuffling forward as the line moves up the block.

"Shhhh." Eli pushes his forefinger to his lips. "We don't ask questions in New Orleans. We just eat."

I can't help but laugh. Whatever made his eyes go wide clearly isn't bothering him anymore.

The line moves quicker than I expect. We step into the restaurant and are through the ordering line in ten minutes flat. The building is so cramped that it's hard to move around. Tables are scrunched together in the little dining room. When a new group enters and orders, the host yells to them to find a seat in the back. The brick walls are covered with pictures, thank you letters, awards, and certifications.

Once people receive their orders, all talking ceases. There is nothing but their mouths and the sandwich. I order what Eli suggested, and soon enough a waitress brings out our food and places a hulking mass of meat and bread in front of me. Brown liquid has soaked into the bread and onto the plate; pieces of meat fall onto my stack of French fries.

"Um Eli, what did you make me order?"

"What did I tell you? No questions. Just eat the po'boy." He catches my eye and holds the gaze a little too long, but then his sandwich steals his attention as he stuffs it into his mouth, tearing off a gigantic bite. I look from his sandwich to mine. I rip one half of the sandwich off my plate and bite into it. My tongue explodes as it attempts to decipher all the different flavors: ham, roast beef, gravy, and mayonnaise. Each bite gets better and better. I ignore the fries completely and rapidly devour my entire sandwich to the amusement of my friends, who are taking their sweet time.

"Did you eat a little fast there, Cheyenne?" Mason asks, peering at me over the remaining half of his po'boy.

I glare at him, my hands resting on my protruding stomach. "Eat your sandwich and hush." Everyone smiles, quietly turning back to their food.

By the time everyone else finishes, most of my food has digested, and I am pretty sure that moving may now be a possibility. I start to walk toward the door we entered, but Eli grabs my arm and swings me toward the back past the cashier and the last few tables. I barely notice a tiny exit sign near the ceiling, only visible unless someone was really looking for it. I carefully move my arm out of his grip, stealing a side-glance at him. The corners of his mouth hook into a smile. "Only tourists go out the entrance. Don't be a tourist, Cheyenne." I roll my eyes as we exit the restaurant and wait for Anne and Mason to follow us.

"So what's next on the agenda, Mr. Ashford?" Mason asks. I turn my back to them staring out at the busy city. Lunch crowds are emptying restaurants as the afternoon grows later: almost three o'clock.

"Whatever it is, it has to be quick. I have to be home soon," I say turning back to this group whom I now consider friends.

"What about the Museum of Art? It's free entry on Wednesdays," Eli suggests, looking to me.

"I don't know; that's pretty far away. And to get through the whole museum..." Anne says doubtfully. I turn away from the group when my phone buzzes in my pocket and find a message: "Change of plans. Rove got in early. Come home now."

"Sorry guys. I actually have to get home. My cousin just got in. Bye!"

"I'll call you later," Anne yells to me as I hurry down the sidewalk to the streetcar. With one hand, I shoot a thumbs-up back at Anne, and with the other, I respond to Thomas: "On my way."

"Mind if I join you?" Eli appears beside me, hands stuffed in his pockets.

"I'm in a hurry." I speed up, but he keeps pace with my brisk walk.

"Well, you're not going to get home quickly with the street car. Why don't we get a taxi?" He stops in front of me and holds his hand up to hail a passing cab. He opens the door for me with an "after you" wave of the arm. I slide in and give the driver my address as Eli climbs in next to me. I press myself against my door, putting as much distance between us as possible. The driver barely shifts out of park before Eli cuts to the chase.

"So why do you not like me?" His gaze is steady, calculating. I stare out the window at the passing city. We are out of downtown now, moving closer to the Garden District. "Cheyenne?"

I turn around slowly and cross my arms over my chest. "It's not that I don't like you."

"Then what's the problem?" He slides his hands out of his pockets and moves closer.

"It's that I *can't* like you." My fingers twist together in weird contortions as I shuffle through the words in my head.

"That doesn't make any sense."

"Eli…" My mouth parts. His eyes are sharp, determined.

I drop my own to the floor, unable to keep eye contact with him.

"Here we are, Missy. That'll be fifteen, please," the driver calls. Eli pulls a twenty out of his back pocket and slaps it into the driver's hand. He slides out first and offers his hand to me, which I painfully ignore.

"Good bye, Eli." I turn my back on him, not looking back, and jog up the stairs. I grip the handle just as the door swings open. Thomas stands on the other side, his charming face darkened by a sharp glare.

"Get in the house." He grabs my arm and pulls me through the door, his eyes blazing at Eli. "Who is that?" He shuts the door, careful not to bring any attention to himself.

"Just a guy. I don't know. I went to high school with his brother." As soon as the door is closed, Thomas throws me against the wall, his face threateningly close to mine.

"You stay away from him. Do you hear me?"

"Why?" I struggle beneath him as he presses my shoulders to the wall. "I'm allowed to be friends with humans," I mutter through gritted teeth.

"He's not just some stupid human, Cheyenne!" He growls, "Can't you sense it?"

"Sense what?" I finally shove him off of me.

"The magic! He's a witch, Cheyenne!"

My jaw drops, literally drops. That would explain what happened in the cemetery, but no, there's no way. Witches belong in history lessons, not my real life.

"Come on, Thomas. Are you paranoid?"

In an instant, he's on me again, pressing me to the wall with his anger. "No, I'm not! Witches are monsters who killed our people, our families. And you've led one straight to our home. If I see you anywhere *near* him again, I'll..."

"Thomas, is she home?" Kara interrupts him before he says something I'd hope he'd regret, but I'm just not sure these days. Thomas turns on his heel and stalks to the living room. He's determined. I know he's going to do something, but I have no idea what. The dark room is silent except for the uncomfortable shuffling of feet. Only one light has been turned on, and paired with the room's deep maroon color, everyone in it looks absolutely morbid.

"Hey, Munchkin!" Rove jumps off the lounge and flits over to me, wrapping his lanky arms around me.

"How was the flight?" I ask and switch on the light beside me.

"Quick. I slept the entire time," Rove smiles.

"Typical."

"So, did you have a nice time with Anne?" Kara asks as we settle into chairs, ignoring the tense air between Thomas and me.

"Yeah, we went to this place called Mother's for lunch, and it was good. We heard a band play for a little while." *No need to mention whose.*

"Well, do you have any plans to entertain Rove tomorrow? Thomas and I have a doctor's appointment. We find out the sex of the baby!" Her eyes squint as she smiles, like they always do when she's excited.

"I'm sure Anne will find something for us to do." I force a close-lipped smile.

"Well, before you show Rove to his room," Thomas starts, "let me just go over a few ground rules." I feel Rove tense beside me, and I can practically hear the eye roll.

"You don't go anywhere without my permission. You are to stay with Cheyenne and Anne during your entire visit. When you need blood, come to me. When you have a problem, come to me. I know you're only here for a few days, but knowing you, I need to outline these things."

The anger rolling off Rove is intense. I feel like he's going to pop something. If Rove opens his mouth right now, who knows what would pop out, so he just nods. "Good," Thomas smirks. "I'm your alpha. You better get used to it." He's starting to piss me off now. "Cheyenne, why don't you show Rove to his room? We're glad you're here, Cousin!"

"Come on, Rover." I grab one of his bags at the side of the couch and carry it up the stairs on my back. I push open the door to the room opposite mine and sling his bag and myself onto the bed.

"Holy crap! I want to punch that guy in the face. Is that allowed? Does that follow his rules for me?" Rove roars, slamming the door shut. "What is that dude's problem? Gotten a bit power hungry, maybe?"

I don't say anything because I'm getting accustomed to the stick up Thomas's butt.

"So was that guy outside the house the same guy we met at Lily's? The jackass's brother?" Of course he saw Eli.

"Rove..."

"Cheyenne Marie Lane, are you dating a human?" Rove springs to a seated position, one slender eyebrow rising to a point.

"No! He just hangs out with the same people I do."

"Well, he's clearly into you, and you can't tell me that

you're not enjoying it."

"You don't know the full story, Rove."

He lies down again so that we are head to head. "Well, then tell me." His hands link over his stomach as he settles in for what he assumes will be a long story.

Thomas's words thunder through my mind: witch. Is it possible? And if Eli is a witch, is Erik one too? "What do you know about witches?"

"Just what the 'rents feed me during lessons. Why?"

"Well, Thomas seems to think that Eli is one. He said he could sense the magic on him."

"So, let me guess the rest of the story. Witches are our mortal enemies. They killed our ancestors. There is *no way* that you can ever hang out with him again. Am I getting any of this right?" he asks, sideways smiling at me.

"Verbatim. I'm having déjà vu right now," I say sarcastically.

"So what are you going to do about it?" he asks, leaning up on his elbow, staring down at me inquiringly.

"What do you mean, 'what am I going to do about it'? I can't do anything. If Thomas is right..."

He looks over at me. "Jeez, Munchkin! No need to look so uncomfortable." He bumps my tense shoulder and chuckles.

"He's just different. And he kind of seems to care about me. He's almost, I don't know, protective."

"Protective? Why? What's he protecting you from?" He sits up instantly, the brotherly instincts kicking in. I roll my eyes at his protectiveness, brushing it away without a second thought.

"Nothing really. Erik just showed up at the cemetery.

It's not a big deal." I can tell he wants to say more, but he bites his tongue and moves on.

"Cheyenne, you are working way too hard to talk yourself out of this. If you like this guy, live in the moment and suffer the consequences later."

"He already has two strikes against him. One—he's *Erik's* brother." My teeth clench together at the sound of his name. "And two—he might be a witch. I can't just ignore all that. I'm not like you."

Rove makes a mouth with his hand and sticks it in my face. "Blah. Blah. Blah. That's all I'm hearing."

I'm ready to snap back when Thomas yells up the stairs. "Rove, Cheyenne, be ready to leave in twenty."

Seven

Rove and I follow blindly behind Kara and Thomas through the Garden District. They've already flitted a few times, leaving me behind without even realizing it, but they come back eventually. Rove and I keep our distance per their request. As Kara said, they "have some business to talk about."

"So how's Jillian?" I ask.

"Fine, I guess. Haven't talked to her much since summer started."

"That's probably a good thing. I mean…"

"Let it go, Cheyenne." I can feel his glare on my back. "It's not like I'm going to marry the girl. Let a guy live, would ya?" he huffs. "Are you this much of a pain around Eli?"

"Would you stop it? Don't bring him up around Thomas."

He rolls his chin against his chest in silence. "It was just a simple question."

"No, I can't exactly be myself around him. And why do you keep bringing him up? It's not that big of a deal." I cross my arms and try to speed up, but he has longer legs.

"It's just that I may never get to tease you about a boy again. I'm simply seizing the opportunity while it's in front of me."

"Well, you need to drop it. Please? You'll have plenty

of chances to mess with some of the other cousins later in life."

"Yes, but this is now, and you are too much fun to mess with."

We stop suddenly, just short of running into Kara and Thomas. I glance up at our stop and see nothing. We are standing in front of a house, a drab, dull yellow house with a broken porch. The streetlight beside it is out, and all of the plants wrapped around the balcony are dead.

"Um, Kara, where are we?" I whisper into her ear, stretching on my toes to rest my chin on her shoulder. She doesn't answer me as we watch Thomas knock once, twice, three, four times on the cracked maroon door. With a quick swipe, a small box opens in the middle of the door at mouth level.

A thick pair of lips, cracked and partially covered by a mustache appears in the opening. "*Mot*?" the rough voice asks, the lips barely moving.

"*Vieuxsang*," Thomas whispers the French word for "old-blood" in a husky voice as a wisp of smoke escapes through the opening before it shuts. Thomas looks back at us and smiles reassuringly as we wait. Kara patiently, Rove and I in confusion.

"Kara…" I step up beside her and slide my arm through hers. She rubs my arms covered with goose bumps until they start to melt away. A moment later, the door swings open, and Thomas steps through with a slight tip of his fedora. We step into a narrow hallway covered in coat hooks. Thomas removes his hat and sets it on a free, rusty hook.

We see the Lip's face for the first time: a clean shaven, thin face. The man stands taller than all of us, his tattooed arms crossed over his broad chest. He wears black on top of black and stares at us through his small green eyes, his choppy black bangs shielding some of his view. I glance closer at the tattoos on his arms. They're all French or Latin words looping across his arms in graceful swooshes and curls. The man bows to Thomas, one hand across his chest, the other curled into a fist behind his back. Rove looks back at me, a spark of fear tangled with excitement in his eyes. I swallow and follow Kara through another door. The man closes the second door behind us, locking us into a busy room resembling a club.

Luxurious booths and wooden tables fill one side of the room with a long, elaborate bar on the other. I expect to smell alcohol, but instead, I'm greeted by the welcoming scent of fresh, warm blood. Waitresses go back and forth from the bar to the tables carrying trays of blood to thirsty patrons. Electric music reverberates through the walls, and I can feel it in my chest.

Rove moves to stand beside me, watching the onlookers who gaze at us in a dreamlike state as we move through the crowd, past the bar and the dance floor, to a small room in the back of the club. The techno beat dulls as the waiter closes the door behind him, leaving us alone in a densely carpeted red room, dimly lit by an elaborate crystal chandelier hanging in the center of the ceiling. The adults walk casually over to the luxurious velvet booth, leaving room for Rove and me on the end. Kara slides in beside Thomas. He rests his arm on the back of the booth and smiles at us.

"So what do you think of the place?" he asks. I glance around at the cherry wood and the scarlet walls, as I sink into the cushioned, crimson booth. The waiter walks in again with a tray of glasses filled to the brim with blood. "Thank you, Michael," Thomas nods to the young waiter.

"What exactly is this place, Thomas?" I ask, suddenly realizing that I'm the only one without a glass of blood. A moment later, another waiter walks in and hands me a single glass, nodding once at me and again at Thomas.

"Just a little secret club for Deuxsang. The vampires created it, and now we run it. We can drink here safely without the worry of humans seeing us," Thomas says, taking a long gulp of his blood.

I glance at him as I take my first sip. I don't know if I'm beyond thirsty or I'm just nervous, but that first sip sends an electric shock through me. I down the rest of the glass in a second, and before I can even ask, the same waiter places another one in front of me.

"This place is really wonderful, Cheyenne," Kara says, relaxing beside Thomas. "You and Rove should go dance!" she exclaims, clapping her hands together. "I can't, so I have to live vicariously through you." Thomas nods his head in encouragement, and Rove shoots me that stupid grin that can get me to do nearly anything that I'll most likely regret. Without a second thought, I follow him out of the private room.

The flashing dance floor is crowded to capacity with writhing bodies pressed too close together to be comfortable. My drink is the only thing I can find pleasure in here. The music's too loud and scratchy, the dancers have no respect for personal space, and the employees seem strange. A pasty white Deuxsang stumbles off the dance floor, nearly smashing my glass into my chest. He stops just short of me and smiles lazily, eyeing me with a disturbing hunger in his reddish-brown eyes. I lean instinctively away from him. The guy takes a step closer, his wolfish grin taking up the majority of his face.

"Hey, sweetie," he whispers, pressing his cold lips against my ear. I shove him away with my free hand and take a step closer to Rove.

"Get lost, dirt bag," I say. He stares at me another horribly long moment before turning away to his next victim. "Maybe we should go back to the room?" I ask Rove, staring around at the freak show around me. You would think such an exclusive club as this would have a bit more decorum, but apparently not. The black light disco ball illuminates the graffiti covering the walls. Trash fills the floor, and people simply crunch it under their feet without a second thought.

"It's not that bad! Get into the beat." Rove starts bouncing around, eyeing all the girls. He looks away when he catches me looking and pretends to stare at the disco ball.

"You have a girlfriend," I remind him.

"I have a *human* girlfriend. Besides," he smiles as someone else looks back at him over her bare shoulder, "it's just one dance." That goofy twelve-year-old grin appears on his full lips, and he dashes out to the dance floor, not hesitating to see if she is remotely interested. He just pushes her other partner—a guy much shorter and much bulkier than Rove—away, and places his hands on her swaying hips. I scoff and turn away, not willing to watch my cousin act like an idiot. The sooner I get out of here the better.

The waiter from earlier approaches and hands me another glass as I set my empty one on the counter—my third glass. I need to stop. I know I need to stop. I'm limited to two at home. Before I know what I'm doing, I have downed my cup. Every color in the room becomes more vivid, every movement sharper. I press my finger to my cheek and giggle as a ripple of electricity sparks beneath my skin. I notice a guy staring at me from the other side of the bar. His white blonde hair reflects in the light of the disco. His fuzzy, chocolate beard seems inviting and warm. I set my glass down in one swift movement and walk up to him, a charming smile plastered on my face. He smiles back, and before I know what I'm doing, I throw my arms around his neck. "Hi, there," I giggle.

"Hey, I'm Bentley." His muscular arms circle around me, conjuring more giggles.

"Cheyenne," I manage to utter. He smiles pleasantly, slowly starting to move me toward the dance floor.

"Would you like to dance?" he asks. I glance over at Rove who is still dancing with his partner, but I notice that they're now much, much closer than they were before.

"I would have...sorry, *love* that!" I giggle at my mistake as he leads me out to the dance floor. We weave between the mass of dancers until we reach the center of the floor right under the glittering disco ball. I find myself mesmerized at the spots that appear on Bentley's flawless face. He pulls me close against him.

Everyone around us is jumping on the balls of their feet, shouting and throwing their fists in the air. Bentley's arms wrap all the way around my waist. I become very hot very fast. The heat paired with my three glasses of blood, sends me into a frenzy. I press myself closer to Bentley, swaying my hips against his. My eyes glaze over as everyone moves around me. Sounds are dulled. Sights are fuzzy. Even Bentley's charming face right in front of me is blurred. A slow song comes on, and he pulls me so close that it seems like we're connected. My chest presses against his. His hands roam farther down my back, and I don't want him to stop.

Suddenly a couple bumps into us, knocking us out of the center of the dance floor. I'm pulled from my partner's arms and pushed systematically through the crowd until I'm off the dance floor. In a snap, I want to be outside. I crave air even though I don't need it. I feel alive, and I want to expand as far as I can. So I scan the room, spot the entrance guarded by two massive guys dressed in all black, and make a beeline for the door. They see me coming and push the door open before I crash through it.

I stumble onto the sidewalk, embracing the cool breeze that blows through the deserted street. I suck deep breaths into my body. Beads of sweat roll down my cheeks. I spin around and let myself fall to the ground laughing. With my back resting against the wall, I pull my knees into my chest and wrap my arms around my legs, resting my head against my knees.

"Cheyenne?" I glance up at a familiar voice, matching it with a blurry picture in my head: Eli. "What are you doing here? Are you okay?" I look beside him at the girl hanging on his arm. Her wavy beach hair falls like a halo around her face as she stands next to him. A rock suddenly forms in the pit of my stomach. Eli drops her arm and kneels down beside me, pushing my damp hair behind my ear.

"I'm fine." I shove his hand away and scoot nearer to the door, hugging my knees closer. "What are you doing here anyway?" I glance over his shoulder at his perfect date.

"We got a little lost on our walk." He follows my gaze toward the girl and grimaces. "Are you okay, Cheyenne?"

I walk back to the door without answering, painfully aware that Eli is following me.

"Cheyenne, where are you going?" He presses his hands against the door to keep me from opening it.

"I'm going back inside my friend's house. She's having a party, and I just needed a breath of fresh air," I stammer awkwardly as I fumble with the doorknob.

"Eli, she's drunk. Just leave her, please!"

I stumble as I spin on my heel, point at the new girl. "Why don't you mind your own business, Blondie?"

Eli puts his arm around my waist when I start charging toward her. "Crystal, can you just give me a minute?" She scoffs at him, but when he doesn't let me go, she walks away to lean against a wall across the street.

"Let me go, Eli!" I jerk away from him and collapse onto the sidewalk. When his face appears above me, I laugh. "Why can't you just leave me alone?"

"Cheyenne, come on." He pulls me to my feet but doesn't let go.

"No, I'm not going anywhere with you. Get away from me."

"I can't leave you like this." He grabs my wrist when I try to pull away, and in a flash, faster than I've ever moved before, I have him pinned against the brick wall.

"I told you once to leave me alone. I'm not going say it again." His hands are up in surrender as I slowly back away. "Leave. Now."

Eli's movements are cautious as he meets Blondie across the street. I watch as he turns around several times before finally disappearing from my sight. But I can still hear their footsteps miles away. My senses are heightened even beyond Deuxsang ability. I've never felt so powerful. I feel in control, like no one can tell me what to do or make me do anything I don't want to. It must be the blood. I like it, but I don't understand it at all.

That's when I spot the eyes staring at me. Ten red eyes. I swear I'm not crazy. But then they're gone. Like they'd never been there. So maybe I am crazy?

After a few deep breaths, I knock on the door and two bouncers open it for me. I clench my hands into fists behind my back and step back into the vibrating room. Rove has apparently finished dancing with his girl. He's slouched beside Kara, a dull absence in his clear, blue eyes. He glances up as I shut the door behind me and shows a hint of concern in his otherwise emotionless face. Thomas and Kara are engrossed in their conversation and don't even notice my entrance. I tiptoe over to Rove, pointedly sitting farther away from him than before. He glances at me over his shoulder, sighs, but says nothing.

For the rest of the night, I sit in silence while the rest of my family chatters away. I don't know what happened to me, and I don't know how to ask, let alone explain it. Eventually, we stumble out of the club. I keep my arms wrapped around myself the entire walk home and stare at the heels of Kara's shoes.

The rest of my family jokes with each other easily, giddy from all the blood. I can't even count how many glasses we've all had. When we reach the house, they walk into the living room laughing so loudly that they're waking up the entire neighborhood and don't even notice that I abandon them for my waiting bed, which, though it doesn't have the answers I need, is more comfort than they will ever be.

Eight

Early in the morning—too early for any sane person, like 10:00 am—I hear an annoying knock on my door. "Wake uh-up!!!" Rove's singsong voice cuts through my peaceful, deep sleep. He throws the curtains open, allowing the bright rays of the sun to pry my eyes open. I curl into a ball and burrow under my comforter, grateful for its thickness. "Munchkin! Come on, the day is beautiful; the sun is practically calling you! Can you hear it? 'Cheyenne!'" he throws his voice in an off-key falsetto.

"Get out of my room. Now." I shove the blanket away from my face in exasperation and sigh. "I will kill you." I glare at him through sleep-filled eyes.

"I highly doubt you have the guts," Rove shrugs his shoulders, a smug grin on his fuzzy face.

"Go shave," I grumble. "You look like a Yeti." I kick the covers off myself as he slumps out of the room muttering something about how having facial hair makes him look...I don't know. I don't really care either. I reluctantly roll to my side, glancing at my phone. Five texts from Anne, all saying the same thing: "Are you up yet?" or "Get up."

"Get a grip, Anne. We're not meeting you until noon."

"But knowing you, you'd sleep until 11:30. I was just covering my bases." I know she can't see me rolling my eyes, but I'm sure she knows its happening.

I smell the blood before I see it. Thomas has a tray set out on my desk, the most ironic of combinations—toast and a glass of blood. A healthy, balanced breakfast for your average Deuxsang. Except it's not. It's just for me. And I'm not complaining anymore. I drink the blood and enjoy every last drop. This stuff is better than anything I ever had at home.

Before Rove comes back in here yelling at me to hurry, I brush the blood out of my teeth and off my tongue. My hair, standing up in its typical every-which-way, I rip through without a care about what it's doing to my hair. Unprovoked, I feel this quiet rage bubbling inside me, and I just want to punch something. Or someone. Or just scream. I'm going to lose my mind if I can't shout and rip something apart.

"You ready, Munchkin?" Rove pops his head into my room, looking his usual carelessly attractive self in pre-distressed jeans and black shirt. I try to shake off the mood swing, but I'm still on edge.

"No, God. Just give me a minute."

"Whoa, what crawled up your butt?"

"Get out, Rove. I can't get ready with you barking at me."

"What the heck, Cheyenne? What's your problem?" He steps all the way into the room, shutting the door carefully behind him. Not that it'll help at all. These walls are paper-thin.

"Everything's my problem. You! Eli! My parents! Kara! Eli! No, you know what? Thomas is my problem! Him and his freaking power complex." I collapse onto my bed, a weird sense of exhaustion hitting me.

"Now that last statement, I can totally support. He's being an ass. I think everyone can agree on that." When I don't respond, he picks up my phone and holds it above my face. "Get dressed. I want to go meet your friends, slash be away from the freak show."

I snatch the phone out of his hands just before he flits out of the room.

By the time I make my way downstairs with my empty glass, Rove is prancing by the doorway, anxious to be out of the house and away from Thomas. I slip my glass into the kitchen, sneak past the dining room, and we almost make it out the door before Thomas flits in front of us. "Where exactly do you two think you are going?" He crosses his arms, blocking the door.

"We're meeting Anne for lunch. I talked to you about this the other day." I try to hold back my sigh, but I'm obviously not successful when I see his nostrils flare. "Thomas..."

"I don't recall you asking permission, and if I remember correctly, you're going somewhere else after lunch?"

"If you already know all of this, then why are we still standing here?" Rove asks, leaning lazily against the doorframe.

"I would remind you to watch your mouth, kid. I can send you home just as quickly as you came." A weird sense of unease washes over me when Rove stands up straight, mirroring Thomas by crossing his arms. And for a moment, they have a staring contest. Who is alpha enough to hold the gaze longest, I guess. Thomas stands to his full height, which definitely beats Rove, so that he's looking down at him. And I'm just standing there, waiting to leave.

I can feel my phone buzzing in my pocket from Anne's constant texts. We're definitely going to be late if Thomas doesn't get over his power complex really fast.

"Where are you going this afternoon, Cheyenne?" Thomas mutters again when Rove finally looks away, frustrated.

"I don't know, to some fair that's going on. Anne knows the details. I'm just following her."

"When you get there, you'll let me know where and what it is. We clear?" Thomas looks down his nose at me, and I have to push away the urge to smack him.

"Of course, your majesty." With that, Rove grabs my arm and pulls me out the door before Thomas can come up with another reason to delay us.

We don't get a minute of rest. Anne's waiting outside the house, hand on hip. "Oh, my gosh! I was about to come charging in there. I thought your sister was holding you hostage or something! You weren't answering your phone; you didn't meet me at the restaurant, so I figured I might as well come over here and make sure you were still alive. Thank goodness, I don't want to go to this thing by myself!" She throws her arms around me when Rove and I get down the porch stairs. "Oh, my gosh! You must be Rove. Cheyenne's told me so much about you in that she's told me that you're her cousin, and you're not a jerk."

"Well, both of those are compliments. I'm glad she didn't share any of the bad stuff." He winks, which is returned by a curious eyebrow raise.

"I said you aren't a jerk most of the time. This is one of those times that you are," I elbow him in the gut, mouthing an apology to Anne. "So where are we headed? New lunch place?"

"No, it's a little too late for lunch. We're going to meet Mason and Eli for gelato. You're going to love this place, Cheyenne! It's the coolest."

Glancing out the corner of my eye, I notice Rove's smile and want to punch him. Fingers crossed he doesn't say anything to Anne. "Now, I've met Eli before, but who's Mason?" he asks, grinning at me like an idiot.

"Oh, Mason's my boyfriend; he's in a band with Eli. That's how I met him." Rove's face falls ever so slightly, but it's only visible to me. Anne is already walking away. "Come on, they're waiting on us!"

We rush after her. I have to take extra giant steps to keep up with Anne's fast pace and Rove's long legs. "So what are we doing after gelato? You never really clarified that."

"The band has a gig for a benefit carnival in City Park."

"What's the benefit for?" I ask, as we turn onto the heart of Bourbon Street. The place is dead, but I can hear the preparations going on inside all the clubs and bars. Come tonight, this place will be filled with people.

"Breast Cancer. Mason's mom has been battling it for five years now." Rove and I exchange a glance behind Anne's back.

"Is she okay?" Rove asks.

A shiver runs down Anne's spine as we wait for her answer. "Yeah," her voice cracks. "She'll be fine. She's in remission right now. You'll probably actually get to meet her, and you are in for a treat! Before she got sick, she was this badass government agent. She's traveled all over the world and speaks like ten languages. She has the absolute best stories, the ones she can share that is. Plus, she's the sweetest lady you'll ever meet in your life."

Nine

Twenty minutes later, we turn into a small gelato shop, PoGels. The place is empty except for two familiar faces sitting in a corner. The textured walls are painted the shades of sunset, starting at the ceiling with a pale pink, transitioning to midnight blue at the bottom of the walls. Hanging over the gelato menu is a square black board with a quote written in neon blue chalk. "*The course of true love never did run smooth.*"

Mason and Eli stand up to meet us. Mason throws his arms around Anne and smiles at me. "Hey. Who's this?"

Rove comes to stand beside me. "This is my cousin, Rove. He's visiting for a couple of days. Rove, this is Mason, and you remember Eli." Rove shakes Mason's hand, once he releases Anne, and grabs Eli's hand for one of those typical guy handshakes, something I've never, nor will I ever, understand. I don't meet Eli's eyes, no matter how hard he looks at me.

"Good to see you again, man! How've you been?" Rove smacks Eli's back as they follow us up to the counter. A girl stands at the cash register waiting for us to order. Her bullring and eyebrow piercings match the colorful tattoo sleeve running down her left arm.

"Eli, where's your truck?" Anne asks as she roams the menu board.

"We left it at the park and took a cab over here. It'll be

too busy when we're ready to head over there."

The girl behind the counter just glares at us, bored with our conversation. "Before you order, if you can guess the poet," she boringly points to the quote above her head without looking at us, "you get a free small gelato."

"Shakespeare," both Eli and I shout at the exact same time. I glare at him as he smiles confidently at the cashier.

"Well, aren't you cute?" the girl grumbles as she grabs two small blue cups. She turns to me and asks, "What kind do you want?"

"Chocolate, please." She plops two tiny scoops of dark chocolate into my cup and thrusts it at me. Cranky, much?

I find a table outside while everyone else orders. Eli is the first to join me, thankfully not saying anything as he chooses the seat across from mine. We just stare silently at each other, scooping bites of gelato into our mouths with our spoons sized for mice. He smirks at me once, then suddenly sucks in his lips and looks down into his cup. "What?" I ask. "What's wrong?" He shakes his head without a word, smiling into his cup. All the animosity from last night is gone.

Rove walks over a moment later with a large cup that contains way more sugar than he needs. He snorts as he pulls out the chair next to me and says, "You got a little something on ya, Munchkin." He rubs the right side of his mouth and the tip of his nose. I quickly wipe my arm across my face, a knot forming in my stomach. Pulling my hand away from my face, I turn to Rove for approval, but he just shakes his head, chuckling, and touches his nose again. I scrub viciously at my nose until it feels raw. Suddenly, Eli pulls a white handkerchief out of his pocket and hands it to me.

"You carry a handkerchief?" I ask, taking it carefully out of his hand to avoid any contact.

"Always have, always will," he says proudly. "Call me old fashioned, but I'm always the one prepared for instances like this." Eli smiles at me, a crooked, half smile that forms butterflies in my stomach. Once they confirm that the chocolate is gone, I toss the handkerchief back to his side of the table and lean back in my chair to finish the rest of my gelato.

This is a beautiful little alcove. Outside the parlor, the patio is covered top to bottom in vibrant green ivy. They've hung oil lanterns on wires and strung crystal lights through the ivy. I look down at the concrete below my feet and gasp at the beautiful chalk drawings on each tile: the Mona Lisa, Van Gogh's Starry Night, among others. I'm sitting on a sunset that splays the rich colors from the walls of the gelato parlor.

On a small table in the corner sits a box of worn down chalk. My fingers begin to itch, a feeling I haven't felt in a long time. I glance up at Eli, who is gracefully slipping a bite of strawberry gelato into his mouth, then at Anne and Mason, who sit closely together laughing at something private.

I stand silently and pull the chalk lid open. I choose colors and walk over to a blank concrete square near the front of the courtyard. Kneeling down, I pull out the black chalk and trace the silhouette of two people, a boy and a girl, their hands interlocked. When I'm satisfied with the silhouettes, I fill in their bodies until the chalk is no more than a stub. Behind the figures, I begin smearing in the colors of sunrise starting with pink to orange to light blue, dark blue, and finally finishing out with a deep violet. The pink splays just high enough to outline the couple and show their faces turned toward one another. I don't realize what I'm drawing until it's in front of me.

Four pairs of feet tiptoe over to me as I set the final stub of chalk back into the box and lean back to look at my picture. I dust off my chalked hands and stand in the middle of my friends who are all staring down at my art.

"Just like riding a bike, huh?" Rove whispers in my ear, and I nod in agreement, smiling at my creation. The last time I drew anything was before my Ascension. I sketched all the time and was quite good. But after I ascended, I don't know, the imagination just disappeared. For a long time, I would just sit with a pencil in my hand and a notepad on my desk, but nothing came.

Eli grabs the white chalk and kneels down by the corner. He leans close to me as he scripts out my name across the bottom and dates it. Come rain, the picture will wash away. But right now, it feels as permanent as the concrete itself.

Ten

"So are you having fun yet?" Anne asks Rove as we walk around Carousel Gardens Amusement Park. Rove is definitely in his element, while I'm still reveling in the beauty of the magnificent moss covered oak tree that stands 60 feet tall with a trunk as wide as two of me. We've been here for over two hours and have done basically everything Rove wanted to do. He even convinced me to ride their Tilt-A-Whirl, which I'm never doing again.

"Of course I'm having fun!" Rove yells. "We don't have anything like this back home. I hate to tell you this, Anne, but your new friend is from a very boring town where nothing ever happens. We live in a bubble."

"Well, that's depressing. It's something we'll just have to fix. We have another forty-five minutes to kill. What do you want to do?" Anne asks right as we walk up to a bottle-shooting booth. Rove smiles at me, and Anne begins to giggle.

"No, this is not a good idea. One of you idiots is going to hurt someone," I say, reluctantly following them to the counter. A tall man in a striped hat forces a strained smile onto his thin face.

"How can I help y'all on this beautiful day?"

"Three please," Rove says and hands him six dollars. The man snatches the money out of his hand and slams his palm against the start button.

"Good luck," he steps away into the shadows of the booth and stuffs the money into an envelope. Music blasts through invisible speakers as the game begins to whir to life. I lift my rifle, standing between Anne and Rove, and turn to watch my cousin.

"Wanna make a bet?" he asks, grinning impishly at me. "If I beat you, you have to ask Eli out. And if you beat me, which is not likely, I have to..."

"Drop the topic forever and always." I settle the rifle under my right arm, aiming at the middle bottle in the bottom row and shoot. All the old, glass coke bottles come tumbling down in succession. Beside me, Rove shoots three times, managing to knock off only the top bottle from his pyramid. Suddenly, the music stops, and the man steps up to the counter.

"I do believe the young lady has won a prize!" he announces, smiling at people walking by. "What's your prize, m'dear?" I look up at the wall of stuffed animals and rinky-dinks, finally settling on a simple mood ring that barely fits around my pinky finger. "Thank y'all. Come again."

Rove sulks behind Anne and me as we walk away from the booth. I admire my new ring and smile back at Rove. "You know, I technically think you cheated," he grumbles. "You're supposed to start at the top of the pyramid. Everybody knows that, Cheyenne."

"I think you're just a sore loser. Besides, if you start at the top of the pyramid, you have to take them out one by one. Start at the bottom, and you kill them all with one shot," I snicker and turn away. "So, what do you wanna do next? More firing practice?" I can just feel Rove roll his eyes as Anne tries to stifle her laugh.

"You're so mean to him." She loops her arm through mine, and we stumble into the two guys in front of us. They whip around and, being much taller than both of us, glare down at Anne and me.

"Watch where you're...oh, come on!" Erik says, backing away from me. The man beside him looks quizzically between the two of us but doesn't say anything.

"Well, maybe you should walk faster," I say. Rove steps up beside me, standing as tall as Erik. The guy with him stares patiently at the three of us. His long blonde bangs do little to hide the gruesome scar that runs diagonally across his face. He stares at me with green eyes as a slow smile appears on his full lips.

"You must be Cheyenne." The guy steps forward, extending his hand. "I'm Lucas, Eli and Erik's brother." I look down at his hand, then at Rove, not quite sure what to do. Rove nudges me forward, and I accept Lucas's hand. A shadow passes over his face for a brief second, and my stomach does a cartwheel. His gaze is piercing and analyzing, as if he's sizing me up but worse. Suddenly his look changes to recognition and certainty, then his charm reappears. "Obviously, you know Erik. Unfortunately, he's not in the greatest mood today, so if you'll excuse us, it was lovely meeting you." He squeezes my hand gently once then turns away, pulling Erik with him.

"What was that about?" Anne asks, stepping in front of me. I shrug my shoulders, trying to appear calm. He knows. He can't. But he does. Somehow, he knows what I am, which probably means that Eli knows, and Erik. The brothers disappear in the midst of the crowd as we push forward in an attempt to distract ourselves. "How about face painting?" she asks, steering us toward the left side of the path where a tall booth is set up. The line curls around itself as children leave the booth with intricate designs or a full-face paint.

"Um, how about somethin' else?" I ask, eyeing the line impatiently.

"Don't worry about that. I've got connections," she winks at us and leads us past the kids along the side of the booth. Under a tall pink tent, ten tables are lined up in neat rows. The painters display their baldheads proudly as they smile at their eager customers. Anne weaves to the back of the tent, past a woman covering a boy's face with the orange and black stripes of a tiger.

We approach a frail woman sitting in the back corner. She looks up when she hears us, a warm smile on her face. She's beautiful. Her eyes are an even mixture of sky blue and grassy green. Every feature is perfectly defined if you ignore the shadows under her eyes and her sunken cheeks.

"Hey, darling! I was hoping you'd come to see me." The woman carefully pushes herself to her feet and slowly walks toward Anne, folding her in a warm hug. Rove and I stand a few feet away, taking in the woman in front of us.

"Rose, I'd like you to meet my friend Cheyenne and her cousin Rove." Anne motions to us as she unfolds herself from the woman's embrace. "Guys, this is Mason's mom, Rose." Rose smiles at me as we step closer, meets me halfway, and pulls me into the same warm hug that Anne just received.

"I've heard so much about you. I'm so glad you're able to come today. It's an absolutely beautiful day for a carnival, don't you think?"

"Yes, ma'am, and you have quite the turnout," I say, glancing back at the lengthening line.

"Oh, yes. The people of New Orleans have always been good to us and our fundraisers." She pats my hand gently and leads us to her table. "So how about a painting—on the house?" She pulls me into the seat across from hers, smiling up at Rove, and grabs a paintbrush. "What'll you have?" I glance down at her chart, but I already know what I want.

"I'll just have the ribbon, please." She smiles to herself and dips the tip of her brush in light pink paint. Turning my head to the left, Ms. Rose places the cool brush against my cheek and begins tracing the outline. I shudder when she fills in the ribbon and try not to wriggle as a tickling sensation bursts against my cheek.

"There you go, sweetie pie. Looks wonderful." I stand up to let Anne sit in my place and tilt my head toward the wind to dry the paint. "Are you excited to hear Mason? He's been working on some new songs, but he hasn't let me hear them—says he wants me to be surprised."

"Oh, I think you'll enjoy 'em, Rose. He's worked really hard," Anne says. "And Eli's been a big help." Rove glances over at me for a moment as he smiles to himself.

"That boy is so sweet. He's been such a good friend to Mason while all this has been going on. My boy's got it good," she chuckles softly as she finishes the pink ribbon on Anne's cheek. "And what about you, sir? May I paint you a pink ribbon somewhere?" She smiles at him and pats the seat in front of her.

He holds out the underside of his forearm to her.

"How about here?" With a quick swipe of her brush, the ribbon is painted as boldly as a tattoo. He holds out his arm to let the wind dry it.

"Hey, Rose, it's about time for the band to play. You wanna walk over there with us?" Anne asks while Rose begins cleaning her station.

"Sure thing, honey. Hold on just a minute." She throws her plastic brushes into the trashcan and wipes off her paint-stained hands with a wet baby wipe. Her large apron swallows her small frame as she unties the ribbon and places it over her chair. "Alrighty, let's get this party started!" She loops both her arms through Anne's and mine and pulls us out of the tent toward a path, which finally leads us to a concert space named Pavilion of the Two Sisters.

The band is set up in front of the fountain that houses a towering statue: Enrique Alferez's famous "The Flute Player," Anne explains. A giant crowd of people is seated in folding chairs in front of Mason's battery-operated speakers. Mason tunes his guitar and taps the top of the microphone. Their saxophonist blows scales into his mouthpiece, while Eli raises his cymbal a few inches higher. Mason has reserved seats right in the front for his mom and us, so we lead her down the aisle between the large crowd of people that's already seated. Color forms in her otherwise pale face as she eases herself into the chair, and Mason smiles at her, his matching blue-green eyes meeting hers.

A tall woman in a pink "Save the Girls" t-shirt approaches Mason's microphone, smiling at the growing audience. "Hey, everyone! Thanks for coming out today for our fundraiser. I hope y'all have had a great time.

The last act will be a performance by the son of one of our very own cancer warriors. Please put your hands together for Monde Musique!" she claps loudly, stepping away. Mason approaches the microphone, his acoustic guitar ready, his eyes focused on Anne and his mother. He first strums harmonic chords and the saxophonist joins in with a few sparse notes. Eli runs what looks like a small metal rake across the top of his cymbal just as the pianist and saxophonist delve into an upbeat juke. Eli bounces a repetitive rhythm into his snare, and Mason busts out lighthearted lyrics. They've gotten better since the first time I heard them a couple of weeks ago.

After awhile, Mason finally stops to take a breath and introduce the band. He turns back to face the crowd and holds out his hand. "And now I'd like to bring my girlfriend and manager, Anne Lacroix, up on stage to sing this next song with me, which, by the way, we co-wrote." Anne releases Rose's hand and takes Mason's as she stands beside him.

The two stare at each other as the music begins. Mason pushes his guitar to his back, holding onto her hand. The audience is gone to them—whenever they look at each other like that, everyone else disappears. The song is beautiful: soft melodies with an eerie undertone, hollow chords and sporadic saxophone runs. Anne ends the song with a miraculously high note that puts the audience in a state of awe. After several minutes of applause, Anne rejoins us, smiling from ear to ear. Mason concludes the set with his newest piece. He hands the lyrics to his mother as the saxophonist packs up and joins the audience.

The song is perfect. "*You Give Me Hope*" talks about

the inspiration his mother has given him: how brave she's been, how calm. They are each other's rocks as they deal with her illness on their own. He's an only child, and his father left the picture a while ago, Anne told me. None of their family lives anywhere near New Orleans. He's her support system, but he's only nineteen. I don't see how he forces himself to be so strong. I'd be an emotional wreck. But the song isn't about their struggles—it's about his mother's victories.

I look over at Rose, and tears are pouring down her cheeks but a smile on her beaming face. Anne's crying, too, but she's doing a better job of hiding it. Mason sniffles as he concludes the song and turns from the audience to wipe away his tears. The crowd bursts into applause, cheers, and whistles as the band moves into a line and bows. Eli grabs Mason's shoulder, giving it a tight squeeze. Mason bites his lip as Anne rushes up to him, and he falls into her open arms.

The woman who gave the introduction returns to the microphone. "Well, wasn't that just wonderful? Why don't we give Monde Musique another hand?" Anne rubs Mason's back as they turn around to accept the second round of applause. "Thank you, Mason and Monde Musique, for performing today. It's much appreciated. And that, Ladies and Gentlemen, brings our event to a close. Thank y'all so much for coming out to support us today. We hope you've enjoyed your experience and have a great rest of your weekend." The applause continues as she walks away, and the band begins to pack up their instruments. Rove and I walk Rose to where Mason is packing up and then back away as he wraps her in a bear hug, forcing a smile onto his face.

"That was nice, wasn't it?" Rove asks. He nudges me, and I straighten my tilted head.

"Huh?" I watch Eli complete Mason's packing as he talks with his mother.

"Eli," he whispers. "He's a good friend." He nudges me again, and I scoff as I walk away from him.

"Need any help?" I ask Eli, who is bent over Mason's guitar case.

He glances up, startled. "Yeah." He straightens himself. "Actually, I do. You can help me carry this stuff to my truck." I lift two of the speakers and slide a cymbal case under my arm, ready to follow him. He glances back at me, two drums in his arms. "You know this is going to take two trips, right?"

"I'm good." I follow him through the park, watching as he carries the drums under his arms with ease.

At the back of the park, we come to a beat up Ford F-150. Its black paint is beginning to chip off, and the bottom half looks like a pig in a mud pen.

Eli opens the bed of the truck and pushes a pile of junk hidden by a tarp toward the back, and I could swear the drums just float onto the truck. I blink once, twice. He wasn't even touching them. My mouth drops open. He just used magic right in front of me! In front of everyone! I glance at the crowd slowly leaving the park, but no one is paying us any attention.

When I look back at Eli, he's staring at me. "Something wrong, Cheyenne?" Not responding is my best chance of keeping my thoughts to myself. "Well, alright then," he sighs. "Ready to get the second load?"

I nod my head, setting my drums beside his, and follow him through the park.

"How long have you and Mason been friends?" I ask.

"Um, wow it feels like forever. Must be since middle school? I caught a couple of our classmates teasing him about his dad leaving. I made them regret that decision. We've been friends ever since."

"You're a good friend, Eli. Mason's lucky to have you."

He stops, a smile creeping onto his lips. "I'm sorry, but did you just say something nice to me?" He stares at me in awe.

"You should really learn to take a compliment and shut up." I walk past him, arms crossed over my chest.

"Oh, come on, Cheyenne, don't put the wall back up. I'm sorry!" He jogs to catch up, grabbing my shoulder.

"I don't have a wall!" I shake off his hand and keep walking. People are dispersing, and I have to push through them as they make their ways to the streetcar stop.

Eli follows behind me the rest of the way, hands shoved into his pockets. Rove has already packed up the rest of the equipment, and as we approach the group, Eli brushes past me to grab two amps and a cymbal. I stop beside Anne and smile at Rose, but my eyes stay glued to Eli's back, his muscles coiled like a snake ready to strike. Rove plows behind him, carrying a load that would drag down an ordinary person.

I turn back to Anne, Rose, and Mason as the guys disappear into the crowd. Rose follows my line of sight and then turns back to me, concern clouding her pale face. But that concern vanishes with a blink of an eye. "So are you two taking Cheyenne and Rove to the museum tonight?"

Ms. Rose asks, her easy smile returning.

"Well, it was going to be a surprise." Anne avoids looking at me as I glare at her.

"How can it possibly be a surprise, Annie? She's got to get ready, doesn't she?"

"I'm sorry, but what exactly am I getting ready for?" I place my hands on my hips and turn to stare at Anne.

"Annie, you might as well tell her." Rose smiles at me, nudging Anne with her arm.

For a moment, Anne says nothing. She simply stares at the ground, formulating a plan in her mind. It's scary how close we've become in two weeks. Suddenly, her head shoots up, back straight, eyes narrowed, chin high.

"Cheyenne. You have absolutely nothing to worry about. Mason and I wanted this to be a surprise, and it's going to stay that way. You're going to come with Rose and me, and we'll get you ready while the boys all go together. I refuse to allow my surprise to be spoiled!" She grabs my wrist and pulls me away just as Eli and Rove return, both of them staring after me, mouths slightly open as if to say something.

HANNAH RIALS

Eleven

"Oww! Anne, you're stabbing my eyeball." I dodge the pencil aimed in my direction, watching her arm carefully. "I swear, if you come at me with that thing one more time."

"Calm down, Cheyenne, it's just eyeliner, not a stake. No need to be so melodramatic," she scoffs, grabbing my chin and tilting my head toward the sky. I feel the urge to move, but she's got a tight grip. "There, but if you don't sit still, your perfect hairdo is going to fall out, and I don't think Rose would appreciate that very much." Anne smiles at her as I let myself relax, painfully aware of the liquid foundation plastered on my skin and the numerous bobby pins jabbed into my scalp.

"Am I done yet?" My back slouches into the cushioned chair as I cross my arms over my chest.

"Your hair and makeup are done, but you have to wait to put your dress on until I'm ready. And Rose, will you please keep her away from all mirrors until I return. Thank you!" Anne floats out of the room, a triumphant smile glued to her smug face. The wicker chair creaks as I roll my neck back and forth across the top of it, working the nerves out of my neck. I don't know why I'm nervous. I've gotten dressed up before. The only difference is that I actually knew what I was dressing up for.

Rose sits silently on a bed that looks as old as the house.

It's a small house with a purple exterior, which means that the first owners most likely spoke French. The floors are a deep oak that matches the rest of the ornate furniture. The bed is canopied with robin egg blue drapes cascading down the sides and tied with ribbons against the bedposts. The ceiling looks like an imitation of Michelangelo's Sistine Chapel. Everything in this house seems artistic and antique. There isn't a room without a painting, and the walls that aren't covered in paintings are covered with shelves of books—more books than I could ever read in my lifetime.

My eyes land on a red vase filled with gorgeous white roses in full bloom. I look down at the vase once more, the bright crimson vase. The color stirs an unbearable ache in my throat, and I'm now painfully aware that I'm alone with an extremely weak, ill human. I glance at Rose out of the corner of my eye, watching as the vein in her neck throbs. *What's wrong with me*? I've never had a thought like that before. I would never *ever* consider a human as food. That's so wrong. Not to mention, the Council would probably flay me if they could read my mind. My heart pounds, and an awful cough racks my body, leaving my throat a tunnel of fire. Rose turns to me calmly, a knowledge that I can't recognize in her tired eyes.

"I'll be right back, Cheyenne. Don't worry." She slowly stands and tiptoes out of the bedroom. When she returns, she's carrying two full bottles of cold blood, just like the ones the Council delivers to every Deuxsang residence once a month. Panic rises in my chest. I bite my lip and sit on my hands as they begin to shake.

"Oh, honey, don't worry. I've known for a while. Anne

can't keep a secret from me." I swallow, not sure what I'm supposed to say. Anne completely disregarded the most important covenant that our kind made with the Council: Keep the secret. I can't believe this! My best friend is risking unspeakable punishment for us and everyone we know all for a stupid human boy. Now that I know, what the hell am I supposed to do?

Rose steps closer, her eyes never straying from mine. She takes one of my hands and places it around the bottle. "Cheyenne, take it." I watch her as she backs away and sits on the edge of the bed, her head turned away. I stare at the bottle, silently suffering as the smell infiltrates my nose and makes my mouth water. I'm getting that feeling, the feeling that everything is about to go terribly wrong.

I could be paranoid. I could be, but I'm not. This is big. This is all wrong. This is not how the world is supposed to work. Deuxsang aren't supposed to date humans, and humans are *not* supposed to know about us. Plus, witches are supposed to be in hiding, not doing magic tricks to impress me.

I glance back at Rose. The smell of the blood stokes the fire in my throat, and another fit of coughs racks my chest. Slowly, carefully, I bring the bottle to my lips, allowing just a drop of blood to fall on my tongue, but that's all it takes. In a matter of seconds, I've drained it. I notice this doesn't taste like the stuff we have at Thomas and Kara's, but that's the least of my concerns right now. It's still blood, and I just drank in front of a totally aware human. I lick my lips and wipe off the rest that my tongue can't reach with the sleeve of my robe. I rub my tongue over my teeth to clear away any residue.

Rose finally turns back to me, smiling in relief. "Do you need more, Cheyenne?"

"No, thank you. That was enough." We stare at each other in uncomfortable silence. I flinch as my extended fangs sink back into my gums. I never even noticed that they had dropped down.

I can tell that she wants to say something. The words are on the tip of her tongue, but the door bursts open, and Anne is standing on the threshold, her red hair pinned up in 1940s victory curls. Her lips are redder than cherries, and her black polka-dotted dress twirls with her as she spins through the room.

"Well? What do you think?" She lands on the opposite side of the room, a dizzy smile on her lips. She blinks a few times to focus her eyes and stops. Her face falls along with her raised arms. "What's wrong? What's happened?" She walks back toward us, a hesitant hand gripping the bedpost. I glance at Rose out of the corner of my eye and then look down. Nothing could make this situation any worse. Might as well rip off the band aid.

"How could you tell a *human*, Anne?" My eyes meet hers, and I feel the weight of both of their gazes. "How could you break *that* rule?" She looks back at me with her wide, green eyes, her made-up face unable to conceal her shock.

"How?" she starts.

"Blood, Anne! She offered me blood! You have a human stocking blood for you! Are you insane?" I'm beyond controlling myself.

Rose, on the other hand, chimes in as if we're all having a nice girly chat. "Cheyenne had a bit of an episode, so I grabbed some of your supply to help her."

"Are you okay now?" Anne asks, looking back at me.

"I'm fine. I just—I think I need to go home." I start to stand up, untying my robe and throwing it over the back of the chair. "Thank you for your hospitality, ma'am."

"Wait, Cheyenne. You can't leave before we talk." Rose pulls herself to her feet. I stand by the door, my hand resting against the frame. When I don't move, she continues. "I'm not just any human, dear. I'm a witch, and I knew about Annie long before she ever worked up the courage to say anything to Mason and me."

My nostrils flare. If Mason knows about Anne, then he probably knows about me. Anne flinches under my gaze. "We can sense each other. And now that you know, you'll be able to do it too."

But when I look up at Anne, her jaw touches her chest as she tries to comprehend Rose's words. "Wait, back up. What do you mean you're a witch? That's not possible, is it?" She looks to me, and I know she's experiencing everything that I've been dealing with the past couple of days.

"I'm sorry, I know this is difficult for you. I am a member of a very old coven, and our history is closely linked with yours."

"So does this mean... Is Mason a witch too?" Her chest is heaving. She looks like she's about to pass out.

"No, that is not his path." I don't see why it would make much of a difference. Either way, she's screwed. She can't possibly continue seeing him with this knowledge.

"So I don't get it. Why are you telling us this?" I ask. "And why haven't I run out that door yet?"

"You're quite fiery for a Deuxsang, aren't you?"

Hearing the word come out of her mouth is a slap in the face. "I'm telling you because it's time. I knew the moment I saw Cheyenne checking out my carotid artery." I think I'm going to be sick. But she's laughing!

Anne turns to me in horror. "Cheyenne, you didn't!"

"Of course not," I lie, forcing myself not to look down in shame.

"Shh, don't worry about it," Rose coos. "But it is strange, definitely uncharacteristic for Deuxsang. I believe it's a sign that something is happening."

"What are you talking about?" I snap. This is getting out of hand.

"Cheyenne, please sit down. You're making me anxious." I didn't realize I was pacing until Anne throws out her arm to stop me mid-step. I look up at her, but she won't meet my gaze. Reluctantly, I sit back down by the vanity as far away from the both of them as possible.

"We, my coven that is, have known for ages that the vampires are planning something, but we've never been able to discover exactly what. Vampires' mental abilities are impossible to penetrate. Our magic has never been able to get information from their minds. Deuxsang are another story. With only one instead of four abilities, your minds are not so different from humans. Our psychics have learned a great deal about your world by getting close enough to read your energies."

"So is that what you're doing?" I exclaim. "Getting close enough to Anne and now me to steal information from our 'energies'?" My sarcasm does not go unnoticed.

"As a matter of fact, no," Rose responds with attitude to match my own. "I don't know why our paths have crossed in the way they have, but I'm sure there's a reason. May I please continue?"

I shut up, angry with myself for wanting to know more.

"Our high priestess has charged us with learning as much as we can from the Deuxsang, but unfortunately it does us little good. The vampires have you under their thumb and completely in the dark about their doings. Sometimes I wonder why we even do it, but I must trust her wisdom. Each high priestess passes down clandestine knowledge to her successor, some of which the rest of us never learn."

"Sounds like we're not the only ones kept in the dark." Surprisingly, this snide comment comes from Anne. Rose ignores her and keeps speaking.

"What we do know is that several generations ago, the path of our coven crossed with that of the vampires. Things went badly, as you might expect from dealing with the undead. The records from that time are sparse, but we have reason to believe they stole some magic from us. We must find out what they have done or plan to do with it."

I've reached my breaking point. "Was this before or after a bunch of you slaughtered a town full of Deuxsang?"

For the first time, Rose is the one who looks taken aback. "Excuse me?"

"Oh, what? Your 'psychics' didn't tell you that we know all about how witches massacred our people two-hundred years ago and how the only reason any Deuxsang still exist is because the vampires stopped you before you took out the children?"

"Where did you hear that?"

I'm completely exasperated. I look to Anne for backup.

She replies calmly, "It's one of the first lessons we're taught after we ascend. That's where Deuxsang history begins."

"Begins? What about where you come from? What are you taught about how the Deuxsang came to be?"

I've never considered that before. I didn't learn that story. Anne is unperturbed.

"We were an accident, a fluke of nature. A nameless vampire mated with a nameless human. The vampires are our protectors. They keep us safe from humans, who always seek to destroy what they do not understand."

"That's quite a spiel," Rose interjects. "Sounds like you've been studying for your Affirmation interview." She stares at us, but we remain silent. "Remind me, this massacre supposedly occurred two-hundred years ago? So early 1800's?"

"Yes, and what do you mean supposedly?" I shout.

"Oh, I can say without a doubt that it never happened. But seeing as you've been indoctrinated to the point of recitation, I think it's pointless to argue the fact right now." I start to yell at her some more, but she raises a hand to stop me. Weak as she is, the gesture is extremely intimidating. "My High Priestess is currently traveling. When she returns, I will speak with her, and hopefully we can find some answers. In the meantime, I might approach the rest of the Ashfords."

"Whoa! Eli's a witch too?" Anne shrieks, throwing herself away from the doorframe. "Cheyenne, did you know about this?"

I shrug. "Only recently."

"But, now that everything's all out in the open, you can talk to him about it." Rose attempts a smile, but it turns into a frown when she doesn't get a reaction out of me.

"I should be getting home now. Thank you for the... drink." I stand again and move toward the door.

Rose stops me again. "Don't be silly. You're still going to the museum."

Dumbfounded, I pivot wildly. "You expect me to still go along with this, knowing that you all are witches?"

"Oh, please. If we witches were out to get you, would I really be lending you my make up? Or letting *you* make out with my son?" She looks pointedly at Anne, who bites her lip and grins awkwardly. "Yes, I expect you to go have a good time with your friends. Like I said, we'll talk more when we know more."

I can't look at either one of them yet, but I know Anne is already on board.

"Cheyenne, please come with me. I've had this surprise planned for a while, and I think you're really going to enjoy it. Please?" Anne holds her clasped hands up to me in a prayer.

I sigh, defeated. "Okay, just for a little while." Anne shrieks and throws her arms around me, bouncing on the balls of her feet.

"I promise, you will *not* regret this!" I can't understand her giddiness, but I force my smile to match hers. "Let's get you into your party dress, shall we?"

Twelve

Anne and I share a silent cab ride to the museum. I keep feeling her eyes on me, but I stare steadily out the window, watching the sun set over the city. I've no clue where we are. Anne's never taken me to this part of town. The straps of my shoes are digging into the backs of my heels. Bobby pins feel like needles stabbing into my head.

Anne's finally built up the courage to say something to me. She turns in her seat just as my phone buzzes in my purse. I don't turn around as I answer the phone, expecting Thomas or Kara.

"Hey, my girl! How are you?" A familiar booming voice comes through the receiver.

"Dad? What's wrong?" I ask, trying my hardest to ignore Anne's glare. I don't exactly want to talk to him, but at least it's a distraction.

"I'm checking in. Your mom and I haven't heard from you, and we want to make sure everything is alright." I can hear the underlying accusation behind that calm voice. I'm in trouble.

"Sorry, Dad. I'm just busy."

"That's not an excuse, but I'll let it go. So where are you now?"

"Somewhere with my friends. Not exactly sure. All I know is that I look like I just walked out of the forties," I say, glancing down at my red dress that comes up to my collarbone. "But Dad," I look over at Anne, head hung, hands crossed, "I'll call you back. I think we're almost there."

"Hey, tell Kara to call me."

"Bye." I hang up and finally turn to face Anne. "I'm sorry, Anne, but I have a right to be mad. You know that we're not supposed to tell them about us, even if they aren't really them at all," I whisper, glancing at the cab driver. "What you did was bad. If the Council finds out..."

"I know, okay? I just wanted someone to talk to other than my parents. They don't care about me, about what I do. All they care about is that our family keeps up its stupid appearance. Rose didn't judge me when I told her. Someone was taking an interest in me and trying to understand me, okay?"

"Anne, I understand your need for someone to support you. I swear, I do. But you've got no idea how dangerous this is. They could blab, and you'd be killed. Didn't you think about any of this?"

"Of course I did. You just don't understand, okay. If you were with Eli, you'd have told him, too."

"Oh, no. This isn't about me. This is about you and your mistake."

"Come on, be honest with yourself. You care about him, and you know it. And now you know what he is, but that doesn't mean you can't still be together. If you'd just give him a chance..."

"Anne, you're insane. I'm in enough trouble just knowing." I cross my arms over my chest, unconsciously biting my bottom lip.

"Cheyenne, I'm so sorry I brought you into my messed

up life, but I think you're wrong about Eli."

"Can we drop it, please?" I ask, staring at her incredulously.

"Sure." Her half-smile looks absolutely pitiful. "So we're good?"

Why do I always feel like the bad guy? "Yeah."

"I probably should've told you that they knew about us. I still don't know what to think of all this *stuff*."

The cab driver suddenly parks. "Here we are, ladies. New Orleans' very own World War II Museum. Enjoy your night." Anne slips some cash into his hand, and we slide out of the cab and step right into a line of people running out the front door of the Museum. Two huge windows make up the front of the building, displaying fighter jets and B-52s. Tank statues face the building, pointed up at the planes, on the front lawn.

Everyone around us is dressed in the same forties style. My ankles wobble in my stupid heels, and a cool breeze sends chill bumps down my bare back. "Anne, what are we doing here?"

"Every Sunday in July and August, the museum hosts a free forties swing dance party. Tonight is the opening night!" She's glowing as she stares into the museum, probably looking for the boys. In a second, she starts waving madly to them.

"Hold on a second, are you telling me that I have to swing dance?" She nods once, avoiding my glare. "Anne, you suck."

"Hello, ladies!" Mason wraps his arm around Anne's waist, planting a big kiss on her cheek. Rove whistles, smiling at me.

"Well, looky here. Looks like my little cousin *can* get dressed up, after all." Rove applauds, bowing slightly.

"Would you shut up?" I start to punch his shoulder but stop as Eli approaches with the same blonde beanpole from the other night attached to his arm. He looks like a member of the Rat Pack. A pinstriped fedora sits on top of his head, tilted slightly downward to cast a shadow over his eyes. His hair's been slicked back with gel. A full-fledged smile is beaming on his handsome face.

"How's the gang doing tonight?" he asks, tipping his hat to us. "I'd like you to meet Crystal Johns. Crystal, these are my friends Rove, Mason, Anne, and you remember Cheyenne." He forces his smile, directed at me.

Anne steps forward to shake the girl's hand. "Nice to meet you." Crystal gives her a once over as she limply shakes her hand. Rove glances at me but doesn't say anything. "So do you go to school around here?"

"No." It speaks. "I'm just visiting for the summer. E and I go way back." She links her arm through his, grinning from ear to ear with her perfectly white teeth.

"E?" Mason snorts, smirking at Eli, who only rolls his eyes. Anne nudges him in his side, and he bites his lip. "Sorry." The line begins to move, and I walk to the front of the group. Anne jogs to catch up with me, leaving the boys to gawk over Eli's date.

"So we're going to have fun tonight, right?" she nudges my shoulder. I ignore her. The sooner she lets me leave, the better.

A man in a pinstriped suit stamps my hand, allowing me entrance into the museum. The group follows me into a room where colossal planes and jets hang from the ceiling.

Many of the floor displays have been pushed against the walls to make room for dancing. A live band stands on the stage at the back of the room, smiling down at the dancing crowd. Every inch of the floor is covered in feet kicking, spinning, and tapping. Men lift women, swing them from side to side, and finally slide them on the floor between their legs.

Without hesitation, Mason pulls Anne into the middle of the crowd. I see Anne's red shoes fly up in the air, her high, distinctive laugh audible over "Hooked on Swing." Eli and *Miss Crystal Johns* follow suit while I sit back and watch. Rove walks over, smiling into the crowd.

"Let's go dance!" he says. I stare at the girls' spinning dresses, the boys' twisting feet. I hum along to the popular song, nodding my head to the beat. He repeats himself, successfully gaining my attention.

I look up, startled. "I'm sorry, have you ever seen me dance?"

"I've seen you *try* to dance," he smirks, amused.

"There's no way I'm gonna dance like that in front of all these people. I don't even know how to swing dance. Uh-uh. Not happening. Go find yourself someone else." I shoo him away and continue to watch the crowd.

"You'll never know how if you don't try. Come on!" He grabs my hand, pulling me out of my chair. I tug on his hand, trying to wriggle my wrist out of his grip, but his strength matches my own. He locates Anne and Mason, with Eli not too far away. I meet Eli's green eyes for only a second before I glare at the floor. Anne laughs as she spots us and claps her hands. "Hooray!"

I roll my eyes as Rove positions my lifeless body and

takes my hands. "Follow what I do." I bite my lip as he pulls away from me, still grasping my hands, then pulls me to his right side as he comes up to my left. We switch and pull apart again. We repeat this move several times before, without warning, he grabs my hips, lifting me off the ground, and swings me from side to side. "Swing your legs." I stare straight at him. "Just do it." I do as he says, swinging my legs from left to right, building more and more momentum. Finally, he pushes my lower body even higher in the air, then slides me against the floor between his legs, letting me go to grab my wrists and pull me back to my feet. I wobble on my heels, laughing hysterically.

"That was amazing!" I yell over the music. "How'd you learn to do that?"

He shrugs his shoulders. "I watch movies." He grabs my hands again, and we dance for the rest of this song and begin another. I laugh as we spin, twist, and swing across the dance floor. Suddenly, I bump into a couple behind us. I turn around to apologize but bite my tongue. Eli's smiling at me, an "I-knew-you-would-like-this" kind of smile—completely irritating. Rove looks between the two of us and at Eli's date who is huffing and crossing her arms.

"Hey, Eli, mind if I steal your date? I'm tired of Cheyenne stomping on me with her two left feet." Rove holds his hand out to the girl, and she takes it, smiling spitefully at Eli. Before he can even reply, they disappear into the crowd. Eli looks after them for a moment before turning to me. We stare silently at each other as he stuffs his hands in his pockets while I pull at my fingers.

"I'm gonna go sit down." I motion over my shoulder, watching Eli's shoes very carefully, and turn on my wobbling heel.

"Cheyenne, wait." Eli grabs my arm, and a warm tingle shoots from his hand. I gasp as a fire sparks in my throat, and I turn painfully to face him. "Come on."

I look from side to side. "I'd hate to upset your date."

He chuckles. "She's not my date. Crystal's a family friend." He reaches carefully for my hand, as if he's afraid that I'll pull away.

I let him pull me close, stiffening my body as the fire in my throat grows. He takes both my hands in his. I look at him then back at the crowd. I gulp, as I turn back to him, eyes wide, palms sweaty. He smiles at me with that perfect half smile that doesn't quite show his teeth. We begin to do the same movements that I did with Rove, but this time it's different. His eyes stay locked on mine. I don't think about what I'm doing, I just do it.

Suddenly, Eli grabs my hips, lifts me into the air, and spins me around until the room spins with me. He slides me on the ground between his legs, his hands slowly sliding up the sides of my body before he grabs my wrists to pull me up. He catches me around the waist as I collapse against his chest, laughing. His crooked grin turns into a full-fledged smile. We finish off two more songs, laughing, spinning, and yelling into each other's ears. I've nearly forgotten about my throat. Every time he touches me, it sparks, but I push it out of my mind.

My laugh echoes through the room as the band starts playing a slow song. We stand apart, hands clasped, smiling like loons. He's slowly pulling me closer.

"I need some water." I drop one of his hands, but he holds onto the other.

"Cheyenne, just one more?"

I meet his eyes. I'm afraid to talk for fear of how my voice might sound. I glance at all the partners pulling each other close, twirling around in slow circles. The fire grows stronger and stronger. I need blood. Now.

My head spins. I look back at Eli's blurred face, feeling my hand slip out of his as I sway. "I…" My feet carry me away. I elbow my way through the crowd, my throat tightening as I peer at empty faces, searching for Anne. There are too many redheads.

Faces blur in front of me. I hear Eli call after me. The heat from his hand seems to seep into my throat. I squeeze my eyelids shut, trying to focus my eyes. I stumble into a dancing couple and try to apologize, but I'm not quite sure what comes out.

Someone grabs my shoulders and shouts my name. "Cheyenne? Are you okay?" I look up into Anne's face as she steadies me.

"Help. I need…" Anne slides herself under my arm, and Mason follows as they lead me off the dance floor to a quiet corner. I sit down in a chair, swaying, barely listening as Anne tells Mason to pull something out of her purse. I cough, my body shaking, and close my eyes. Anne pushes my mouth open and brings the bottle to my lips. Bless Anne for her recklessness. The first drop of blood on my tongue sparks frenzy. I snatch the bottle from her hands and gulp it down. I hold out my hand for another, but she shakes her head.

The fire dwindles. The room focuses. I swallow the last bit of blood and lick my lips. I don't mean to sigh, but I do. "Are you okay now?" Anne asks, staring at my eyes.

"Yeah, sorry."

Eli comes jogging up to us. I hate myself for thinking it, but even sweaty, he's still perfect. "Are you okay? I couldn't find you anywhere."

"I'm fine. Just a little over-excited, I guess." The band's still playing a slow song, and I stare uncomfortably at my shoes.

"Well then. May I have this dance?" He holds out his hand, waiting for me to accept.

"Of course you may!" Anne says. She takes my hand and places it in his. Eli carefully pulls me to my feet but thankfully doesn't lead us too far onto the dance floor. I have no clue what I'm doing. Eli looks like he's waiting for me to make the first move, but I don't know what to do. I glance at the other couples as he steps up to me, placing one of my hands on his shoulder and the other in his left hand. His free hand rests on the small of my back. This is one of those moments when I'm glad that I can't blush.

"So I excite you?"

Really glad I can't blush.

"No. I just didn't know how much I liked to dance."

"With me. You didn't get overexcited dancing with Rove."

"Ew, he's my cousin."

He pulls me closer, and I bend my arm as I try to keep my hand on his shoulder. His arm slides all the way around my waist, and the fire in my throat is suddenly back. A sharp, stabbing sensation forms behind my canines as my fangs pierce through my gums. I run my tongue over their pointy edges, swallowing deeply as I suck in my lips. Slowly, I let myself move closer to him. My arm slides around his shoulders. Even in heels I only come to his nose. I turn my head to the side. The warmth from his body seeps into mine until I feel like my whole body is flaming. And he smells so good, like wood and air from the gulf. I inhale deeply, stiffening as he drops my hand and clasps both his hands behind my back.

I feel him smile as he takes my limp arm and puts it around his shoulders. "You really are new to this, aren't you?" he whispers in my ear. I smile but don't say anything.

The song ends and couples step apart to applaud as the lead singer signals the end of the set. I cough into my hand and accidentally bite down on my lip. My fang pierces it, opening a small puncture wound, but no blood comes. Eli glances at me, smiling from ear to ear. I suck in my lip but not before he sees. I turn my head to the side and walk away with him following close behind.

"Wait!" He pulls me around to face him. I cover my mouth with my shaking hand, but when his hand reaches for mine, I let him gently reveal my fangs. I'm trembling all over. "You don't have to hide from me."

I want to melt when he says that. I want to forget about everything that I've learned tonight—to be a human girl who likes a boy. But I can't. I'm a Deuxsang, and he's a witch. I open my mouth to respond to him, not even knowing what I'll say, but I can't say it.

I drop his hand, turn my back, and walk out of the museum. I don't look to see if he's following behind me, or if anyone notices me leaving. I fight off the tears burning my eyes and keep walking. The massive crowd bulging through the museum's doors covers what I should be hearing: the nearly silent footsteps behind me. I quickly slip into an empty alley and wait for the footsteps to pass, but they don't.

A moment later, Eli materializes in front of me. First his feet, then his body, and finally, slowly, his face. I stand speechless, immobilized. He's magic.

"Cheyenne."

He takes a step closer to me. This is unreal.

"Please don't run away from me. I'm tired of chasing."

I suddenly realize that I'm pressed against the wall, that there are butterflies twisting up my stomach. A deep, completely different burn forms in my throat as my fangs drop again. The tips peek out between my lips.

"So stop chasing me," I whisper. My hand shakes as his body moves closer to mine, our faces nearly touching.

"I asked you first." I watch his hand as he brushes a strand of hair away from my face, his fingers leaving a trail of fire. My throat aches, and I feel myself leaning forward, anchored in.

Then his lips are on mine. He's kissing me. All that fire that was in his touch, in my throat, transfers into his lips. I lean into him as my arms circle his neck. His hands drop my face and wrap around my waist, pulling me even closer to him. All my thoughts are cloudy as his lips push harder against mine. We fall back against the wall as he pulls away from me with shallow breaths.

"Cheyenne." He smiles, that wonderful Eli smile. I want to smile back, to respond, but I can't. His pulse is driving me crazy. I can hear the blood rushing in his veins. His heart is beating out of his chest. And the smell, the intoxicating smell. I can't think straight. His touch only makes it worse. His face becomes a blur. All I can see is his neck, where the vein protrudes as he swallows.

Suddenly, he leaps backward, gripping his neck. "Ow!" I blink out of my trance, psyching myself out. What the hell? He releases his throat, rubbing it. "What was that? It felt like something bit me. Hard."

My eyes open so wide I'm sure they'll pop out of my head. "Oh, no. No, no, no, no, no, no, no." I did that. I made it happen. *I hurt him*. After years of trying to access my ability, it has to come along with my first kiss. I'm an inflictor.

"I can't do this," I whisper, and then I take off. In a moment I'm running faster that I've ever done, faster than humanly possible. The world rushes past me in a haze as I work through the city. And now I'm suddenly flitting too. When I slow down, it's an out of body experience. My body stops in less than a second, but my vision and mind are still rushing forward. My eyes clear, and I can tell I'm miles away from where I started.

I calm down as the scent of Eli's blood fades. That can never happen again.

I hold myself up against a light pole when I notice him standing a few feet away.

"I thought you were done running away from me." Eli's voice slows my mind down, and I'm able to stand on my own. How did he get here so fast?

"Eli, I can't do this. You know I can't do this. And why do you want to? I just hurt you!"

"That was you? That's a pretty cool power. Scary, but cool."

"Yeah, a pretty cool *brand new* scary power that I can't control. You need to stay away from me."

"You know, I have powers too." He gives me a flirtatious look. Could this guy be any more stubborn? But I have to admit, I am curious.

"Okay I'll bite. What are your powers?"

"Well, there are some things that all witches can do with practice. Scrying, shape shifting, astral projection. I've actually been working on that last one. I'm trying to communicate with ancestors on other planes."

I really wish he'd stop getting more and more interesting. "Wow, you can do way more than I can. I don't even know what any of those things are."

He doesn't drop his eyes from mine as he moves closer. "I know you've been trying to avoid *this*," he gestures between us, "But why won't you just give me a chance?"

I appreciate that he's keeping a respectable amount of distance between us, all the while hating that I want him to move closer. If I can just kiss him one more time, I can let this stupid crush go and move on. Then we'll be the witch and the Deuxsang, because that's what we are. He's a witch, and I'm Deuxsang. We're on opposite sides of a very wide, treacherous river. There's no way I'm crossing that.

"I can't. You don't get it! There's just too much on the line. I just...you don't understand."

"Then explain it to me." He's closer to me now. "Can we please just talk?" I open my mouth to object, but he stops me. "If you're not satisfied with everything afterward, then okay, I'll stop. But you have to talk to me first." I hate those stupid green eyes. If he'd just stop looking at me, I could say no, flit away, and be home in a matter of seconds. Then I could avoid him for the rest of my existence. But he won't look away, so I can't say no.

Without thinking, I grab his face and kiss him. I pull back quickly before my mind starts fogging up too much. "Talking. We're supposed to be talking."

"You're the one that kissed me," he smiles.

"Can we just…don't you…gah," I mutter. When he leans away, just a little bit, and drops his arms. I glance at my phone, at the five missed calls from Thomas and the four from Kara. I'm so dead when I get home. "Okay, Eli." I look up at him. "What do you want to talk about?"

"Well, we could just beat around the bush for the next ten minutes, or we can just say it. Hi, I'm Eli Ashford, and I'm a witch." When I don't say anything, he nods at me, rolling his hands around each other. I just stare at him, despite the scream going through my head right now. "Alright. 'Hi, I'm Cheyenne Lane, and I'm a Deuxsang,' " he says in what he thinks is my voice.

Hearing him say it, my breath catches in my throat and sticks there. I can't move, no matter how much I want to. "Eli, this is a horrible idea. I can't talk to you about this."

"Yes you can."

"Eli," I sigh, looking at him so hard I think I might burn a hole through his face. "There's just no way I can see this ending well. I'm not going to deny that I'm attracted to you, but I also can't deny that there's something about you that sets my nerves on end, that makes me thirstier all the time, even during the day."

I can tell he wants to say something, but I can't stop now. I'm on a roll. "If the Council found out that I wasn't following their rules to the letter, I'd be in serious danger. They could take my entire family. I need you to understand that." He opens his mouth, but I cut him off. "And not only that, but you could die. You and your entire family. I can assure you that the vampires will be gunning to get their hands on witches, so it's just safer for both us and our families to keep our distance." He's looking at me with those green eyes again. And it looks like nothing is getting through his thick skull. "Eli."

I don't get a chance to say anything else because he's kissing me again, and I'm letting him. He's gentler this time, like he's completely sure this won't be our last kiss. My fangs drop instantly, and that intoxicating scent blocks my nostrils again. But I'm so distracted by his lips, those soft, gentle lips that I can almost ignore the blood. Almost.

I pull away first, but not too far. His warm hand still cups my cheek as he smiles at me, and I hate that I smile back. I feel him looking at my fangs. But he doesn't scream or cringe or pull away; he just looks back at me.

"I don't care about all of that. Why can't we just try? Besides, for all we know, I could get sick of you." My eyes double as I shove him away, laughing.

Thirteen

The next morning I'm yanked out of my dream by the obnoxious ring of my cell phone.

"Where are you?" Thomas asks.

No "*Hello,Cheyenne! How are you*?" That would be too polite for him.

"I'm in bed. Why?"

"I need you to pick something up for me. An attorney downtown is holding some papers for me."

"Can't Kara do it? I just woke up," I groan.

"No, she can't, and I wasn't asking, Cheyenne. I need the papers."

I wish he were here to see my glare. I fight off the urge to piss him off with a snide comment. "Where do I go?"

"The Law Office of Barret and DuBois on Main Street. It's a tall, tan stucco building on the east side. You can't miss it. Ask for Mr. DuBois."

"Got it. Bye, Thomas."

"Leave now, Cheyenne."

"Good bye, Thomas." I hang up the phone, knowing I won't be leaving right now. After taking my time waking up, I throw on some clothes, and find that I'm able to flit toward Main Street. It's amazing—even through the haze of flitting, I can still hear the sounds and smell the scents of the city: jazz music on every corner, beignets, fresh seafood, honking cabs, and bike bells.

I stop a little ways onto Main Street, smiling at the thriving city around me. I look to my right, noticing the man hunched over something, spray cans lined up all around him. I take a step closer and glance over his shoulder. The man's hands are caked in spray paint, and he's sponging orange onto a canvas, blending it in with vibrant pinks and reds. He drops the sponge, dissatisfied with the texture, and spreads the paint with his thumb. The beach stares back at me. I feel like I can jump into the canvas and be there.

The artist notices me when my shadow gets in the way of his sunlight. He turns, his eyes squinted at me. "You want?"

"No, sir, just looking." He tips his hat to me and turns back to his cans, spraying a deep shade of purple to the top of the canvas.

I stroll down Main Street, admiring the antique buildings, some with beautiful stained glass windows, when suddenly a wave of unease washes over me. I look to my left, my right, over my shoulder. Nothing. People are minding their own business, going about their day. I'm just paranoid. On my left, a little way down the street, I see the law office.

A sign hanging from the second story window reads in elaborate script: Barret and DuBois Law Offices. The sign swings gently in the breeze, creaking on its hinges. I cross the busy street and pull open the large glass door. The front room seems cold with its concrete floors and walls. A wooden desk sits to the side of the door, but it's empty. "Out to lunch" is written on a sticky note set on top of the messy desk. A dim light comes through a cracked door that says DuBois. Behind it, there's a stairwell leading to the basement.

My hand searches for a banister, and I sigh when it lands on something warm and wooden. The first step screeches under the weight of my foot. Eventually, three dim lights along the side of the wall guide me down to a small, warm sitting room closed off by a steel door. I jump a little when I think I hear the sound of footsteps.

Suddenly, the door at the top of the stairs slams shut, and I jump ten feet out of my skin. I sprint up the stairs and yank on the handle, but it breaks off in my hand. No big deal. Mr. Dubois can help me get out. Back downstairs, I knock on the closed door that must be Mr. DuBois's office, but there's no answer. I knock again before gently pushing the unlocked door open a few inches. The room is dark as I step inside.

"Hello? Mr. Dubois? Anyone here?"

I walk farther into the room, allowing my hand to release the handle. I touch a lamp on his desk and turn it on, noticing the "out to lunch" sign. Who leaves their office completely empty?

The office walls are lined with books and chests of files. One labeled "Private: DS" attracts my attention. The drawer squeaks as I pull it open, fingering over the long line of files with names written in bold sharpie.

I come across one labeled "Lacroix" and yank it out. I flip the file open, and the first thing I see is a picture of a guy who looks exactly like Anne. Stamped across his picture in large red letters reads "Deceased." Anne has...had a brother? Carefully, I place the file back in its spot and keep searching. Lane isn't in here. Neither is Burns.

I shake myself, stand up, and gently kick the drawer closed. Thomas said that I was supposed to pick up papers, so maybe Mr. DuBois left them out for him. I pull my cell phone out for extra light and shine it over the room. I walk back to his desk and find a file with Thomas's name on it. As I reach for it, I hear a creak coming from the outer room.

"Hello? Mr. DuBois? Is that you?" I grab the file and walk around the desk just as the steel door swings closed. I'm not fast enough to catch it. Again the handle breaks off in my hand. I bang my fist against the door, screaming at the top of my lungs. Turning back to the room, I shine my phone around. My eyes adjust to the darkness, seeing only vague shapes: bookshelves, a desk, and a chair. A dank smell surrounds me— mildew and kerosene. Something thick and black is crawling up the concrete wall in the corner. I gotta get out of here. The smell of kerosene grows stronger, making me dizzy. I press Kara's speed dial and wait for her to pick up. Damn it. Voicemail.

A lump grows in my throat as I dial Thomas's number, and my body chills when he doesn't answer. I bang on the door again, my throat growing hoarse and sore. I swallow hard, forcing the pain out of my throat as I scream louder and louder.

My senses begin to yield to my vampire instincts. I can smell the humans walking on Main Street, and I'm nearly able to taste their blood on my tongue. I hear the sounds of the city and smell smoke. A distant crackling noise sparks in my ears as smoke floats in through the cracks around the doorframe. The smoke rises quickly, forcing its way into my nostrils, mouth, and eyes. My eyes water, and I drop onto all fours and crawl away from the door, my phone to my ear. I catch movement outside the door, a shadow. I hear footsteps.

"Hello!" I flit to the door, putting all my strength into banging on it and yelling "Help me!" I convulse from coughs and drop to my stomach, looking through the bottom crack where the door meets the frame. Just on the other side of the door, I see light and shiny brown, wing-tipped leather shoes.

Suddenly, the door is shaking from the other side. Someone's trying to help me. "Hurry, please!" I shout. The person yanks at the door until I hear a snap, but nothing happens. I look down between the door and the ground, and, in a single breath, the shoes disappear.

"No! Please!" I hit the door one last time, startled by the hoarse cry that escapes my throat. I crawl on my knees through the dark room, collide with the desk, and lean against it to dial Eli's number.

He answers on the first ring. "Hey there! What's up?"

Before I can answer, I hear Erik's voice in the background, "Eli, man, I messed up. I need your help."

"Hold on a minute, Erik. Cheyenne, what's going on?"

"It's important!" Erik yells, and I can hear Eli muttering something to him.

"Eli, I'm trapped in a basement at the Barret and DuBois Law Office on Main Street. The building is on fire, and I can't get out. Please!" The line goes dead without a response, and I drop my phone on the floor, tears of anguish pouring out of my eyes. The room is already filled with smoke, blurring my vision.

I push myself onto my feet, gripping the desk as

the world spins around me. I slam my back into the door again and again, and it groans under my weight. I try pushing with my arms and ramming my shoulder into the steel. I finally lie on the floor and kick the door with all the energy I can muster, and that's when the door weakens. I jump up and ram the door one more time with my entire body and nearly cry when it gives.

I collapse with it and fall into a room of fire. Flames roar around me, reaching almost to the ceiling. I roll off the door as it singes my skin. Coughs rack my body. I'm surrounded by the flames—red, orange, blue, and black. I lie on the steaming concrete floor, absolutely helpless. I try to pull my body up, but a burning plank from the stairs drops beside my arm and scorches my hand black. My eyes close again as the flames dance around me. Far off, I hear a quiet voice, almost inaudible over the roar of the fire, but it grows louder, coming closer to me. I can almost make out my name.

"Cheyenne!" The voice is right by my ear, but I don't want to move. I can't move. I want to call out, but my voice is gone. "Wake up!" A cool hand touches my face, contrasting sharply with the heat from the fire. I blink my eyes open, staring up at Eli's blurry face. "We have to go. Come on." I close my eyes again as his cold hands reach for mine. He lifts my arms around his neck, pulling me up and over his shoulder. As he jogs up the stairs, taking them two at a time, my head bounces against his back. I watch the flames chasing after us. My eyes water and thunderous coughs rumble through my body.

He sprints through the open door and runs out into the street. As soon as we reach the sidewalk on the opposite side, the flames lick up around the sides of the building. The roof falls in, and the stained glass window shatters. Sirens blare down the street, and men are standing on the tops of trucks, hoses ready. Through my blurred vision, I think I spot Erik hiding in the crowd, but then I black out.

...

Ash. In my nose. On my tongue. In my eyes. Just ash. I blink my eyes open and cough up a black cloud. My bed is warm, warmer than it's ever been. I look down, expecting to see my comforter, but instead find myself staring at a blue afghan. The room is different. The walls are white. Where are my bookshelves? Am I in a hospital? I blink again, hoping this is all a dream, that I'll be back in my room any second now.

"Feeling any better, Miss Lane?" I open one eye, hesitant of this new, unfamiliar voice. But I know him from somewhere. I've met this man before. His green eyes remind me of—

"I'm sorry, I'm being rude. I'm Eli's older brother Lucas. We met at the Carnival." He doesn't extend his hand. They remain clasped together behind his back. He's tall. Taller than Eli if that's possible. The only resemblance between him and his brother are their green eyes, though Lucas's are more guarded.

"I remember you, but why am I here?" I keep looking at the door, waiting for Eli to come in.

"After the fire, Eli brought you here since I'm the healer of the family. Too bad my mother wasn't here when Eli got your call. She would've put the fire out in no time."

Lucas smiles grimly at me, his scar twisting his face into a weird contortion. "Those should be good to go in a day, maybe a little less."

"Thank you," I mutter, glancing down at my burns, already starting to heal. "Do you mind if I ask you a question?" I eye him warily as he stands rigid by the desk.

I can tell he's nervous. "Of course."

"Why are you helping me?" I ask.

He sighs, apparently expecting a much worse question. "I don't share the sentiments of my youngest brother, or our father, from whom Erik learned his hatred."

So maybe Erik's vileness isn't just a personal vendetta against me. "Your father? Why does he hate us?"

"You'll have to excuse me. I'm a bit exhausted from healing you." He rises to go. "I'll leave you to rest."

"Lucas, are you bothering her? She just woke up." Eli steps through the white door, his smile beaming. Something inside my chest jumps a little. Then I realize how stupid I'm being.

Lucas looks at his watch. "It's late. You should probably be getting home, Cheyenne."

I shoot up in bed. "Late? How late?"

"About 5:45."

Panic surges through me. "I have to get out of here! I've been gone all day. Thomas is going to kill me!" When I try to stand up, the dizziness hits. I press my palm against my forehead, only to find a layer of green goop on my hand. I pull my face back in surprise.

"It's a salve," Lucas explains. "For your burns."

I flex my fingers and form a fist in amazement. "It doesn't hurt at all."

Eli gazes at me, his eyes a mixture of amusement and concern. Those eyes can distract me from just about anything except the mess that's waiting for me at home. I'm dead meat. It's not like I can tell Thomas I was saved by witches. As far as he's concerned, I've been gone all day and never got the papers to him. I don't even have the papers now. I have probably missed a hundred calls.

As if on cue, my phone rings. Thomas booms through the receiver. "It's nearly six o'clock. Where the hell have you been all day? I sent you out seven hours ago!"

"I'm sorry, Thomas. I had some trouble at the office. Did you not hear about the fire?"

"If you're going to lie, make it convincing. Get yourself to the club, now. We'll meet you there."

"Yeah, okay. I'll see you in a little bit."

Eli winks at me and grabs his shoes from the corner. Looks like we're going for a walk.

Fourteen

"So how is this supposed to work?" I ask as we work our way down Canal Street. His elbow brushes mine, sending shivers up my arm. "We didn't really talk about that during our *talk*."

He shrugs slightly. "Maybe we can actually go on a real date? You know, I pick you up; we eat lunch and maybe go to a movie?" He looks down at me, his green eyes even greener in the setting sun.

"Sounds great." He grabs my hand, interlocking our fingers. "But can I just meet you at a restaurant? You and my house are not a good combination."

"Mason's then. I'm sure Anne will want to help you get ready. Wednesday at 11:30. And dress in your best."

"You don't dress up for lunch." I look at him like he's crazy.

"Yes, but this will be more like a dinner date, since that's not an option for us. It's going to be magical." He waves his fingers in front of my face, little sparks flying out of his fingertips. I watch, mesmerized, as they disappear in midair.

The Quarter is starting to pick up pace. More bands are popping up on street corners and restaurant lines are growing longer. A few blocks away from the club, I spot the same group of homeless children from the cemetery huddled together in an alley. They look up when we pass, staring at us through their red irises. *What*? I squeeze Eli's hand. "What?" he asks, following my eyes.

When Eli glances their way, they blink their eyes, and the red dissolves to a muddy brown. "Never mind. I thought..." I glance at their brown eyes one last time before we pass the alley. "Never mind."

As we reach the corner before the club, I pull Eli to a stop. "What's wrong? We're almost there." He looks back at me.

"I know. But they have bouncers, and I don't want them to sense you?"

He laughs at my awkwardness. "Cheyenne, I'll be fine. Don't worry about me." He walks again, his right foot turning the corner. I don't let go of his hand, and he stops when I don't move. "Cheyenne," he groans, looking back at me.

"Eli, I need to go alone. It's just safer if we say good bye here."

He grabs my other hand, smiling like he has a secret. "Good night, not good bye."

I smile. "Right, I'll see you later."

"Wednesday, I believe." I laugh at his impish grin and nod my head. "Good night, Cheyenne." He pulls me close. I glance at his lips, perfect, inviting. He leans closer, close enough that I can feel his warm breath on my face. His mouth parts as he tilts his head to the side and presses his lips against my cheek, the corner of his mouth touching mine. I exhale as he walks away, holding my fluttering stomach. I turn around, but he's gone, disappeared completely.

With a deep breath and a burning throat, I round

the corner, the smell of blood strong in the air. Two bodyguards stand watch at the door, tall and intimidating in their black. They tilt their sunglasses down, peering over the rims, as I approach the door.

"Mot?" The low rumbling voice pulls out a clipboard, waiting.

"Um, I don't remember *le* mot, but I'm with Thomas Burns." I tilt my head back to look at his face, shaded by his long, dark hair.

"Of course, ma'am. Excuse me." The other guard swings the door open and knocks twice to the guard in the entry room. I nod at the men as I pass. The man in the next room leads me past the crowded dance floor and opens the door to the back room.

What was a few weeks ago a small, quiet family gathering has transformed. As I walk through the door, a wall of noise from a thousand conversations meets me. Strangers fill the room, mulling around in little groups, and they're all families. I squeeze my way through the groups until the back booth is in sight. Rove spots me first, an amused yet relieved look on his furry face. I stumble up to my family's table. Their laughter stops as they stare at me.

"Well, look who finally decided to show," Thomas says, his arm slung over Kara's shoulders. What is his problem?

"What's all this?" I glance around the room as I take my seat next to Rove.

"We're just having a little party, getting acquainted with some of the other families in town," Thomas says. "Who knows, maybe you'll make some friends."

"I have friends, Thomas."

"Maybe it's time for some better ones," Thomas snarls.

"Here, have some blood." He sets a full glass in front of me, watching and waiting for me to drink. I down the cup in seconds, and before I can blink, he sets another glass in front of me.

"Could you slow down, please? I just got here."

"You look parched, Cheyenne. You need blood. Drink." His eyes never waver from mine. I sip slowly from the cup, despite the urge to gulp it down. My body is on fire, all senses painfully acute. When another glass appears in front of me, I glare at Thomas.

"I think I'm good for now." He doesn't argue with me, especially since I finished my second glass without realizing it. I scan the families as they glance around at each other with a mixture of disdain and recognition. My vision is sharper than normal. I try to distinguish one Deuxsang from another, but they all look the same down to every last detail. Servers are milling in between them, carrying trays of blood. The pounding music and loud conversations are giving me a headache.

"So, Sis," Kara chimes into my thoughts. "Since I didn't get to see you last night, we have some good news to share!" Her grin might be able to split her face in half. "We're having a baby boy!" She screeches over the music, doing nothing for my headache.

I smile, despite my mood. "Congratulations, Kara! I'm so happy for you guys."

"Yes, we're quite pleased." Thomas looks so proud and conceited all at the same time. I want to slap him really hard.

"Have you guys thought of names yet?" Rove asks, looking at me curiously.

"Yes," Kara sings, "but I don't want to give it away yet. It'll be a big announcement." Her voice is like nails on a chalkboard in my head. I want to scratch her eyes out.

"Thomas, I'm not feeling so well. Can I just go home?" I groan, massaging my forehead as I stare out into the sea of partygoers.

"Nonsense, you're fine!" Thomas laughs.

Kara eyes me suspiciously. "Sis, what's that on your neck?" I self-consciously cover the burn with my hand. "Maybe she should rest. She looks awfully weak," Kara grabs Thomas's hand, looking at me with concern. "Why don't I walk her home? I'll be back soon, huh?" She begins to scoot out of the booth, but Thomas holds onto her.

"Just give it an hour, Cheyenne. If you're still not feeling well by then, we'll leave," Thomas says as I down the glass in front of me and nod my head. "Now go mingle." Thomas shoos me away, my head pounding even worse after my third glass, and Rove follows, his strong hand steady on my shoulder.

I plaster a smile onto my face as we pass the families and nod. A few people small talk with us, eyeing us like we're new and shiny. I swear I can almost hear their thoughts. *Her hair is a mess. I wonder who she belongs to. Oh no, my glass is empty. Where's the waiter? That new guy has to be full of it. I'll believe in this so-called leader when I meet her. His tie is crooked again. Council coming next week. Better call the cleaners. Ooh yum.* A girl our age passes by Rove, looking at him with hungry eyes and bumping into him not so accidentally. When we reach the back corner of the room, we lean against the wall, shoulder to shoulder. Rove glances at me several times as he chews on his bottom lip.

"Do you want to talk about what happened with Eli?"

"You know what I really want?" I ask, resting the side of my face against the wall as I turn to look at him. He shakes his head. "I want you to take me home." He glances back at our table. Thomas is engrossed in a conversation with a man in a pinstriped suit. Kara looks at us once before turning to the man's wife. Rove puts his arm around my shoulders and leads me out the door into the even louder club. The room shakes as we pass the dance floor. Rove opens the door, nodding at the guard behind it. He knocks on the wall twice, and the next door springs open. The two bouncers bow to us as we stumble out the door and rush into the busy streets of the Quarter.

"So how much trouble are we going be in when Thomas realizes we're gone?" Rove asks as we stroll arm in arm. Jazz music emanates from clubs lining the streets. The pressure in my head releases as I breathe in the fresh night air. The strings of lights hung on balconies glitter like stars roaming over the city, and the actual stars feel incredibly close. In fact, nothing seems out of my reach in this moment.

"I don't really care." I take a deep breath and close my eyes, letting a warm breeze wash over my face.

I can feel Rove's eyes on me. "So, Eli?"

I cannot hide my smile no matter how hard I try. I open my eyes to look at him, at his smug, smirking face. "I don't think that's any of your business."

He opens his mouth, an I-told-you-so on his lips. "Spill."

"Eli is taking me on a date Wednesday." I look at him

out the corner of my eye.

He nudges me playfully with his elbow, gloating. "Did this happen last night?

"No, actually it happened today after he saved me from a burning building."

Rove pulls me to a stop in the middle of Canal. "I'm sorry. What?"

"Thomas asked me to pick something up for him at some law office, and when I went, no one was there. I went into the man's office and got trapped. Then the building caught on fire. I guess I passed out because I got burned a little." I tilt my head back so that he can see the burns on my neck and show him my hand. "Eli got me out."

"Why am I just hearing this now? Does everyone else know? Why didn't you call me?"

"I dunno. I tried to tell Thomas about it, but he didn't want to hear it. So I guess if you don't know, no one else does. And I did try to call, but you didn't answer. And let's be honest, you would've had no idea how to get to me."

"I would've figured it out. So do you think Thomas like set this up?"

For a moment, I don't even process what he's saying. "What? Of course not, Rove! How can you even suggest that? He's my brother-in-law."

"I'm sorry. It's not completely out of the question. You have to admit, the guy's a little…" I stare at the side of his face like he's absolutely insane.

Rove drops the conversation as we arrive at the trolley stop. We shuffle to the back of the car and lean into the wooden benches. In ten minutes, we're at the Garden District stop. Rove follows me off the car, saying good night to the exhausted driver. We walk down the silent street without a word. I find the spare key under the mat. The key slips in the lock easily, and the door swings open under my weight.

The house is silent. Rove follows me into my room, but I don't turn on the overhead light, just the small lamp next to my bed. Maybe Thomas won't come roaring into the room if he thinks we're both asleep.

Rove collapses into my lounge chair, stretching his neck from side to side. I grab my pajamas from the edge of my bed and change in my bathroom, brushing out my hair, splashing my face with cold water. My eyes feel heavy like bricks. All I want to do is sleep. I rub lavender lotion over my hands and bring them up to my nose to smell. I'd give anything not to smell ash. I plait my hair down my back and push the door open. Rove's nearly asleep on my chair.

"Rove, get up." I push his shoulder as I pass. He grunts, rolling his head to the side. "Go to bed. I'm tired."

"Well, then shut up and go to sleep." He curls up into a ball on the chair. I don't see how those long limbs of his can bend like that.

"Rove!" I kick his leg until he moves, thrashing his arms like a wild animal.

"Alright, alright! I'm going. Chill out." He stomps out of my room, closing the door behind him. I crawl into bed, and the moment my head hits the pillow I'm out.

Fifteen

Miraculously, I'm never disturbed. After I fell asleep, the world just melted away. I doubt that Thomas could've woken me even if he'd tried. I was dead.

But the amazing part is that no one woke me up at all. With my eyes partially closed, I roll over to the side of my bed and glance at my alarm clock: 10:30.

I roll out of bed, listening for movement in the house. Kara has taped a sticky note to my door: "Remember that we're painting today, wear some old clothes please. K." I groan as I stretch out my tight muscles. The smell of ash is still faint in my nose, but the burns have all but disappeared. There is only a small red spot on my neck where black was yesterday. After slipping on a t-shirt and a pair of old overalls, I flit down the stairs, stopping at the front door. I follow my ear to the sitting room where Rove and Kara are talking quietly. "Good morning, Sunshine." Rove smiles at me as I take a seat beside Kara.

"Feeling any better, sis?"

"Yes, much better." I force a smile at my shoes, avoiding Rove's eyes.

"Well, you definitely look the painting part." Kara pats my back. "Hopefully, we'll be able to finish before Thomas gets home from work."

"He's gone?" I ask, looking up at my sister. Her belly grows every day, faster than normal. She's glowing.

"Yes, he said that he wanted to work on his lesson plans today. He wants to make a good impression, of course, so let's surprise him with a freshly painted room for the baby, shall we?" I nod my head, her cheerful attitude annoyingly contagious.

"Well, I should head out." Rove stands. "Thanks for putting up with me for a few days." He steps around the coffee table to hug Kara, careful not to push on her stomach.

"Are you sure you can't stay a few more days? It's been great having you here." Kara holds onto him, her nails digging into his shoulders.

He laughs, gently pushing her away. I heave his bag onto my shoulder and lead them out to the front door. When I turn around, he wraps his arms around me, and I'm already regretting him leaving. He has made living here bearable.

"Thank you, Rover, for everything." I wrap my arms around his waist and squeeze.

He squeezes back and chuckles. "Keep me updated. I don't want to be left in the dark." His chin rests on top of my head for a moment before he pats my back and releases me. "Take care, Munchkin." He ruffles my hair and takes his bag from my shoulder, loading it into the back of the cab. He rolls down the window from the back seat. "Bye! Don't forget, Cheyenne." And then the cab moves away. Kara and I wave, watching the cab disappear down the road. Kara slips her arm through mine as she pulls me down the sidewalk.

"What did he mean by that? Don't forget what?" she asks.

"How should I know? He says weird stuff all the time."

Kara shrugs as if that's a perfectly acceptable answer. "Why don't we walk to the paint store? The fresh air will do us some good."

"Why don't I go? You can stay here and rest."

"Nonsense—you don't know what color I want. Besides, I'm quite well rested, thank you very much." She hasn't said anything about last night, which is weird. Plus, with Thomas gone, I don't have to drink blood this morning. I'm not complaining, but double weird.

When we stop in front of the paint shop a few minutes later, I hesitate. *He's here*. I can sense him. "Hey, I'll race you to the door!" I call while flitting down the walkway, swinging the door open, and skidding to a stop. Customers turn to stare at me as I scan the room for Eli. A moment later, Kara pulls the door open, yelling my name.

"Cheyenne, what's wrong with you? We're in public," she hisses. She stops when she notices all the eyes on her and smiles. "Sorry," she whispers, holding up her hand as she turns to glare at me. "And since when have you been able to flit?"

I shrug my shoulders. "A few days ago. Just kinda started happening." I bit my lip. I'm not lying.

She rolls her eyes but bites back whatever she was going to say. "Go get a paint pan and don't forget the liner, please." She walks up to the counter to order the paint. I keep my eyes peeled, afraid that Eli will just pop up out of nowhere.

I weave my way through the aisles, half-heartedly looking for the pans. The man at the counter hammers the lids onto two cans of paint and places the paint dots on the centers. Kara walks to the other end of the counter by the cash register and looks back at me, tilting her head to the side and motioning with her eyeballs to hurry. I walk down the aisle a ways before I feel something brush my arm. I turn my head, but there's nothing behind me. I walk again but stop when something rubs my lower back.

I spin on my heel, and a voice appears by my ear. "Boo!" I jump, my breath catching as Eli materializes in front of me, beaming from ear to ear. "Oh, you Deuxsang have nothing on witches," he chuckles.

"You need to leave." I push him toward the front door.

"Only if you come with me." He grabs my hands from his chest. I glance back at Kara, who's thankfully distracted by the cashier.

"No, you have to go. My sister's here. She'll sense you." He glances over my shoulder at Kara, completely unperturbed.

"We set for tomorrow?" He looks like a little boy when he grins like this. I glance over my shoulder, and my heart plummets to my toes as Kara spots Eli. She storms over to our side of the store. Eli tries to step in front of me, but I throw my arm out to stop him.

"Not unless you want to die," I whisper. I hold my hands out as Kara approaches. "Kara, calm down."

"You! You stay away from my little sister. I don't want you anywhere near her!"

Eli steps back, his hands raised.

"Kara, stop. Eli and I are—"

"Friends, ma'am," he cuts me off. I clench my jaw, wishing he'd just keep his mouth shut.

She glares at him, a snarl gurgling in the back of her throat. She takes a threatening step toward him. Suddenly, her fangs drop, and he flinches.

"Kara!" I yell, taking a step back toward Eli.

"We're leaving." She grabs my hand and drags me out of the store, the two paint cans in her other hand. Eli follows us onto the sidewalk, calling my name, but I wave him away. Not a word is spoken the entire way home.

Kara routinely checks over her shoulder to ensure that Eli's not following us, giving her a reason to glare at me. When we reach the house, Kara drops the paint cans and drags me upstairs. I follow her into my room, my head bowed. She slams the door as I take a seat on my bed, waiting for the eruption, but she stares at me for several excruciatingly long minutes.

"Are you crazy? Have you absolutely *lost* your mind? You realize what he is, right? You realize what his people did to us?" Kara bursts, her face red from holding in all that anger.

"Yes, Kara. I'm not an idiot."

"Oh, well that's a shame. I was hoping you were going to plead insanity. That would have made me feel better. Well, if you're not stupid, and you're not crazy, then what are you thinking?"

"I'm thinking that Eli is a nice guy, and we have a good time together." I tilt my head up in defiance.

"You are risking the entire family's safety! I can't *believe* how selfish you are!"

"Hey, now."

"We're not just talking about a human here, Cheyenne. He's a witch. Do you realize that your relationship could restart the violence, Cheyenne? You're going to get all of us killed."

"I think you're being a little dramatic," I answer, although I know it isn't outside the realm of possibilities.

"Wake up! Do you have any idea what will happen if the Council finds out about this? You are putting our entire family, our entire kind, in jeopardy all for a stupid summer fling!" She stops, resting her hands on her bulging stomach. I watch her gently lower herself into my armchair. Her tightly braided hair is falling out, little fringes collecting around her face.

I stare at her feet, shamefaced. "What if it's not a stupid summer fling?" I whisper, pulling on my fingers.

She laughs, a bitter, exhausted laugh as she tilts her head back against the neck of the chair. "Cheyenne, I can tell you don't fully comprehend what I'm saying, but hear this: There are things in this world that matter more than feelings. You are just one girl. And he is just one boy. So let it go. Now."

Sixteen

I stare in the mirror, trying to find myself through all the makeup. Anne has my gold eyes lined with delicate browns and greens, making them look even more cat-like than they already do. My cheekbones look higher from the blush. Then there are my lips—full and stained a shiny red. The top half of my hair is pulled back, interweaved with small, nearly invisible braids, primarily for the purpose of keeping my hair out of my face.

Anne's dress fits me perfectly, hugging my waist and showing off my shoulders. The deep purple compliments everything about the look. The wavy bottom of the dress just brushes the tops of my wedges, which I'm not quite sure I can walk in.

Rose knocks on the door, peeking into the room. "Hi, sweetie. He's here."

I turn around as she steps into the room, a beaming smile on her weak face. "Do I look okay?" I ask, self-consciously staring down at the dress and heels.

"Cheyenne, you look absolutely beautiful, but if I were you, I'd wear those flats you have in your purse." She winks at me. I change shoes quickly and follow her down the stairs. Anne and Mason stare up at me from the bottom of the stairs, absolutely beaming.

Mason offers me his arm and leads me around the corner where Eli is waiting. This is so ridiculous.

I suck in a deep breath and hold it in, an attempt to calm the butterflies soaring through my body. He stops when he sees me, his hands dropping to his sides. I smile at his red bow tie and shiny black shoes. His hair is combed to the side, away from his face. I watch his green eyes travel from my face to my toes, his mouth slightly parted. Mason drops my hand and walks over to him, nudging his shoulder and whispering something.

Eli's head snaps up, smiling at me. "Ready to go?" He steps forward and offers me his arm, which I gladly take. He's warm, and he smells like hickory wood and soap. Rogue curls pop out at his temples. My throat burns standing so close to him, and I can't help my fangs dropping. When I turn to face him, he smiles down at me, a genuine, excited smile that sends shivers down my arms and back.

Eli leads me out the front door to his old beat-up truck and opens my door. I grab onto the handle at the top of the door and pull myself up in one swift movement. He slides into the driver's seat and smiles.

"So where are we going? I'm not overdressed, am I? 'Cause if I am, I'm going to kill you."

"We're going to Commander's Palace in the Garden District. Great food!" We pull away from Mason's house and head toward the Garden District, toward my house. *Perfect*. Eli reads the expression on my face.

"I know that it's risky, but you just can't miss out on this restaurant. I want to be the one to see your face when you first try it," he smiles, his hand resting beside mine.

"Are you sure this is such a good idea? Maybe we can just forget about the date." I turn to him as his hand brushes mine, just for a moment.

"Cheyenne, do you want to spend time with me?" We come to a stoplight, and he turns in his seat, piercing me with those green eyes of his.

I stare back at him, running through all the consequences and dangers in my head, but then his face blocks all my rational thinking. I can't see anything but him. I know what I'm doing is wrong and dangerous, but right now, I don't really care. He raises his eyebrows at me. "Yes, I do," I say in a sigh.

"Good, because I really want to spend time with you." He places his hand on top of mine, pressing the gas when the light turns green.

A few minutes later, we arrive in front of an enormous, sky-blue building that looks more like a Victorian home than a restaurant. Eli parks across the street, and before I can even blink, he disappears in his seat, reappears at my side of the car, and opens my door, offering me his hand. I take it, reveling in the warmth, as we cross the street and stare up at Commander's Palace in all its elegant glory. Eli holds the door open for me, following me to the hostess's desk.

"Hi, reservation for Ashford at noon." His hand stays linked with mine as the tall, elegant woman scrolls down her computer screen.

"Ah, yes. Two?" She looks up at us, the skin on her face pulled back by her tight ponytail and places her hand on two menus. Eli nods, and we follow her through the beautiful dining room, set with white linen tablecloths, golden chairs, and crystal chandeliers. Soft classical music is playing in the background beneath the quiet chatter of the customers. The hostess leads us out to the veranda. Eli pulls out my chair before taking his seat opposite me.

I open my menu as a man in a tuxedo pours my water. "May I get you anything else to drink?" He glances between the two of us, a towel hung over his left arm. We both shake our heads and smile as he walks away.

"So what's good here?" I ask, perusing all my options.

"Well, the shrimp and grits is my personal favorite."

"What's shrimp and grits?" I ask.

He stops, dropping his menu and jaw. "Are you serious? I thought you were a Southerner."

"Shrimp isn't really a staple in Virginia." I shrug my shoulders.

"Well that's what you're having!" he exclaims, sitting back in his seat.

The waiter returns, forcing a smile onto his face a few feet away from the table. "Are you ready to order, or shall I come back?" He turns to me, waiting for an answer.

"Well, I guess I'm having the shrimp and grits." I smile at Eli as he grins to himself.

"And you, sir?"

"I'll have the same, thank you." He hands the waiter our menus, not turning his eyes away from me, and waits for him to leave. "I never told you how beautiful you look."

I gulp. "This is a really pretty view." I turn my head quickly and bite my bottom lip.

"Cheyenne, can't you take a compliment?" he asks, reaching for my hand across the table. My instinct is to pull away, but his hand is so warm. I look up at him and feel like melting.

I enjoy about twelve seconds of bliss before I spot him. At the far end of the veranda, Thomas and two other men are seated at a table set for eight. The other two are in suits, hair slicked back and wearing custom-made shoes. Thomas takes the seat next to the head of the table, leaning back leisurely in his chair, waiting for someone. My head spins as I search for the nearest exit. Eli turns around several times, trying to see what—who—has startled me.

"Cheyenne? What's wrong?" he turns around again, his eyes searching the veranda.

"My brother-in-law is here with two other Deuxsang. We need to leave now." I rip my napkin off my lap and scoot my chair out.

"Hold on a second."

"Eli, believe me, I want to stay, I want to try shrimp and grits, but I'd rather try it somewhere else and live than stay here and die." When Thomas turns this way, I turn my body to face the river. "Eli, please?"

Eli glances back at Thomas and the men with him. Who are these guys? They don't exactly look like the college-professor type.

He's spotted us. Every muscle in my body stops when he focuses on Eli. Suddenly, he shoves his chair out from under him and storms in my direction.

"We have to go—right now." I pull on Eli's hand and sprint down the stairs. Thomas takes off after us, screaming my name as we race down the sidewalk. I don't turn back.

"Cheyenne," Eli huffs, "why don't you just flit? We'll be out of here in no time."

"Because I can't do it with a passenger. Can't you just poof us out of here?" My shoes fly off my feet as I push harder and harder into the concrete, willing myself not to slow down. Thomas glares at me as I glance back at him and pushes himself faster.

"Cheyenne!" Thomas growls just feet behind us. My hand constricts around Eli's, and suddenly we disappear. He jerks me to the side, out of Thomas's path. We watch as he stops, spinning in circles, seething. He growls, low and menacingly, baring his fangs. Eli squeezes my invisible hand. We wait for Thomas to give up, to go back to his table. Instead, he sniffs the air. I feel Eli stiffen beside me as Thomas walks right in front of us, staring into my face. Then everything disappears into darkness. Thomas's face evaporates before my eyes as we are sucked into a black hole, away from the street, the restaurant, the world.

Eli's fingers are interwoven tightly with mine, and I feel his arm slide around my waist, pressing me to his invisible body. My head spins as we travel through nothingness and land back in the real world. The concrete slams against my feet, sending a painful shock up my legs. I reach for Eli's shoulder to steady myself as the nausea dissipates. I blink one eye open, then the other. Eli's truck sits in front of us across from the restaurant. He reappears beside me, his hand still locked with mine. He tries to laugh, but it comes out as a sigh.

"I actually did it," he whispers, mostly to himself. I release his hand and lean against the truck, inhaling deep, calming breaths. "Wow." He looks down at me, a mystified smile on his face. "Are you okay?" I look back at him, speechless. "Cheyenne?" He steps in front of me, his hands hesitating beside my face. I glance at him then at his hand. He presses his palm against the side of my face and rubs his thumb across my cheek, leaving a burning trail in its wake.

"That was too close, Eli," I whisper, actively forcing myself not to lean into his hand. I swallow the fire in my throat and run my tongue over my fangs.

"I know. I promise, I won't let it happen again." He steps closer, the heat from his body radiating against me.

"You can't possibly promise me that." Tears well up behind my eyes, and I bite my lip harder, willing the tears away.

"Cheyenne, everything will be fine. I won't let anything happen to you, okay?" He tilts my face up so that I am staring into his eyes. I blink and nod my head. As he looks down at me, I have the feeling that I'm being studied. He looks me over: my hair, eyes, nose, lips, and chin. He breathes in, rubbing his thumb across my cheek. His face moves closer to mine, and I know what's about to happen.

Gently he presses his lips against mine. My eyes shoot open as a bolt of electricity zaps through my body. My knees buckle as his lips press harder. I give under the pressure, my mouth parting beneath his. His hand slides behind my neck, pulling me against him. Suddenly the fire in my throat becomes too much. His lips are dangerously close to my fangs. I push myself away, my hands resting on his shoulders. He stares at me, gasping to catch his breath. "We should go." He opens the car door, his fist closing around the metal frame. I watch him as he jogs around the hood of the car, jumps into his seat, and starts the ignition. He glances at me, plastering on a brilliant smile.

I don't know how much more I can take.

Seventeen

Rose's porch light shines through the dusky sky as we pull into the driveway behind Anne's Cadillac. We walk to the door and face each other.

"Are you sure I can't drive you back? I'll park a block away." Eli asks.

I shake my head, staring down at my shoes. "That'll only make it worse."

"What's going to happen when you get home?"

I shrug my shoulders.

He bobs his head and squeezes my hand. "Well, you'll call if you need me?" He smiles down at me, his eyes meeting mine. "Good night, Cheyenne." He leans down and presses his lips against mine one more time, sending another shock through my body. I gasp as he pulls away and walks down the porch steps to his truck. He waves out the window and speeds down the street, leaving my head spinning.

The front door swings open the moment his car disappears. Anne and Mason stare at me, jaws dropped. I push past them, unable to address their bombardment of questions. Ms. Rose has a bottle of blood waiting on the living room table, which I immediately grab and gulp down in seconds.

She brings in another just as Anne and Mason appear in the room. I down the second bottle, letting the cool blood work its magic on my burning throat. I can still feel his lips: warm, soft, and gentle. I press my fingers to my mouth, leaning back on the couch. Anne and Mason sit in chairs across from me while Ms. Rose waits beside the couch. I don't say anything and just stare at the wall. Anne's face turns a stark red, her mind a gasket bubbling with questions and ready to burst.

Eventually, she can't handle it. "Well?" she explodes. "How'd it go?"

I smile at her lack of control and smooth the skirt of my dress. "It was nice. Until my brother-in-law arrived and saw us," I reply.

"What? Wait, how'd that happen?" Mason asks, leaning forward in his seat.

"Well, Thomas came in the restaurant with a bunch of men. He turned his head, saw me with Eli, and charged us."

"What did you do?" Anne gasped.

"We ran, of course."

"I don't get what the big deal is," Mason says, resting back into his chair.

After a while, Anne and I finally head home. I can't put it off any longer. Anne gets a ways down the street before she begins her questioning. "So is that really what happened?"

"What, Thomas? Yes, he was really there. Yes, he really chased us down the street. Yes, I'm really going to die when I get home."

"What happened after the restaurant? Did Thomas follow you?"

"We hid at the movie theater. The movie was awful.

We ate popcorn. We talked. We came home." I shrug my shoulders, my eyes focused forward.

"Did he kiss you?" she whispers, even though she already knows the answer. I can't keep myself from smiling. She giggles when she glances at me. "Ooooh!" she shrieks.

All our giggles and smiles drain out of us as the house comes into view. Only one dim light is on in the living room. Anne stops along the side of the street, staring up at the shadows looming over the front yard. I grab my backpack out of the back seat and slowly stumble out of the car.

"I'll get the dress back to you tomorrow," I whisper. I feel like even the trees are watching me. The wind probably carries my voice into the house so that they can hear what I'm saying. A shadow passes in front of the dimly illuminated curtains—a tall, hunched shadow.

Anne nods and glances back at the house. "Good luck. Call me if you need some back up." I smile and wave as she pulls away and disappears down the road. With steel resolve, I turn to the house. The wind whistles through the trees, a cold, ominous whistle that sends goose bumps up my arms. I walk up the sidewalk and into my doom.

"Join us in here, Cheyenne." My knees shake when I hear Thomas. I reluctantly follow his voice to see Kara waiting, pacing in front of the window. Thomas's face is smooth as stone as he looks me over, an unspoken threat in his eyes.

"Take a seat."

I do as I'm told, sitting on the edge of the sofa. Kara chews on her nails, a habit I thought she broke years ago, while Thomas stands by the window, staring at me. I wish Rove were still here. I wish Eli were here. I wish this wasn't a big deal. I wish that he'd say something.

"Thomas," I start, growing uneasy of the silence.

"Don't make things worse for yourself, Cheyenne. I thought I made myself clear that you cannot see him ever again. I'll make sure I get the wording right this time." Oh, no. Thomas is going to compel me. I won't be able to disobey him. "Because I will not allow you to get in our way."

"Thomas, what are you talking about?"

"You think you're in your own little world, but you're not. You're blind to the forces that govern your life, but not for much longer. Things are changing. You need to know who you are—what you are." He steps toward me, his face shadowed in threats.

"I know what I am." I stand to leave the room, but Thomas grabs my shoulders and shoves me against the wall. "Get off me."

"It's not that simple. If you're a Deuxsang, you better start acting like one. *Stay away from the witch*," he hisses in my ear, pressing my shoulders into the wall. It's done. He's compelled me. My will is bound. He leans away, his irises fixed on me. I swallow my fear and spit in his eye. He grits his teeth as he wipes away my saliva and raises his hand in the air.

The backside of his hand strikes my face. I drop to my knees, holding my throbbing face. He stares down at me, and I think I hear a snort. I rise to my feet, staring him in the eyes. He glares down at me, the muscles in his shoulders coiling. I scream and leap for him, dragging him down to the floor. I jam my knees into his stomach and claw at his face as he wriggles beneath me. He catches my hands and throws me off.

I land a few feet away but jump to my feet quickly when I see him stand. I race at him, but he simply stands there, glaring at me. When I collide against him, he pins my arms behind my back and jerks me to my knees. "Enough, Cheyenne. You're acting like a child." He pushes me away, and I stumble to regain my balance.

Thomas and Kara stare after me as I limp into the entryway. I glance back at my sister. Two tears quiver in the corners of her eyes as she stares back at me, her hand raised to her mouth.

"If you think I'll ever forgive you for just standing there, think again."

Kara opens her mouth to speak, but I flit up the stairs and into my room before she can utter a word. I kick the door shut and fall onto my bed. My back and shoulders ache, and tears pour down my swelling face.

I need to get out of here. I can't be here anymore. I pull my phone out of my pocket and dial Dad's number. He answers on the first ring. "Finally, you call. I was about to be angry. Rove told me you'd call once he got home. What have you been doing?"

Before I can get any words out, a sob erupts from my mouth. "Daddy..."

"Cheyenne, stop crying. What are you saying? Pull it together."

My nostrils flare as I try to calm myself. "Thomas just attacked me." I hate that my voice quivers, but that's the best control that I can get.

"What did you do?"

For a minute, I can't respond. Did he actually just say

that to me? I just told him that someone hit me, and he automatically believes it's my fault. "Are you serious?"

"Well, he wouldn't have done anything if you didn't give him a reason to." I can't believe this.

"Goodbye." Before he can respond, I snap my phone shut and then the sobs start again. I can't control my body when it starts shaking. I'm trapped.

Just then, I hear a rattle against my balcony door. I slowly raise myself off my bed, acutely aware of my groaning muscles. The bloodless welt on my cheek pulls at the skin. I glance out and see nothing. Suddenly, a pebble flies up at me and smacks into the door in front of my nose. I open the French doors and step out onto the balcony, peering down into the backyard. Eli materializes, illuminated by the lights embedded in the lawn.

"Eli, what are you doing here?" I hiss, my hands gripping the balcony.

"I came to make sure that you were still alive," he calls, smiling slightly. "May I come up?" He glances nervously at the back door then back up at me.

"Are you crazy? They will know you're here."

"I've got it covered," he assures me, pulling a small bottle from his pocket. "Cloaking potion. My brother's a genius with herbs."

A small gust of wind suddenly whips through the back of the house. I blink several times as Eli is raised into the air and placed gently on my balcony.

"Well that's a new one." I lead him through the double doors into my room. But wait, Thomas compelled me to stay away from Eli. Doesn't this count? I guess not, since he didn't compel Eli to stay away from me.

"Air is my element. Are you okay?" he asks, standing in front of me, looking at my tearstained face.

"You can sit down if you want." I turn my head to look at my lounge chair, and that's when he stops me.

He closes the distance between us, gently holding my face. He turns my head to the left then to the right, observing the bruise forming on my cheek. "Did he do this to you?" He gently brushes his thumb along the top of the bruise, and I wince away, nodding. He jumps to his feet. "I'll kill him."

He charges the door, but I pull him back. "Eli, no, you can't go down there. If you do, he'll kill you."

"Cheyenne, I can't just let him get away with this." He stares back at me with a mixture of vengeance and helplessness.

"You have to."

"Well, what does that mean for us?" he asks, staring down at our locked hands.

I smile, the pain from the fight slowly starting to wear off. "It means we need to get better at keeping secrets."

Eli runs a finger through my hair. "You're a bad girl, Cheyenne Lane," he whispers, a smile in his voice.

"It's your fault." I smile as I wrap my arms around his neck, and he pulls me against him. His arms tighten around my waist, and my head rests in the soft crook of his neck. We stand like that for some time, just holding each other. My fangs extend, and I don't feel ashamed. My throat is on fire, and I relax into the heat, letting it consume me.

Eighteen

"Anne, do we really have to do this? I mean, I like Rose and all, but I really don't want to spend the evening being lectured on witch and Deuxsang culture."

She glares at me from the driver's seat, her hands gripping the wheel. "Rose wants to celebrate my birthday with me. If you didn't want to come, you should've said something earlier." The sun is falling over New Orleans as we drive farther into the music district. As it gets later, the smell of humans becomes more prominent to me. Rose had better be well stocked.

"Besides, she doesn't get to come to the Affirmation party, so this is our make up." She's no longer glaring at me, but at the road. I'm already dreading my Affirmation party the way that Anne's described planning it. It marks the year that our Ascension is complete, and we begin to age as slowly as the rest of our family. It's kind of like a coming out party. We are fully accepting our Deuxsang nature and being presented to society with a highly overdone social event. But we also have our final interview with the vampires, and if I thought my Ascension interview was bad...

"I know you don't want to do this party Anne, but..."

"It's not even MY party! It's just for my parents so that they can schmooze with the Deuxsang elite and show off how good of a Deuxsang their daughter is. No one I care about is invited."

I smile at her frustration and try to hide my laughter. "I'm sorry, that sounds terrible. So does that mean I'm not invited, since I'm not an important person who you don't care about?"

Her frown breaks into a grin. "Of course you're invited! You're my only hope of not having a completely horrible night. Mason and Rose can't be there, so it's down to you. My happiness rests on your shoulders."

"I'm so glad I'm your third choice," I snort.

"Whatever. You have to come. Please promise me you're coming." She's stopped looking at the road, pleading at me with those big eyes of hers.

"Yes, Anne I'll be there. Just watch the road." I sigh, loosening my grip on the door. "Besides, I'm sure my social-climber of a brother-in-law wouldn't miss an evening like that."

When we pull in front of Rose's house, Anne shuts off the car. "Did Thomas do that?" She's looking at the bruise. Thomas must've hit me real good. It should be gone by now.

"Yeah, last night when I got home. It's not a big deal, Anne."

I can see her visibly fighting off whatever it is she wants to actually say to me. "Did you tell Eli?"

"Yeah, he came by the house later, and it's not like I could hide it."

"Right. What about your parents? Didn't they say anything?"

I don't say anything. I just stare forward. She takes the hint. "Got it. Well, let's get my party started!"

The car unlocks, and in a heartbeat, Anne flits to the front door. I follow after her and plaster a smile on my face when Rose opens the door.

"Hello, my lovely girls. Come in, come in. We have a full night planned." She shuffles us into the house-turned-spa. Candles are lit all over the room, nearly masking the smell of her blood. She has a facial station, nail station, and a foot soak. A movie is already running on the TV, but I don't recognize it. It's some sappy Rom-Com that Anne probably loves.

"Oh, Rose, this is so sweet of you! I can't believe all of this." Anne looks like she's about to burst with joy.

"Well, I know I can't be at your party, so I wanted to do something for you, and for Cheyenne. I'm only here to help with the spa treatments, then I'm leaving you girls to have some friend time. You're always around the guys, so I thought you'd like to spend some quality time together." I start to waver under Ms. Rose's warm smile. I don't want to trust her. She knows so much, and I'm sure there's plenty that she hasn't shared, but I can't really hate her for that.

"You mean you're not staying the whole night with us?" Anne asks.

"No, no. You two need time to talk. I have you a stock of good movies that Mason said you like, and a fridge full of blood that should keep you for the night." I wince as she speaks. I still can't handle hearing someone outside the Deuxsang community speaking about blood. "So, where do you want to start? Nails, facials, massage?"

"I'd kill for a facial right now," Anne sighs, dropping her purse by the door and kicking off her shoes. Rose leads her over to the couch where she lies down.

She's got a bunch of herb concoctions that I can't even name. I head to the kitchen, grabbing two bottles of blood. When I walk back into the living room, Anne swipes hers out of my hand without even opening her eyes.

I settle by the television, combing through the stacks of movies that are pulled out, only half of which I recognize. All of these look like movies Anne would mush over, so I guess Rose knows what she's doing.

I feel her watching me, her eyes hard on my back. "I know we haven't gotten to talk a whole lot, Cheyenne. So if there's anything you'd like to ask me, I'm open for questioning." She stares boldly at me as she continues to cleanse Anne's already flawless skin.

"Nope. No questions." I say, pulling my knees to my chest.

"Eli really cares about you, you know? He thinks you're special."

I hesitate before responding. I shouldn't say anything. I shouldn't be talking to her about this stuff. "Being special isn't really something I should be proud of."

"Ah, yes. The Deuxsang Creed: Control and Conformity," she chants, a hint of amusement in her voice. I nod against my knees, despite myself. A new smell enters the room as Rose begins to exfoliate Anne's face. I'm surprised Anne hasn't chimed in yet. "It's okay to be special, Cheyenne. You've got a voice. It's okay if that voice doesn't sound like any you've heard before."

"Maybe in your world," I snap.

"No offense, Rose, but I'd love a more cheerful topic." Anne wakes from her stupor. "Anything but Deuxsang, witches, or the upcoming disaster that my parents call a party." Her eyes close again as she relaxes into the couch, her face mask hardening.

"Sorry, hon. More cheerful. " She pauses, trying to think of a cheerful topic. "Well, Anne, I know you don't want to talk about your party, but I also know you're excited about your dress. Why don't you tell us about that while I do Cheyenne's nails?"

Anne considers a moment as I walk to the dining room table, choosing a teal polish. "Can you do my toes?" I whisper to Rose. "I don't really like anything on my fingers." She smiles at me as Anne begins to ramble about her fabulous dress. I curl into myself on the chair, resting my chin on my knees as Ms. Rose paints an undercoat on my toenails. We listen patiently to Anne, until two coats and a topcoat later, she sighs, signaling the end of her spiel.

We switch places, and Ms. Rose finds some safe, unimportant topic to talk to Anne about. I zone out as she goes through the different stages of a facial. My skin tingles beneath the different herbs working. Before she moves to do Anne's nails, she hands me another bottle of blood. I didn't realize how thirsty I was until now. The blood's gone in a matter of seconds, and I become aggravated by the scratching in my throat.

Watching Rose, I see her growing tired. Her movements are more cumbersome. Light shadows are forming under her eyes. Anne sees it too. She watches her carefully, her hand ready to catch the nail polish if it starts to fall from Ms. Rose's shaking hand. We exchange a glance, and I nod. "Rose, I think we're good down here. Why don't you go lie down?" Anne suggests.

Ms. Rose nods, a weak smile on her lips. "I think that's

just the medicine I need. Didn't realize how tired I was until you said something, Annie." She wraps her shawl around her thin shoulders and pushes herself to her feet. Anne stands with her and leads her to the stairs.

"I'll be right back, Cheyenne. There's more blood in the fridge."

I nod as they start up the stairs. "Thank you for everything, Ms. Rose. I enjoyed the spa stuff."

"Of course, dear. I'm glad you liked it." Her voice is no more than a whisper now. I walk into the kitchen and open the fridge. Most of it is normal food, which I expect. But there are two shelves on the door stocked with full bottles of blood. It's weird seeing this. I've never gotten my own blood. Dad gave it to me at home, and Thomas gives it to me here. I don't even know where he keeps his supply.

Anne's already settled into the couch when I come back with two bottles. She's looking at the TV, but her mind is somewhere else completely. I curl into the opposite corner of the couch, turning toward her. "Anne?"

"Hmm?" She asks, zoning back into reality and turning to face me.

"What's wrong?" I ask, forcing myself to take just a sip from my bottle.

She shakes her head, rubbing her thumb over the top of the bumpy lid. "Nothing. Why do you think something's wrong?"

"Well, the only time you've really opened your mouth all night was to talk about your dress. I know you've got more going on up there than just a dress, so talk."

"It's nothing really." She won't look at me, just at her

hands. "My parents are just killing me right now. It's like they have surveillance cameras set up or something. They're always asking where I'm going, who I'm seeing, when I'll be back. They're scrutinizing me now more than ever." I can tell that's not what she wants to say. There's something there.

"Well, you are dating a human" I smile, nudging her with my foot.

She smirks, but she's holding back. "At least he's not a witch," she passes a sly glance at me.

"Yeah, what's up with that? Humans. Witches. The world's going to shambles, Anne. Next thing you know, we'll be catching werewolves." I try laughing to lighten the mood, but she's not having it. "Sorry."

"I don't really see why you're laughing. You're a part of this too." She snaps, still not looking at me.

"I know. I was kidding." I bite my lip, thinking. There's something I've been wanting to ask her ever since the fire. "Listen, Anne, does any of this stuff going on with your parents...does it have anything to do with your brother?"

Her head snaps up, finally looking at me. Her eyes are wet with tears she's trying to hold back. "What do you know about my brother? *How* do you know about my brother? I've never told anyone about him, not even Mason."

"You remember that law office I went to? The one that burned down?" She nods. "Well, I was being nosy, looking through files before the fire, and I saw your family name. So I opened it, and it had a picture of your brother that said— "

"Deceased?" she guesses. I nod. Now I'm the one not

looking at her. "I don't know the details. I wasn't born yet. I'm sure my parents weren't going to tell me, but I was snooping when I was little and found some old stuff of his. When I asked my parents about him, they told me he died. They've never given me specifics though. Have you ever known a Deuxsang to die? It's totally bizarre. You'd think they'd explain it, but no. If something doesn't look good for our family, we don't talk about it."

I feel like she's waiting for me to say something, but I don't know what. "That's what I hate about this stupid culture. Everything has to look good. Image is everything. We're always trying to prove ourselves to the vampires, but they don't care about us. All they care about is that we keep our mouths shut and stick to the status quo."

"You're right," I whisper, meeting her eyes.

"Of course I'm right. My parents and your brother-in-law are up there with the worst of them."

I feel like I should be offended. Family first and all, but I'm definitely not. "Yeah, he's pretty much a nightmare."

Eventually she continues, "Cheyenne, I'm really sorry I'm in a bad mood. My family just has this ability to get under my skin. I really don't want to talk about them anymore."

"Alright." I shrug. "What do you want to talk about?"

She thinks for a minute, then a disturbing smile stretches across her face. "Eli."

"What about Eli?"

"What's going on there?" She laughs.

"I don't know. So Thomas basically threatened me last night, and I don't know. I'm just over it. I've always been the perfect child. And now that I do one thing wrong, I'm going to lose my life over it? I don't think so." I shake my head.

"I'm so proud of you. You're a delinquent like me!" She leaps across the couch and throws her arms around me. "This is great! Oh, did you tell Rove yet?"

"What? Why would I tell Rove? He doesn't..."

"You just don't want to prove him right," she laughs. "Come on, call him. You can use my phone." She pulls her phone out of her pocket and hands it to me, grinning and wiggling her eyebrows. "He deserves to know, Cheyenne."

Rolling my eyes, I snatch it out of her hand and dial Rove's number. I wait. And wait. And wait. "He's not going to..." I start.

"Munchkin? Are you okay?" Rove's voice is husky.

"Yeah, I'm fine. I hope I'm not interrupting anything."

"Put him on speaker phone!" Anne yells, grabbing the phone from me and switching him to speaker. "Hey, Rove!"

"Is that Anne?" he asks. It's weird, like he's re-orienting himself. "Hey, Anne. So what's going on?"

I look at Anne, inwardly enjoying the discomfort that waiting causes for her. I open my mouth to respond, but Anne beats me. "Eli and Cheyenne are dating!" She screams at the top of her lungs. I lean away from her, covering my ears.

"Will you lower your voice, please? Rose is asleep upstairs." I grab the phone from her and take it off speaker. "Hey, it's me."

All I hear is laughing. Lots of laughing. "You're telling me that you're actually dating the witch?" Rove manages to get out between laughing spurts.

"Yes, I'm dating Eli." I glare at Anne out of the corner of my eye, but she can't stop smiling.

"Well, that's nice, Munchkin. I'm proud of you. I honestly didn't think you had it in you." He laughs again.

"What's that supposed to mean?"

"Nothing, Cheyenne. I'm just occupied." I grimace when I hear some girl call his name in the background. "I'm happy for you, really. More happy that I was right, but still happy for you. But I really gotta go now." And then he's gone.

"Well that was an interesting conversation." I suck my lips in and hand the phone back to Anne. "Remind me to never call him at this time of night again, please." I grimace, shuddering.

"Wha—ew! Okay, you got it. So, what are we going to watch?"

I check my own phone, sighing at the text message waiting for me. "I'm sorry, Anne. It looks like Thomas wants me home tonight. Would you mind?"

"Not at all. But I'm really starting to hate Thomas. He's almost worse than my parents." She sighs, pushing herself to her feet.

"Yeah, *almost*," I snort and roll my eyes, reaching for my bag. He's definitely worse.

Before we leave, we clean up Rose's spa materials and leave her a note. The ride home is the best part of the whole night. We rag on our families the entire time—how stupid the rules are, how vain they are, how much of a social-climber my brother-in-law is, and how much I hate the way my sister tries to be close to me. Anne doesn't say anything else about her brother, even though I feel like she wants to. I don't push it.

When I walk in the house, everything is dead. I call out to Kara and Thomas, but there's no response. I read in my room for hours before I hear the front door open. Kara peeps her head in my door when they finally come upstairs.

"You're still up. I thought you'd be asleep by now." She smiles, pushing the door open.

"And I thought that you guys would be home since Thomas told me to come back."

"Oh, Cheyenne, don't get all upset. Thomas found out that someone important was going to be at the club tonight, so we had to go. You understand."

No, Kara, I don't. I don't understand why you're so subservient. And I really don't understand why your husband is such an ass. "Yeah, I understand. No big deal. Good night." I turn back to my book, waiting for her to close the door. She hesitates, and I can feel the words she's not saying. Then she turns away and click-clacks down the hallway.

Nineteen

For the hundredth time over the past couple of weeks, I'm sitting on the couch while Thomas stands in front of me, using his compulsion to keep me trapped in this house. My eyes glaze over as he keeps contact, nearly shouting the words, "You will not leave this house under any circumstance."

Kara stands in the corner, gripping her satin handbag and biting her freshly painted nails. When I look at her, she winces.

"Where are you guys going anyway?"

"An event. Nothing to concern yourself with," Thomas mutters as he straightens his bowtie in the hallway mirror. "We'll check in when we return." Thomas offers his arm to Kara, and they walk to the waiting car, Kara's dress dragging behind her.

"You two kids have a great night," I mutter, my arms crossed over my chest as I lean against the doorframe. Compulsion may be my least favorite ability. I mean, inflictors are far more dangerous, but the fact that I'm powerless just because Thomas says so? It makes me want to explode.

Once their car disappears down the road, I head upstairs to my room, grabbing some rogue book off my shelf. I'm only a few pages in when I hear something outside my window. Dang it, Eli.

He's waiting for me below the balcony, smiling like a loon. "Come on down here. We've got places to go, people to see, memories to make, kisses to steal." My eye roll is betrayed by some dumb giggle that escapes. "Come on, what are you waiting for? I've got a gig to get to." He opens his arms as if he's going to catch me. Ha.

"I can't, Eli. I'm stuck here." I stand back from the balcony, not willing to find out what will happen if I lean over it.

"What does that even mean?" he groans.

"Remember how I told you that Thomas is a compeller? Well, he must've assumed that you'd come try to kidnap me, so he compelled me to stay in the house. I literally can't leave."

"So at least try." He shrugs his shoulders like it's the simplest answer known to man.

"Why didn't I think of that?" I narrow my eyes at him. "I *can't*."

"Cheyenne, try for me. Please?" There's that stupid half-smile. I mean, what's the harm in showing him that he's wrong, right?

"Fine," I sigh. Placing my hands on the banister. I lean over, expecting to be thrown back. But I'm not. My upper body glides over the banister until I am parallel with the ground. I spring back up, eyes wide as golf balls. "Whoa."

"See," Eli smiles smugly, arms crossed over his chest. "Just jump. I'll catch you." Excited now, I swing my legs over the banister and push myself off. Eli guides me to the ground on his created wind. "Look at you, conquering compulsion. You're like a superhero!" Eli laughs, kissing me gently.

"Eli, you don't understand. I shouldn't be able to disobey Thomas's compulsion, unless—unless I'm a compeller.

But that's not..."

"I thought you said you were an inflictor. I'm pretty sure I've experienced your ability." He nudges me playfully as I zone out, trying to work my way through this.

"First of all, it was an accident. I've apologized several times. And second of all, I thought I was an inflictor. But if I can't be compelled, then I'm a..."

"Compeller," Eli finishes for me. "Is it possible to be both?" He asks as he takes my hand, leading me to his truck parked two houses down from mine.

"No. Deuxsang all have one ability without exception. I'd have to be a full-fledged vampire to have multiple. They have all four." I slide into the passenger seat after he opens my door.

"Well, maybe you're a vampire," he says in his best spooky voice.

"Very funny, but also impossible. Nice try." His brow knits together as he tries to think this through. I reach for his hand, interlocking our fingers and kiss his cheek as he pulls down the road. "Don't worry about it. So I'm a compeller. It just means I can get you to do whatever I want," I wink, leaning back in my seat.

"Ha, my mind is a steel trap. No use trying to get inside this thing." I roll my eyes but don't respond. "So you're going to Anne's party?" Eli asks.

"I guess I don't really have a choice. Anne'll kill me if I don't go." I rest my head against the window as the Garden District disappears behind us. "Plus she's really nervous about the Affirmation interview."

"What's the interview?"

"Before we ascend, the vampires that monitor our families

interview us on basic knowledge of our culture and people. The Affirmation interview is basically the same thing except way more intense. It's like our coming out into society party. If we don't pass the interview..."

"What happens?"

I think for a second, trying to remember if I've heard my dad tell me anything about a Deuxsang failing the Affirmation interview. I can't. "I actually don't know."

"Too bad you can't take me as your date." He bites his bottom lip, glancing at me out of the corner of his eye.

"You know I wish I could." I glance down at my knees, looking anywhere but at him. His free hand brushes mine, the other hand on the wheel. "I'll go to the party, hate every moment of it, then meet you for the rest of the evening. Okay?" I wrap my arm through his, leaning against him as he drives through the streets of New Orleans.

"You drive a hard bargain, Miss Lane."

"I know. Hey, I wanted to ask you something. Has Rose ever mentioned anything to you about Anne's brother?"

"Anne has a brother?" His brows furrow together in confusion.

"Had a brother. He died before she was born. I was just wondering if Rose had ever said anything."

"No, I don't think Rose would talk about anything that Anne didn't want to talk about. How do you know this?"

"Well, the Lacroix's file was in the law office, and I saw her brother's picture. Then I asked her about it a couple weeks ago. It's not a big deal."

Eli pulls into the closest parking spot he can find. "We can talk more about it later. I'm already late."

I help him carry pieces of his drum set down Canal Street. We work our way through the crowd to get to Preservation Hall. The bouncers lead us through the back door, and I wait backstage until Eli comes back for the rest of his drums. "Thank you." He jogs back out onto the stage, sticks in hand, and smiles at Mason's glare.

I work my way into the audience and take my seat next to Anne. "Things going well?" she asks the moment I sit down.

"Well, Thomas hasn't killed him yet, and I found out I'm a compeller. Besides that, everything's great."

"Don't whine, Cheyenne, and since when are you a compeller? What about inflicting?"

"Guess I'm just meant to boss people around." I start to laugh to myself, but Anne just stares at me with a straight face.

"You think you're funny," her voice is stale, but I detect a hint of a smile.

"And you know I am." I turn to the stage, catching Eli's eye as he straightens a cymbal.

He winks at me before turning away to focus on the music. I shake away my giddiness and look around the room. The temptation to try out my ability is overpowering, even though I'm not supposed to. But who cares? It's not like Thomas is here to stop me.

"Hey, Anne." She looks back at me. "Get some water." As the waitress walks by, Anne stops her and orders a glass of water. After the waitress is gone, Anne turns to me as I try to hide my smile. "Stop it," she glares at me. "I don't insert myself in your dreams. I'm not even thirsty."

I smile, showing all my teeth, but she just shakes her head in mock exasperation.

The Hall is packed tonight. There's no reason for anyone to notice me, but I still feel as though I'm being watched. I scan the room and find just what I was expecting. The group of ragged kids stands in the back corner. Their faces are covered with grime and soot. Their hair is disheveled, and their clothes are full of moth-eaten holes. One, the oldest, looks back at me with what appears to be red irises but turns away before I can be sure. Then I spot another equally disturbing sight—Erik. He stands near the group of homeless children and stares at me until I meet his eyes. He nods his head to the side, motioning me outside.

"I'll be right back, Anne," I tap her hand and point to Erik as he pushes the door open. She nods at me, her eyes glaring in his direction. I push through the crowd easily, almost invisibly, and meet Erik outside. We walk silently past the line waiting to get in to hear the band. Many are holding Monde Musique's flyers, gripping them eagerly in their hands. The band's popularity has really grown since I've been here.

Erik leads me into a side alley—probably not a smart decision on my part. I stand near the entrance, hands on my hips, and wait for him to turn around. He stands facing the wall, his back to me.

"What do you want, Erik?" I ask impatiently, continually glancing around me as people pass the alley.

He spins on his heel, his eyes narrowed to slits. "Stay away from my brother," he hisses.

"Sounds like your issue is with him, not me."

"Don't start with me. If you don't leave him alone, you'll be wishing you were back in Winmore."

"Your intimidation won't work on me anymore."

He stomps forward, pointing his finger in my face. "I'm tired of your games, and I'm tired of hearing your name. Get out of my brother's life before I make you."

"Your brother's a big boy. He can make his own decisions," I glare at Erik as he pushes himself into my face. I shove him backward, a fire roaring up in my throat.

"Watch it, Lane. I don't mind breaking your face again." He walks back up to me, his round face just inches from mine. He pushes me backward, and I stumble, falling to the concrete. I jump to my feet and grab his shirt. He claws at my hands as I throw him against the wall.

Suddenly, he disappears. He knocks my knees out from under me, and I fall to the ground, looking for my invisible enemy through the dusky air. A force slams into my stomach, and I roll to my side. Before he can strike another blow, I push myself to my feet and turn in slow circles, waiting for his next move.

He flickers in front of me, and I swipe my arm in vain. I continue waving my arms like a madwoman until finally I come into contact with something. I ball my fist and slam it into whatever part of him I've found. He gasps, materializing, and falls to the ground. I throw myself on top of him, pinning his shoulders to the ground. I bare my fangs, hissing, and watch as his eyes double in size. Erik wriggles beneath me, but I'm stronger.

All I can see is the plump vein pulsing in his now visible neck. All I can smell is the sweet blood running through that vein. Involuntarily, I lower my mouth to his neck, my fangs just inches away from his jugular. I hover over him, growing more and more thirsty as he thrashes beneath me. Then my head dives, and my fangs pierce skin. Erik shrieks, desperate to push me away. I barely get a taste of his blood before I hear him.

"Cheyenne, no!" Eli's strong arms wrap around my waist and yank me off of Erik. I thrash in his grip as he drags me down the alley and presses me against the wall. I still smell Erik's blood. My first taste of human blood is still on my tongue. It's strangely familiar.

Eli presses my shoulders against the wall. Then he places his hands on both sides of my face. "Cheyenne, look at me." My eyes stare wildly out of the corner of my eyes so that I can still see Erik, but Eli turns my head to face him. "Cheyenne!" I tremble as the frenzy fades away and the smell of Erik's blood dulls. Then I realize what I've done. I curl in on myself, unable to look at Eli, at Erik.

Eli sighs, releasing me, and I fall to the ground. I watch Eli dash over to his brother and kneel down beside him. Erik's still, but I can see his lips moving. "Erik, you need to get out of here. Get to Lucas." Eli grabs Erik's hand and pulls him up to his feet. I can see my bite marks at the base of his neck before he presses his jacket against them to stop the blood. He leans against Eli, his eyes pressed shut. Then he's gone. Disappeared into thin air.

I bit someone. What am I?

I turn my head and see the same group of homeless children. Their red eyes peer at me through ratty bangs. The oldest, no more than fourteen, has his fangs protruding over top his bottom lip.

Eli sees them too. "What do you want?" he yells.

The pairs of eyes blink once, silently. Eli takes a step closer. Three of them hiss back at him, baring their fangs.

I reach for his hand and pull him back, baring my own fangs. "I don't know why you're following us, but stay away," I spit.

The oldest steps out in front of the group, his pointed fingernails tapping his sallow cheek. Suddenly, he's right in front me. "Our leader will be very happy." The boy laughs savagely, displaying his fangs. Then the rest of them step forward, hissing and spitting at me.

Eli suddenly disappears beside me, reappearing behind the child vampire. I watch in horror as he flips the boy onto his stiff back, jumps on top of him, and holds a pocketknife to his neck. The blade pricks his skin, but no blood comes.

"You wouldn't kill me, would you, *witch*? I'm just a boy after all." The vampire stares up at Eli with innocent brown eyes, terror-stricken. Eli freezes, the side of the knife pressing against the boy's windpipe. I look up at the rest of the group. All their eyes are brown again. Eli leaps off the boy, and the vampire stands up, vainly dusting off his mud-coated jacket. "I didn't think so, *witch*," he snarls, grinning back at us. "How does it feel, half-breed? To bite for the first time? I can't wait to share the good news. She's been waiting for you."

In the blink of an eye, the group flits down the road and disappears. Eli drops the knife, and it clatters to the concrete. When he faces me, there's nothing in his eyes.

There's nothing in me, at all.

I search for something, some piece of myself that's still here. There's no language to describe what I've known, what it's like to drink directly from a life source.

"There's no going back from this." The words come from my mouth, and from a million miles away.

Eli hasn't stopped staring. He doesn't move. He must know, though. It's finished. I jump around him, break into a flit, and I'm gone.

...

A few minutes later, I stop in front of the house. My throat feels like an inferno as I slide my key into the lock and push the door open. Thankfully, Thomas and Kara aren't home yet. I rush upstairs to change into my pajamas, making it look like I never left because in Thomas's mind, there's no way I could have.

I just barely slide into bed when I hear the front door open. Thomas and Kara stomp up the stairs.

"Good, you're here," Thomas mutters from the doorway.

"Where else would I be?" I don't quite look at him, or at Kara, but I can feel her heavy gaze.

"Well, we received an invitation to Anne's Affirmation party. You're already planning to attend, I assume." Thomas looks at me down his pointed nose. "We'll be going as a family. There will be several important people there, so dress better than your best."

"Fine, whatever." I slump further into my bed, avoiding Thomas's eyes. "Goodnight." They both stare at me for a second too long before closing the door. As soon as they're gone, tears pour out of my eyes. I stuff the end of a pillow in my mouth and scream as loud and hard as I can. I should have stayed in Winmore.

Twenty

There's no way I can do this. It's not physically possible. She cannot expect me to walk in dangerously high heels while wearing a dress that barely allows me to move my legs. Kara stares back at me, completely satisfied.

"You're magnificent! How do I do it?" she teases.

"Am I allowed to look at myself now?" I ask, attempting to stand taller. Apparently that helps with balance. She nods eagerly, holds my hand, and glides me slowly to the full-length mirror in her room. When I open my eyes, I nearly fall back, and not because of the heels. I look flawless. Kara's masterful makeup has my face coated in every powder, shade, and color imaginable. My hair's pulled back loosely away from my face and up into an effortless-yet-intricate bun.

But the real shock is the dress. This dress is a completely different style from anything I've ever worn before. The thin, rouge fabric hugs every line of my body. Laced sleeves run up my arms and stop just below my shoulders. The front and back of the dress come to a modest v that leaves just enough skin exposed. The dress clings to my body down to the tops of my thighs where it flows to the floor.

Kara comes up behind me and lays a necklace against the center of my chest. The light from the chandelier reflects off the small diamonds that form three connected spirals.

"The *triskele* is supposed to symbolize forward motion, and that's something that I want you to always remember. Sometimes life brings us down, but we have to keep moving forward. We're blessed in ways that vampires and humans will never be. Vampires are immortal, unchanging as the world changes around them. Humans have a short time to live, and they don't understand how to live it until it's too late. We have more time—time to learn and experience—but we also have an end to look forward to. So in this long life that you're given, you always want to move forward."

"And where did that nugget of wisdom come from?"

"Oh, I get one every now and then." Kara smiles as she clasps the necklace along the back of my neck and squeezes my shoulders. I admire the necklace. It's absolutely perfect. I look at myself again, and for the millionth time wish that Eli were here, that he could be coming with me, and that I hadn't screwed everything up.

Once Kara and Thomas are dressed, we ride together in a rented town car to the Lacroix's home. My jaw drops as I see the line of cars pulling up in front of their mansion. It's like we've stepped into another century. Two butlers stand at the end of the path opening doors for fabulous people emerging from limousines. I'm actually glad Kara dressed me. At least I'll blend in.

We wait another ten minutes before our car pulls up to the entrance and a butler in a crisp tux opens my door. He smiles and extends his hand to help me out of the car. I balance on his arm to gain control of my heels. Kara and Thomas follow behind me along the long walk up to the front door. This house is magnificent—pure white stucco with beautiful Spanish iron railings, smooth pillars giving the effect of a Parthenon, and two stone lion heads standing guard before the front doors.

Anne and her parents stand in the entrance greeting all the guests. I see straight through Anne's forced smile, but apart from her mood, she looks absolutely gorgeous. When it's finally our turn to be greeted, Anne's face floods with relief. She throws her arms around my neck, nearly knocking me to the ground. Kara catches me, pushing me upright.

"I'm so glad you're here. I'm dying!" Anne whispers in my ear.

"Ginger! Contain yourself." Mrs. Lacroix whispers, turning a scolding eye on Anne.

"Sorry, Mother." Anne backs away from me to stand in line with her parents. "Do you mind if I go with Cheyenne to show her around the party? I'll be right back."

"No, Ginger, you must stay here and greet the rest of your guests. You may go find Miss Lane when everyone has arrived." Anne opens her mouth to argue, but a look from Mr. Lacroix stops her.

"Yes, ma'am." Anne forces her fake-smile back on as Thomas and Kara compliment her briefly before turning their attention to her parents. I feel a pang of nausea at their overdone praises. I'm the one to push them into the house as the greeting line grows longer behind us. Yet again, my jaw drops. The inside of the house is even more spectacular than the outside, especially with the party decorations, all very elegant to fit the event.

A grand staircase encircles the entranceway, and lights hang from the twenty-foot ceiling, casting a magnificent glow over the room. Pictures of Anne, beginning after her Ascension, line the first hallway leading out to the backyard.

I'm not even sure backyard is the appropriate term. Half of it is covered by crystal blue tile furnished with luxurious porch furniture and two bars. The grassy area of the lot is filled with Deuxsang around my age dancing. A DJ has set up his booth at the back of the yard.

I recognize some faces from Thomas's party at the club, but I've never said a word to any of them, nor do I really want to. Both Kara and Thomas are sporting their society faces. They always have to impress. I'm sure they've ensnared at least half the people here, but there's always another important figure to charm.

"Oh, Kara, there's Mr. Ansel. We need to go talk to him." Thomas takes Kara's hand and leads her away to a very sophisticated man with a glass of blood in his hand.

For a few minutes I just stand awkwardly on the patio, not knowing what to do, where to go, or who to smile at. Several guys my age pass by me, discreetly glancing back over their shoulders as they walk toward the dance floor. This dress must work wonders. Wouldn't Thomas be so proud if a nice Deuxsang boy asked me to dance? I think it might make his night.

I'm finally rescued by Anne. She sneaks up behind me, throwing her arm over my shoulder. "So, I'm already completely over this party. My face hurts from smiling too much. I can't get my parents off my back, and I keep tripping over my dress." I smile at her, at the two of us. We're a hot mess. "Come on, let's go get a drink." She nudges my side, wiggling her eyebrows.

"Yes, please!" I follow her to one of the bars.

The bartender, seeing that it's the girl of honor, pulls out two drinks and hands them to us before we even- touch the counter.

"Ladies, here's the drink of the evening—a tribute to you, Miss Lacroix."

"What is this?" I ask, bringing the glass of blood cocktail to my lips.

Anne smiles, wiggling her eyebrows. "It's like our version of birthday cake. Michael here is a genius. He bartends all of my parents' parties," she smiles at the short, buff guy behind the counter.

After a few sips of blood, I notice that everyone is staring at something. It's not Anne. No one's even noticed us over here. Anne and I stop too, looking to the illuminated veranda, and what I see confuses me more than anything I've seen since I arrived in New Orleans.

Standing like a queen, dressed in all white, is Lilith—tall, proud, smug Lilith.

Instantly my teeth clench together. She's looking down on everybody here, just like she does at family meetings. Before I can compose myself, Thomas and Kara appear beside her with a warm greeting. Everyone's attention is on the three of them, but no one moves, including myself.

"Cheyenne, who is that?" Anne asks, standing defensively beside me.

"My cousin Lilith. She works for the Council." I mutter through my teeth.

"I don't remember seeing her name on the guest list."

"She must have come with the vampires who are going to interview you." My shoulders tense when Thomas motions me over to the three of them. I look to Anne for support, and she links her arm through mine. I want to smack the judgmental look off Lilith's face as she surveys Anne.

"Cheyenne! How's my lovely cousin? You look splendid." Lilith pulls me in for a sharp, painful hug before pushing me away and turning to Anne. "And you must be the lady of the hour, Ginger Lacroix. How very pleased I am to meet you." Lilith extends her hand, her long, manicured nails wrapping around Anne's hand like claws. "I'm Cheyenne's cousin, Lilith."

"Why are you here, Lilith?" I ask, barely opening my teeth to speak.

"Cheyenne, please remember your manners." Kara sighs.

"Kara, it's Lilith, not the Queen of England."

Lilith releases her death grip on Anne to turn to me. There are daggers in her eyes. If I didn't know better I'd think she was inflicting on me. In fact, she seems almost surprised when she returns her attention to Anne. "Ginger, this is a lovely party. Are you enjoying yourself?"

"It's okay, I guess. I don't really know these people, but I'm glad Cheyenne's here."

"Yes, isn't Cheyenne just a lifesaver?" she smirks, that stupid face that makes me want to punch her.

I notice that for the first time this summer Thomas has not said a single word. His eyes are on the ground, and his hands are crossed behind his back. Kara follows my gaze, and when I look at her, she just shrugs, avoiding my gaze. "Thomas, are you alright?" I ask.

He glances up, his face blank as stone. "Of course, Cheyenne. Now if you'll excuse us, I should introduce our cousin to some of our friends." Lilith smiles at Anne as Thomas and Kara lead her away toward a group of official looking men.

"That was weird," Anne says, a hint of concern knitting her brow together. "Whatever, forget her. Let's go dance." Before we even get the chance, Mr. and Mrs. Lacroix appear in the doorway accompanied by five strange vampires. I hadn't even noticed that the sun had fallen.

"Um, Anne." I nod at the house and reach for her hand when I see her go still. "It'll be fine. You know this stuff." I squeeze her hand, and she looks at me and desperately squeezes back.

"What if I fail, Cheyenne? No one knows what happens to Deuxsang who fail. What if that's what happened to my brother?" she whispers, looking back up at the waiting vampires. Mrs. Lacroix looks like she's about to explode waiting for Anne.

"You're not going to fail. Don't start doubting yourself now. Go, and then, because I love you, I'll dance with you after you're affirmed." I smile, nudging her forward.

"You better. It's my party," she mutters as she walks away from me, glancing back once before disappearing inside.

I turn away from the veranda, rolling the tension out of my neck. When I open my eyes, Lilith is staring at me. Thomas stands behind her, chin down, observing us from under his thick eyelashes.

What is my family's problem tonight? I wave at Lilith and glare at her with a smile. After rolling her eyes, she turns back to whatever official man she was not listening to. Maybe Thomas and Kara are trying to set her up or something.

Every nerve in my body is sharp, and I can't take my eyes off my family. I stand on the outskirts of the dance floor, watching people near my age get into the soundless beat of the music. The music gets louder, the chitchat duller. I don't look away from Thomas and Lilith, and Lilith rarely takes her eyes away from me. If I could just punch her pretty face, I'd feel so much better.

I notice Thomas catch sight of the hosts back from delivering Anne to her interview. He immediately steers Lilith toward them, and she plasters on her most sincere fake smile as she shakes hands with Mr. Lacroix. "Why don't we go inside and talk?" Thomas suggests just loud enough that I can hear him, and then they disappear in the crowd. I start to follow them when I smell something. Not something, someone. I turn around viciously combing the veranda for Eli with no luck.

I walk across the whole dance floor and up to the veranda. The scent follows me. I keep checking over my shoulder, but Eli's nowhere to be seen. I lead the scent away from everybody to the back of the yard where no one else can sense him.

"Eli, get out of here. I don't know why you came, but you need to leave," I whisper.

His voice floats through the air. "I have to tell you something."

I back away from his voice, my hands balled into fists. "No, you don't. What you have to do is get out of here before you get killed." I stomp away, but an invisible force holds me back.

"Stop, Cheyenne. This is important."

I wrench my arm out of his grasp and run toward the party in search of Anne, hoping that she's done.

As soon as I approach the house, the five vampires walk out onto the porch floor, followed by Anne, her head bowed. "Attention!" The leader, a woman that looks eerily like Lilith, booms across the span of the yard. "We now present to you the newest member of the community, Ginger Anne Lacroix, dreamwalker."

Everyone applauds as Anne steps forward smiling with relief. Her smile gets bigger when she spots me. The vampire silences the crowd by raising her hand. When she crosses her arms, I'm shocked to find everyone bowing. Slowly, I follow suit, but when I look up, the vampires are looking directly at me. I quickly drop my eyes.

After one minute too long, everyone stands straight, and the vampires are gone. Anne rushes across the lawn to me, throwing her arms around my neck. "I did it! I really did it! I'm going stay young now, and I can peep in on Mason's dreams! Ha! I'm finally a full-fledged Deuxsang."

"See, nothing to worry about. I knew you'd pass." I smile at her, but she senses my anxiety."

"What's wrong?"

I bite my lip, looking around the lawn to see if Eli's shown himself yet. "We have a problem." She looks at me, even more confused. "Eli's here."

That stupid look on her face disappears immediately. "Has he lost his mind? He's going to get himself killed! Why is he here?"

"He says he wants to talk to me about something important." My jaw clenches shut as his scent hits me again.

"Okay, where did you see him?" She looks over the heads

of all dancers, searching for his familiar face.

"Well, I haven't exactly seen him yet."

"But you just said?" She looks down at me, her eyes narrowed.

"He's sort of invisible right now."

Anne groans, rolling her eyes. "Is he stupid or just plain suicidal? Okay, I'll go this way." She points to the veranda. "And you go that way," pointing to the dance floor. "We'll find him."

After a few minutes of pushing through countless dancers, I make it to the other side. That's when I can feel him again. His scent floods over me, and I close my eyes for just a second. "Eli, leave," I whisper, even though I'm moving out of sight.

When we're safe from Deuxsang eyes, he materializes in front of me. I watch as colors start to flicker in front of me. Slowly, starting at his shoes, he begins to take form, except when it comes time to show his face, I'm not looking at him. I'm looking at a stranger. I stagger backward, away from the strange man smiling at me.

"It's me," he whispers, taking a step toward me. His voice matches Eli, but that's not his face. This face looks like he could be related to Anne—fair skin, freckles, and a full head of red hair. He holds his hand out to me. "Dance with me, please."

I gulp, setting my hand in his, and let him lead me to the middle of the dance floor. He pulls me in close for a slow song, and for a moment, I lose myself. I rest my head on his shoulder and relax into him. I hear him sigh and breathe deeply.

"You said you had something to tell me, so talk,"

I mumble into his jacket.

"I've found out some things that you need to know," he whispers, pulling me close again, his lips beside my ear.

"You're not going to convince me to get back together, not that I have any idea why you'd want to."

"Thomas has been feeding you human blood."

I stop dead, and he nearly trips over me. "That's insane, Eli. That is *literally* insane."

He regains balance and makes me keep dancing. "I know it sounds— "

"No, you really don't. You have no idea how closely the Council monitors our consumption of *animal* blood. If the vampires ever caught Deuxsang drinking human blood, they would eliminate us. Not to mention that Thomas cares way too much about climbing the Deuxsang ladder to commit the slightest infraction. Do I need to remind you how violent he got with me over you?"

"So you're saying it's impossible?" He's challenging me.

Of course it's impossible. But I have to admit that the blood he's been serving me at home and handing me at the club did taste different, and I did get a strange high from drinking it. Not to mention that I've developed a strong urge to bite humans and have given in to that urge. "Why would he do that?" My voice is more subdued, and Eli can tell that he has my attention.

"I think it has something to do with you being different."

"Different how?" I scan the dance floor to make sure we aren't being noticed.

"I don't know exactly. But I think you do."

The trauma of my botched Ascension weighs heavily on me. "So what?"

"You say that it's impossible for Deuxsang to have more than one ability. But what if it's not? Have you tried inflicting since you found out you could compel?"

I don't respond, but now I'm certain that Lilith *was* trying to use her ability on me.

"I knew it. You do have two abilities. Maybe more."

"Why are you putting yourself in death's hands to tell me this right now?"

"You're not the only one. I believe Anne's brother is like you, and he's not dead. The Council took him."

"How would you even know all this?" I'm sick of this. My voice is raised, and people are starting to look at us.

"You remember how I mentioned before that I've been practicing astral projection, trying to reach my ancestors?" I nod my head at the unfamiliar face just when I notice Kara speed walking towards us.

"You need to leave," I tell him through gritted teeth. "Now. My sister's coming." It's like I can hear the heavy stamp of her heels.

"Fine, I'll leave," he concedes, "but there's more. Meet me at Mason's house at 10."

I open my mouth to object, but the way he's looking at me stops my words. "Fine! Just go."

"I mean it...10:00. And be careful."

I turn away from him and walk as fast as I can in these ridiculous heels. I glance up and see Lilith standing on the veranda, and she's looking straight at me. Thomas stands slightly behind her, glaring at me then Eli, trying to place his face. I need to find Anne.

And then Kara is in front of me. "Cheyenne, Thomas wants to speak with you for a moment."

"Can he wait?" I search my brain for a reason to stall. "I wanted to give Anne her present. Please? I'll be quick, before she has to start saying good-bye to guests."

Her eyes flicker over to Thomas. "No, now. This will only take a minute." My heart drops to my stomach. I know what's about to happen. I search for Anne, catch her eye, motioning over to the present table.

Kara drags me across the lawn to where Thomas is waiting. "What's up, Thomas?"

His teeth grind at my casual tone, but he doesn't bite back. Instead, he looks directly into my eyes and says, "In ten minutes, you will go home, and you will stay home. No leaving. No questions. Go home and stay home all night." I really hope he can't tell his compulsion is not working on me.

"Aye-aye, Captain," I salute him, backing away before they can stop me. Anne's waiting for me by the table overflowing with gifts from people who probably can't even remember Anne's name.

"Did you find him?" she whispers, turning her back to the crowd.

"He wants us to meet him at Mason's house at ten. I don't like it, but we have to go. He said some things." I look up at her, a stroke of nerves coursing through me.

"What kind of things?" Her head tilts as she considers me.

"Crazy things. He'll tell us all of it when we get there."

"Then of course we're going."

"Thomas just tried to compel me to go home, so at least sneaking out won't be a problem. I have to change out of this ridiculous dress. I'll leave first, then you can come pick me up." She's nodding along with me. "But first I wanted you to have your present." I find my newspaper wrapping near the back of the table.

Without a thought, she rips into the paper. "There's a card, Anne."

"I know, but I have my entire life to read your card." Her movements are rapid as she pulls the paper off the frame, but when she looks at her present, she's still. "Oh, Cheyenne. It's beautiful!"

I smile, remembering the feeling of the script. I pulled out my charcoal for the first time in years to draw her picture: her and Mason's initials locked together. "This means a lot to me," she whispers, looking from me to the drawing.

"Okay, it's just a picture," I shrug.

She laughs, choking back a sob. "I know you don't mean that. Thank you!" She carefully sets the frame down and hugs me tight, crushing my back. "Okay," she says after a moment, "you need to go. Thomas and your cousin are looking at us."

"See you soon," I whisper as we walk past Lilith and Thomas. She turns up the stairs, and I slip out the front door unnoticed. Breaking into a flit, I'm back at my house in less than fifteen seconds.

Twenty One

Leaving my gorgeous dress thrown across my bed, I slide down the banister when the doorbell rings. Anne bounces from foot to foot as I swing the door open and quickly close it behind me. We don't say a word as we race to her car. She's still in her party gown, but she's ditched her heels for flip-flops. As we race through the Garden District, she turns to me, a question hanging between us. "So what do you think he knows?" she finally asks.

"I haven't had time to wrap my head around it." My heart feels like it's galloping across my chest, and my hands are shaking.

"Wrap your head around what? What is going on?"

"I don't know!" I yell, not meaning to. "Just let Eli tell us okay?" I say shortly, staring out the window.

She's silent for a moment, staring out the windshield. "Alright, sorry."

"I'm sorry, Anne. I don't see why he had to come to your party in the first place. Why can't he just leave me alone?" I mutter, crossing my arms over my chest and lean into my seat as Anne steps on the gas.

"Because he doesn't want to." Her voice is quiet as she tries not to look at me. I sigh but don't respond, mainly because I don't know *how* to respond.

A few minutes later, we drive through the Musician's Village and pull into the only driveway with lit porch lights. Mason's been waiting all evening, rocking back and forth in his rocking chair. His eyes open when Anne's headlights scan across the porch. Smiling, he pulls himself out of the chair and meets us in the driveway. He opens Anne's door, holding his hand out to her and pulls her out of the car into his arms.

"You look so beautiful," he whispers into her ear.

She giggles and presses her lips against his. "You're sweet," she says. "Is Eli here yet?" she asks as I step out of the car.

"Nope. He said ten, right? He's still got a couple minutes." His smile is directed at me, and I force myself to smile back. "Well, come on in, guys. Mom's set out some drinks." He leads Anne up the walkway to the front door, but I hesitate.

"I'm just going to wait out here." I lean against the car, staring out into the dark street.

"Cheyenne, that's ridiculous." Mason leaves Anne at the door. "You're not staying outside at night alone." He glances around, into the bushes, at the neighboring houses.

"I'll be fine, but thanks."

"Why don't we stay out here with you?" he suggests, crossing his arms.

"Mason, leave her alone. She'll come in when he gets here. Come on in with me," Anne calls from the porch. She's staring at me, reading something in my face that I don't even know is there.

With a huff Mason turns on me and stalks up to the porch. He takes Anne's hand and walks into the house. I settle myself in to wait on Eli, leaning on Anne's car. I pull out my cell phone and glance at the time. He's five minutes late now. He's never late, but the street is completely empty. I can't hear any motors over the saxophone and blaring trumpet runs from the house next door. The streetlights are faltering. Mason, Anne, and Rose are chatting inside.

I walk out to the end of the driveway and glance both ways down the street, hoping to see the yellow headlights of his old junker. Then again, I could hear that stupid truck coming a mile away and smell the exhaust. I growl and punch a dent into an innocent tree. A splinter lodges in my finger—more like a chunk—and I fall back, holding out my hand as pain shoots up my arm. Very carefully, I take the bottom of my shirt in my hand so as to not touch the wood. I pinch it with the shirt and yank it out. My finger swells. I lean against the trunk of the car, holding my throbbing hand. Time seems to slow down as the hole made by the wood chunk stitches itself together. The pain takes its sweet time in leaving, but eventually, I can't feel a thing, as if the splinter was never there.

As time goes on, I begin to pace. Twenty minutes late. I constantly pull out my phone, waiting for him to call. A knot forms in my stomach. Something's happened to him. I can feel it. My nails suffer through my anxiety as I bite every last one to stubs. My throat begins to burn until I can hardly stand it. Reluctantly, I walk toward Mason's front door with the hope that Eli will honk his horn just as I turn my back. No such luck.

Everyone looks up at me as I walk inside. They stop their conversation, waiting for Eli to trail in behind me. I shake my head and fall onto the couch. Anne hands me a bottle of blood, which I drain in a second. My throat calms for the moment.

All three of them are staring at me. I raise my head as dread seeps in. "I think something might've happened to him. The things he was saying—Rose, what do you think?"

I turn to Mason's mom, curled up in her lounge chair with a blanket wrapped around her. She looks sick, more so than usual. She replies, "I believe you're right, Cheyenne."

"So what should we do, Mom?" Mason asks, his brows furrowing together.

"I'll call Lucas. Mason, hand me the phone, sweetheart," she smiles weakly at her son and holds her hand out for the phone. She dials Eli's brother without even looking up a number. We wait anxiously as three rings pass without an answer. Finally, Rose's face relaxes. "Hi, Lucas, it's Rose. Is Eli at home?" I can already answer that. No. "That's what I was afraid of. He was supposed to be here about an hour ago, and he hasn't shown up." She stops, listening. "Well, I'm worried because he made an appearance at Anne's Affirmation party." Another pause. "See you soon." She sets the phone on the arm of the chair, sighing and leaning her head back. "He and Erik are on their way here. They should be able to find him," she says quietly. I start to open my mouth to object to Erik. I can already feel my blood boiling at the thought of him.

All of us turn when a sharp knock echoes through the living room.

"I'll get it," Anne says, walking to the front door. A moment later, Anne comes back into the room followed by Lucas and Erik.

Rose sits up a little bit, although it's an effort for her. "I believe we all know each other," Rose says.

"What's going on, Rose? What's happened to my

brother?" Lucas doesn't sit down.

"It's her fault," Erik points at me like a child. He makes me sick.

His brother pays him no attention and continues questioning Rose. "Why would Eli go to a Deuxsang gathering?"

"I don't know, Lucas. All I do know is that he was concerned for Cheyenne. He'd seen how her brother-in-law abuses her, and he wanted to help."

"He said he'd been doing astral projection to contact his ancestors," I say. "The things he said seemed crazy, but I guess if he's been taken they must have been true."

Rose chimes in, "His ancestors? Lucas, you don't think he reached *her*, do you? No one's ever been able to."

"What did he tell you?" Lucas demands, visibly controlling his anger.

"That there's something *different* about me." I contemplate saying something about Anne's brother, but I don't think she wants that to be public information, especially in front of Erik.

"Spit it out, Lane!" Erik yells.

"Okay!" I yell right back. "I don't know everything, but I do know that my Ascension went wrong. It hurt like hell. And the vampires all bit me, not just one. They wanted to taste me. I think maybe there's something different about my blood."

Erik nearly erupts, "Whatever. That doesn't make any sense. Let's just go get our brother."

For once he and I are on the same page. We both want to save Eli. I didn't think Erik had these kinds of emotions, and that's unnerving. "Eli also found out Thomas has been forcing me to drink *human* blood. He always did it under unusual circumstances so the effects could be explained away."

"None of this tells us who would want to take Eli," Lucas speaks patiently.

I think for a second. The Council doesn't know Eli exists. There's no way it's them. So there's only one other person. "Thomas." I growl the name with a viciousness I didn't know I had. I stand up, gathering my stuff to leave.

"Wait, Cheyenne." Rose says, reaching for my arm as I pass her. "First things first." She holds my gaze sharply urging me to calm down, but the longer I'm here, the more my throat itches and the twitchier I get. I have to do something. When she knows I'm not going to flit for the door, she looks back to Lucas. "You'll have to do it."

He gazes at her for several seconds, something passing between them. Then he nods.

"You know where," she finishes, nodding over her left shoulder. Lucas walks in that direction and returns with what I can only assume are magic supplies.

Anne, Mason, and I watch silently as Lucas and Erik prepare to track Eli. The first thing they do is roll out a huge map of New Orleans. Erik flattens the map on the floor, pinning down each corner with a candle. A chill runs down my spine when he lights each wick with a snap of his fingers. Then my body runs cold. I think back to the fire, hearing Erik's voice on the other line when I called Eli, seeing his face in the crowd after Eli got me out.

"Did you try to kill me?" I whisper harshly, looking up at Erik. For a second, he's still, looking only at the ground. "You did, didn't you? You set the law office on fire!" I jump to my feet, and he quickly backs away behind Lucas.

"Cheyenne, calm down." Lucas says, holding out his hand to stop me. "Now's not the time."

"You don't get to tell me to calm down! Your brother has been torturing me for years! What did I ever do to him? And now he tries to kill me! How can you stand there and defend him?"

"But I didn't kill you." Erik barely steps out from Lucas's shadow. "I went to get Eli. I just meant to scare you away from him. I couldn't lose another family member to your kind."

"What are you talking about?" I scream, barely containing myself.

Mason jumps into the fray, "Guys, not now!"

"Quick version," Lucas answers for Erik. "Our mother left our father for a Deuxsang. Erik has never forgiven her."

"Because our mother is a..."

"Watch it!" Lucas growls, turning on his brother.

"It doesn't change the fact that you tried to kill me!"

Erik moves farther behind Lucas. "It was just supposed to be a small fire, but then it got out of control. I'm still learning, okay?" He sounds like a child. Rage boils in my chest, and all of a sudden Erik's on his knees screaming.

I hear everyone screaming my name, but all I can focus on is making him feel the pain that he's caused me all these years. Suddenly, Anne grabs me, pulling Erik out of my line of sight. "Cheyenne, stop. Pull it together." I pinch my eyes closed, trying to calm myself down. Erik's still kneeling on the ground, panting.

I fall onto the couch beside Mason, who mirrors my look of shock. He smiles at me sympathetically and puts his arm around my shoulder. I let out a breath, trying to refocus my mind.

"So can we get back to tracking my brother now?" Lucas asks, pulling out a pocketknife. He doesn't wait for our responses, just picks up a crystal and ties it to the end of a string. Mason, Anne, and I shrink back into the couch when Lucas slices the knife across his palm. The burn in my throat is scalding as the tantalizing smell floats across the room. I bite my lip as he takes the crystal in his palm and closes his fingers around it, coating the crystal with blood.

Anne leans over to me and whispers, "I feel like I've seen this on TV."

"You probably have," Lucas replies. He spares a look at us before nodding at Erik.

Lucas holds the bloody crystal over the map, and together they chant, "Blood calls blood."

Ms. Rose is seated in her chair, her feet just inches from the map. Lucas and Erik kneel side by side at the bottom of the map. Leaning forward, Lucas holds the crystal over the city, where it swings back and forth, back and forth, then in circles. The circles are big at first, along the perimeter of the city, and then they start to shrink. Just when I think it's going to stop in the French Quarter—the club, I'd suspect—it quickly shifts to the left and slams itself to the floor. All five of us lean over the map to get a better look.

"It's in the Garden District..." Lucas murmurs.

Both Anne and I lean closer. "It's..." I start to say.

"It's my house," Anne finishes, leaning back, looking more confused than ever. "Why would he still be at my house?"

"Maybe Thomas has him trapped somewhere. I don't know. Who cares? Let's go get him!" I jump to my feet, already making my way to the door.

"Real smart, Lane. It's always a good idea for witches to go uninvited into a Deuxsang residence. Oh wait! That's what got us into this mess," Erik chides.

"Say one more word to me and find out what happens," I growl, taking a step toward him. I didn't realize my fangs had dropped.

"He's right," Anne says, stepping in front of me. "Cheyenne and I have to go in alone."

Twenty Two

Silently, Lucas and Erik climb into Rose's old, beat up Honda. Mason is already in the driver's seat of Anne's car starting up the engine when we follow, Anne in the passenger seat, me in the back. For the first few minutes of the ride, Mason tries to lighten the mood as he always does, but when he realizes that nothing's going to work, he stops talking and turns on his music. I can feel my anxiety levels escalating. All the possible horrible scenarios play out in my mind. I see Eli lying bloody somewhere, Thomas's fang marks on his throat. I see Thomas killing Eli right in front of me. What happened to him being the weird, kiss-up brother-in-law? Does Kara know about all this? Was she a part of this whole thing?

"Cheyenne, your nails," Anne calls, turning around slowly in her seat. I've bitten them down to stumps. If I were any other creature, I'd be bleeding right now.

"Sorry. I'm just nervous." I set my hands in my lap, twisting them in an iron grip. But Anne's still looking at me.

"Eli's going to be fine. Don't worry." She's smiling at me, but I can sense the hesitation. Mason nods his support, keeping his eyes focused on the road.

"It's not just Eli I'm worried about. So much has been going on that I've been completely blind to. How can I be so naïve?" I punch my knee.

"It's not your fault, Cheyenne."

"But if I'd known, then Eli wouldn't have gone and done all this stuff and gotten himself kidnapped. If I had opened my eyes just a little bit."

"Stop it. We're going to get him back. Thomas is going to get his butt kicked. Everything will be fine."

I look at her straight on. "Then what happens after that?" My voice is quiet, almost inaudible. I already know she doesn't have the answer, no matter how much I want her to. Her mouth opens and closes like a fish gasping for water. She's not used to not having the answer either.

And then we're pulling into Anne's long driveway, and every nerve in my body stops. I expected all the cars to be gone, but there are still a few here, parked along the curb of the front lawn. *What is going on here*?

Lucas's car pulls past the house and parks several houses down. Mason doesn't pull into the garage. He just keeps the car parked in the driveway. When he turns the engine off, Anne reaches for his hand to stop him from pulling out the keys. "No, Mason. You know the plan. You stay here."

"Anne, I can't just let you go in there by yourselves." He has that determined look, but Anne's the only person who can calm him down.

"Yes, you can. Cheyenne and I will be fine. Lucas is going to sleep right now. If anything happens, I'll be able to reach him. I need you to stay safe. Please." I look away as they rest their foreheads together. "I need you out here."

"Just be careful," he whispers, pressing his lips against hers. I jump out of the car to give them their moment. When Anne finally follows suit, Mason rolls down the window and calls, "Cheyenne, be careful please and kick some butt." I try to look confident as I smile at him, giving him thumbs up. He nods back, and Anne and I turn to the front door. I have a creeping feeling that everything's about to go horribly wrong.

When we reach the front door, Anne turns the knob and opens it. We're in stealth mode when we enter the foyer. We're hunched over, eyes vigilant, and then we hear the voices—familiar voices coming from down the hall. I follow behind Anne, and before we can even react, we're standing in a living room full of stunned faces: Kara, Thomas, the Lacroixs, couples from the club, and then in the center of it all—Lilith.

I have the urge to run away when Lilith's sharp glare lands on me. "Thomas," her voice is like nails against a chalkboard, "why is Cheyenne not where she's supposed to be?" Thomas looks ready to murder me.

Anne looks around the room, completely exasperated. "What the heck is going on here?" I reach a hand out to stop her, but she only has thoughts for her parents.

"Ginger, we'd thought you'd left with Cheyenne a long time ago," Mrs. Lacroix says, staring calmly at her daughter.

"That's not an answer to the question, Mom. What is all this?" She looks around the room at familiar and unfamiliar faces all staring at us.

"It's just a meeting, nothing for you to concern yourself with, Ginger." This is the most I've ever heard Mr. Lacroix say. He looks up from his linked hands and steadies his gaze with Anne. "Please leave us to our business."

"No. Not until I know what's going on here."

I watch Lilith as she turns to Thomas with a deadly glare. "Thomas, you specifically told me that you had Cheyenne's location secured. She was to be back at your house, yet here she is." She speaks through a façade of calm.

"Did you really think I wouldn't come looking for him, Thomas?" I spit, taking my turn to glare at my brother-in-law. The rest of the men and women in the room are silent, observing the two family feuds.

"Who is she looking for, Thomas?" Lilith won't look at me. She stands tall in her white dress, a frightening power shining off of her.

"Where is he? I swear, if you've hurt him, I'm going to..." I take a step forward, but Lilith stops me with a single look.

A small, creepy smile crawls onto Lilith's face. "Thomas, speak." I look between them, at my once intimidating brother-in-law who's opening and closing his mouth like a guppy.

"It's that damn witch! I compelled her to stay away from him, but I saw them together tonight. He must have found a way to magic through my command. I had to find out how and make him pay. And *you*!" Thomas lunges at me, fangs bared. There's no time to react. I wait for the collision, to be knocked to the floor, but it doesn't come. I open my eyes, and Lilith's standing in front of me, her eyes focused on Thomas as he chokes. Kara's crying, yelling at Lilith to release him.

"You attack when I tell you to attack. You follow my orders explicitly. Are we understood?" Lilith's sigh is heavy and disappointed. Thomas nods as much as he can in Lilith's invisible grip. She releases him, and he crashes to the floor, his eyes narrowed into a glare. Kara runs to his side, fussing over him, but he just brushes her off.

"There is, of course, a much simpler explanation, Thomas. Perhaps Cheyenne has come into her ability. Maybe she's compeller," she speaks looking directly in my eyes.

"That's impossible," Thomas croaks from the floor. "She's an inflictor. Kara saw it in her dreams, and even you said you weren't able to inflict on her!"

I stare at my sister, sick with betrayal. "You've been walking through my dreams?"

She looks up guiltily at me, but her attention returns immediately to Thomas.

"Stop it, both of you," Lilith snaps at the couple. "He's fine. There's no need for melodrama. We have more important things to get to."

Suddenly I remember what the child vampire said, and it makes sense.

"You're the leader."

That creepy smile returns to her face. She sighs, nodding once. "Yes, I lead the Ascending." A note of panic creeps into my mind as I see some of the men moving to block the door and the windows. "I'm assembling the Deuxsang. We're officially organizing ourselves without the control of the Council, but we'll have more time to talk about that later."

Lilith turns away from me to focus her attention on Thomas. His head is bowed in shame, but I can sense the anger radiating off him. Kara, standing behind him, looks nervous to the point of tears.

"Thomas, I gave you two jobs. To recruit and to deal with Cheyenne. Why did you fail me?" The calmness of her voice gives me chills.

"I didn't, Lilith. I was simply doing what I had to." He holds his head up proudly. Anne places a hand on my tense shoulder to restrain me.

"Thomas, you know nothing of the minds of young girls." A few of the men chuckle as Lilith flashes one of her charming smiles. "You tell them they can't have something, and they want it even more. If you'd just let this play out, Cheyenne would've become bored with this silly fling, but no." She starts to move toward Thomas, slowly, the small train of her dress rustling against the carpet.

"But," he gasps, "the witch..."

"I don't care about witches!" The amusement falls from everyone's face as Lilith's voice shakes the walls. Anne and I carefully start moving toward the door still blocked by two men. "And now you've hurt the mission." She's close to him now. His jaw clenches together, his nostrils flared. "I only want to hear one thing from you: Where is the witch?" Her long arms link behind her back as she waits for his response.

Thomas looks up at me. Impatient, Lilith grabs the back of his neck like a disobedient puppy, pulling him closer. "Answer me," she hisses.

"In the office," he mutters, his jaw clamped shut, glaring up at my snobby, pretentious, devious cousin.

I look over my shoulder at Anne, who simply nods at me. The moment Lilith releases Thomas, we both spin around and swing at the two men blocking the door. Caught off guard, they don't even sense the punches until our fists connect with their noses. They fall away from the door, and we rush through, flitting through the main level of the house. The air in the house stirs as the Deuxsang in the room rush into flits after us, but we're already up the stairs and headed to Mr. Lacroix's office.

We stop just before the grand double doors. When Anne pauses, I nearly scream, "What are you doing?" I spin around when I hear someone approach. Anne closes her eyes, bows her head, and suddenly jerks back up. Then she pulls me into the office, locking the door behind us.

"I was telling Lucas where Eli is," she whispers, a pinch to her voice. I don't get the chance to respond. The moment I open my mouth, someone is at my throat, pinning me against the wall. I'm getting really tired of this.

"No one's allowed in here, half-breed," a voice hisses at me. I open my eyes to see one of the homeless kids. Red eyes are staring back at me. His skin is pale, and his fangs are bared, ready to rip out my throat.

"Anne, they're vampires."

"No talking!" The boy slams my head against the wall. The vampire holds my head still, but I can see Anne out of the corner of my eye in the same position as me. The lights are on now. Eli is chained in the corner of the office on the floor, his head slumped against his chest. I resist the urge to scream, to wake him up.

Suddenly, a tunnel of air forms on the other side of the room, and within seconds, Lucas and Erik appear in front of Eli. The rest of the vampire kids rush at them, but when Erik holds his hands up, a wall of fire stops them.

"Lucas, get him out!" I shout before the vampire holding me presses his thumbs into my throat to silence me

Lucas spins around while Erik faces the vampires, putting up an invisible shield. Without even touching him, Lucas makes Eli's chains fall off. He pulls Eli's arm over his shoulder, supporting most of his barely-conscious weight. Eli's eyes blink open, search the room, and land on me. With one look, I regret everything that's happened.

And in a snap, he's gone. The moment Erik backs close enough for Lucas to reach, they jump into the tunnel and out of the room. I fight back the tears forming in my eyes. I can't cry now.

Mr. Lacroix opens the door in the next few seconds, and Lilith, Thomas, Kara, and the rest of them pour into the office, seething. The two vampires holding us remove their hands from our necks and pull our arms behind our backs. I wince when Anne cries out in pain. I look up at her parents. Mrs. Lacroix has a restraining hand on her husband's shoulder, but he looks like he wants to break the vampire in two.

The longer Lilith stares at me, the more I know how much I've underestimated her. "What do you want with us, Lilith?"

She chuckles softly, an eerily menacing sound. "Amazing. You think this is all about you." She looks pointedly at Anne, who's still struggling in the vampire's iron grip, looking pitifully at her parents. "The thing is, you're a problem. Deuxsang are the ultimate hybrid. We have the powers of the vampires, and we can blend in with the humans. We can own the day and the night." She's enjoying this. "And then there's you. The problem we have to fix. And Miss Lacroix—she's just an inconvenience now. You should have stayed away from my cousin, dear," she leans close to Anne, patting her cheek. Menacingly, she talks to me again. "And if we can't fix you..."

"Hold on," Kara steps forward, speaking up for the first time. "You said nothing about killing her, Lilith. This was not part of the plan."

"Oh, calm down, cousin. It won't come to that." She brushes off Kara's indignation with a simple shrug and another chilling grin. "Now, Kara, Gail, take the girls to Ginger's room and don't forget to take their phones."

"No, wait! What plan?" I scream as the vampire wrenches me toward the door behind Anne. Kara and Mrs. Lacroix are close behind us. Lilith ignores me, turning to face her followers. Mrs. Lacroix closes the door behind her and leads the vampires to Anne's room. The kids throw us on the floor as Kara checks the windows.

"How could you do this, Kara?" I yell, leaping to my feet. I want to hurt her so badly.

"I told you to let that boy go, Cheyenne." My sister's face, normally an open book, is completely impassive. "This all could have been avoided."

"Are you blaming me for your insane husband?" My voice jumps an octave as my hands curl into fists.

"Leave Thomas out of this," she mutters through gritted teeth, gripping Mrs. Lacroix's arm for support.

"You can't leave Thomas out of this. This is his fault!"

"He was just doing what he had to. I need you to understand, Cheyenne. We're trying to help you—trying to save our family." Her arms circle around her growing stomach.

I take a long, deep breath, which escapes as a frustrated, frightened laugh. "Really? So what happens if you can't fix me?" I turn to Mrs. Lacroix, looking her right in the eyes. "Are you going let the Council take me like they did with *their son*?"

The calculated calm that I've always seen in Mrs. Lacroix's eyes is gone, replaced with an unrelenting fury. "You don't know what you're talking about!" she hisses, taking a dark step toward me.

"What *is* she talking about, mom?" Anne looks from me to Mrs. Lacroix. "You said my brother died." She grips my arm like a vice.

For a moment, Mrs. Lacroix just stares. "Sweetheart, your brother was like Cheyenne. When the Council found out about him, they took him." Kara slides her arm around Mrs. Lacroix's shoulders in support.

"Why would you lie to me about this?" Anne's indignant, releasing my arm and taking a step toward her mom. "How could you live with yourself?" she sneers, tears leaking from her eyes. "You let my brother be murdered!"

"No!" Mrs. Lacroix bellows. "No, we did not. We tried to get him back!"

Anne shouts through tears, "Get out! Get out of my room!" Mrs. Lacroix takes a step toward Anne, but Anne backs away. "Leave!" Mrs. Lacroix runs from the room crying, her hands covering her face.

Kara follows her slowly to the door. "We all have reasons for what we're doing, Cheyenne," she says softly.

"So what's yours?" I demand.

"You'll understand," she says, more to herself than to me. And with that she closes the door and turns the lock. I flit across the room, slamming my body against the door, screaming. I can sense the vampires on the other side standing watch. I beat my fists and scream until I'm hoarse.

"Cheyenne, stop it. That's not getting us anywhere." Anne's stopped crying, her perfect make up smeared across her face. "We need to think of a plan."

I flit across the room to the window and look down, only to find the rest of the vampire kids hovering below us, watching the street and our window. They look so innocent and pitiful in their ragged clothes, dirty faces. Yet here they are, working for my cousin, ready to snap my neck at her order. And Mason's gone. Lucas must've gotten to him.

"There is no plan, Anne."

Suddenly the door swings open and in walks Lilith, changed from her party dress into a slick black suit. Her heels click against the wood floor. "She's right. Trying to escape is pointless."

"What do you want, Lilith?"

I expect her to smile or gloat. I'm waiting for this all to be an extremely elaborate prank, but her face darkens even more. "You wish to know the mission of the Ascending, so I'll tell you." She pauses, taking an intimidating step toward us. "We are going to take down the vampires." The way she says 'vampires' sends a chill down my spine.

"But why?" Anne asks, speaking up to Lilith, yet I feel her flinch away when my cousin turns her glare.

"Because it is time for the oppression to end. My work with the Council has made this very clear to me. We are their tools. They believe they are better than us, that they can control us, manipulate us. We're forced to give them records of our families. They control our drinking. We're not free." Her words start a rollercoaster in my head.

"So why do you care about me?" I ask.

"The vampires' time is over, and our time has come. Nothing will stand in our way, most certainly not you. The Council wants you for the same reason they wanted Jason Lacroix. I don't know what that reason is, but I know they aren't going to get you. The Ascending will do its best to make you a true Deuxsang, but failure is not an option, so I suggest you do everything to make sure we succeed." I'm no stranger to death threats, but this is the first one I believe.

"And as for your witch," she seems to gain more power when I flinch at the mention of Eli, "I have no particular interest in him. However, if you do not cooperate, I might have to develop an interest."

"Forget about it, Lilith. He's gone. You won't be able to find them."

Another bolt of fear strikes through me when her cold, piercing eyes look me up and down. "I wouldn't be so sure of that. Witches aren't as good at hiding as you, or they, might wish to believe." She moves carefully to the door, every single movement calculated to intimidate us. It's working. "Sleep well, girls."

Anne and I are silent, which pleases Lilith. When she leaves, the door is locked from the outside.

We're prisoners.

~ The Author ~

HANNAH RIALS is a Maryville native and current college student at University of Tennessee at Chattanooga. Hannah began writing her first novel at age twelve. Eight years later, the result is her debut YA novel *Ascension*. When not spending time with her family and playing with her beloved Corgis, Buddy and Noel, Hannah leads a creative writing group, crafts, and cultivates her writing skills.

You can learn more about Hannah on her site:

www.hannaherials.com